Testosterone and a slew of wolfan hormones stormed Rafe's veins.

Burning up all his restraint, Rafe stood perfectly still as Grace moved lithely out of the room with her hips sashaying in an erotic sway that beckoned both the man and the wolf.

God, she was pretty. Long, shiny hair the color of corn silk. Bright green eyes that put polished emeralds to shame. Soft golden skin and an athletic body with just the right amount of curves. None of which he should've noticed. And yet he had, and more.

She had a ready smile, a kind heart toward people and animals. He liked her spunk more than he should.

And she smelled really good, too.

Another time, another place. Another life. She could've been the one.

RESCUED BY THE WOLF

KRISTAL HOLLIS

MILLS & BOON

First Published in Great Britain 2017
By Mills & Boon, an imprint of HarperCollins*Publishers*
1 London Bridge Street, London, SE1 9GF

© 2017 Kristal Hollis

ISBN: 978-0-263-93001-6

89-0317

Our policy is to use papers that are natural, renewable and recyclable products and made from wood grown in sustainable forests. The logging and manufacturing processes conform to the legal environmental regulations of the country of origin.

Printed and bound in Spain
by CPI, Barcelona

Southern born and bred, **Kristal Hollis** holds a psychology degree and has spent her adulthood helping people and animals. When a family medical situation resulted in a work sabbatical, she began penning deliciously dark paranormal romances as an escape from the real-life drama. But when the crisis passed, her passion for writing love stories continued. A 2015 Golden Heart® Award finalist, Kristal lives with her husband and two rescued dogs at the edge of the enchanted forest that inspires her stories.

To all who have loved and lost, and dared to love again.

Although the act of writing may be a solitary endeavor, inspiration is often found far and wide.

To Cam and Scott at New Tokyo Auto Repair, thanks for keeping the Blue Bandit running smoothly so I can attend all those writerly meetings and retreats. A heartfelt thanks to my friend and colleague, John Custis, for sharing your knowledge of baseball. Ann Leslie Tuttle and Kayla King, oh how I appreciate your wisdom and guidance in helping me to shape this story. And, as always, much love, hugs and kisses to Keith— the hero of my heart, thank you for never doubting.

Chapter 1

Boom!

The shotgun blast decimated the midnight calm of the Walker's Run wolf sanctuary. Rafe Wyatt's sure-footed paws faltered. Heart frozen midpound, he dove to the ground, nose filling with the earthy scents of damp dirt and decayed leaves.

A flash-flood of dread and fear rolled tremors through his wolfan body but he didn't feel any pain from penetrating shrapnel.

Then again, three years ago he hadn't felt the bullet that had ripped through him and killed his pregnant mate trotting beside him, either.

Goddamn poacher.

If Rafe had been in his human form, he would've spit on the ground and stomped his foot in it as if it were the dead man's grave.

The hunter hadn't lived long enough to collect his trophy. Rafe, still in his wolf form, had torn him to shreds. A justified killing under wolfan law.

He'd suffered no recriminations from the Woelfesenat, the governing wolf council. Any penance was his own.

Avenging Lexi's death had brought him no peace. His only solace from the loss and longing had come from a bottle of bourbon.

How many times had he drunk himself into oblivion, only to find the sharp talons of reality waiting to shred his heart and soul again the moment he awoke, cold, naked, and alone?

Too many to count.

And it had damn near killed him when he'd blacked out behind the wheel and missed the curve at Wiggins's Pass. Drove right off the mountain. The guardrail, a thick canopy of trees below, and rescue workers had kept his Jeep from plunging to the bottom.

Still, the accident wasn't what convinced him to stop drinking. It had been waking up in the hospital and seeing his father's drawn, pale face, the frenzied panic in his eyes, his ghostly-white lips and the salt-and-pepper hair that suddenly had twice as much salt as pepper. Rafe never wanted to make his father look like that again.

Now, instead of drinking when unbearable loneliness ate him alive, Rafe ran the pack's protected expanse of woods. Only, wolfans didn't use guns to safeguard their territory and the boom ricocheting through the trees was definitely from a shotgun, which meant *poachers.*

A chill frosted his skin. Senses heightening, he focused his acute hearing to pinpoint the direction of the gun discharge. From the echo, the shooter was northwest of him, in the vicinity of Mary-Jane McAllister's farm at the edge the sanctuary.

The wolflings!

Releasing Mary-Jane's potbellied pig, Cybil, and herding her back into her pen without using their human forms had become an unofficial wolfling rite of passage ever since Rafe and his best friend, Brice Walker, had successfully wrangled the ornery sow as teenagers. Their victory had resulted in cracked ribs and massive bruises, but the adventure had been one of the best of their lives.

Rafe suppressed a snarl at the arrogance of youth. Once he'd been cocky and proud. In a time when it felt good to be alive and unstoppable in the face of a nova-bright future and carefree oblivion.

At fourteen, Rafe had believed he was invincible. At twenty-eight, the reality of how wrong he'd been lived coiled inside him like a copperhead, its fangs embedded deep in his conscience, spewing venom into his soul.

The cries of frightened wolflings penetrated his mind. Rafe leaped to his feet in an all-or-nothing run. The nearest sentinels would converge to investigate. Some in wolf form, others in human form dressed as Walker's Run Co-operative security guards. But none were as fast as Rafe.

Paws thundering against the damp and familiar ground, he zigzagged through a dark maze of tall pines. The crisp, cool spring air ruffled his fur as he ran. He covered the four-mile distance in just under two minutes.

Three frightened wolflings darted haphazardly across the farmyard in a confused search for the right direction to run.

"Go on, you damn wolf pups. Get!" Stomping on her front porch, Mary-Jane McAllister—a sturdy woman dressed in a flowered housecoat and tattered slippers with curlers in her gray-streaked hair, waved a shotgun in the air without making any action to fire it again. Although her tongue had delivered a fair share of sharp lashings, she'd never harmed a wolfan and Rafe didn't think she intended to do so now.

"Cybil!" Mary-Jane hollered at the huge pig plowing into the woods. "Be back by morning. I got no time to look for you. I'm plantin' beans tomorrow."

Rafe doubted the pig would return any time soon. Once roused out of her pen, Cybil didn't willingly go back in until good and ready.

She would be safe in the wolf sanctuary. None of the Walker's Run Wahyas would harm one short, coarse hair on her body. The pack considered the big sow family. Besides,

Cooter, the pack's lead sentinel, was sweet on Mary-Jane. If anything happened to that pig, paying the devil his due would be pennies compared to what Cooter would extract.

Mary-Jane trudged inside the house, the screen door slamming behind her. The panicked wolflings fled into the woods. Rafe loped after them to steer them to safety.

Two adult wolves appeared ahead and the wolflings separated.

Rafe nodded to the sentinels, then bolted after the tawny wolfling who'd veered left.

"Alex, stop!" he called telepathically, adding a note of annoyance to his thoughts. Chasing his cousin's delinquent son through the forest wasn't how Rafe wanted to spend the rest of the night.

He'd grown up believing he was the last of his parents' bloodlines. The recent discovery of a maternal relative and her son in need of sponsorship gave him another chance at family.

Not that Doc, his adoptive human father, wasn't family. He was, absolutely and resoundingly.

But Rafe longed for more. The loss of his birth parents and entire birth pack had created a soul-aching need to re-build his family line.

His dream had ended with a single shot from a rifle. After losing Lexi, Rafe had no desire to claim another mate. Since wolfan males could only father children with a female they'd claimed, he would likely never have a family of his own.

Then Ronni and her son Alex, distant cousins through his mother's bloodline, had come along. Looking after them was a far stretch from being a mate and father, but as their only male blood-kin he was responsible for their welfare.

"Alex, I said stop!"

"Rafe?" Even as Alex's startled voice sliced through Rafe's mind, the wolfling disappeared over the ridge.

Damn.

Rafe cut sharply through the budding brush, hoping to catch the wolfling before he reached the old two-lane road.

The soft hum of a motor vibrated through the thinning trees.

Rafe crested the rise and his chest tightened, restricting his airflow like the choke valve on an old carburetor. *"Alex, get out of the road. Now!"*

Paralyzed inside a glaring beam of light, the wolfling didn't budge.

Rafe darted down the embankment, leaped over the roadside ditch, and slammed into Alex. The adolescent wolfan tumbled clear of the oncoming car and darted into the woods.

Dazed and sprawled on the pavement, Rafe stared into the headlights of imminent doom.

He'd spent more than two years drunk and wishing for death. Nine months, three weeks, and five days ago, he'd gotten his life back on track, sort of.

When he quit drinking and resolved to put the past behind him, people said things would get easier with time.

They lied.

Nothing was any easier. At least life hadn't gotten any worse—until now.

The blare of a horn shattered the zombie-like shroud fogging his brain. Pure Wahyan instinct took control. The sudden surge of adrenaline caused a loss of coordination in Rafe's limbs. His legs skewed in different directions, his paws scrambled for steady footing.

Tires screeched from a hard brake, slinging the car into a slippery slide across the asphalt.

"Alex!" Rafe's mind screamed at the wolfling barking frantically from the edge of the woods. Time slowed to a centipede's crawl. *"Look away!"*

A wave of heat from the car's engine rolled over Rafe's

fur. His nostrils stung from the acrid smell of burning brake lines.

His heart pounded furiously, the beat stabbing his chest in a desperate plea for him to get up and run, only his legs wouldn't cooperate. Rafe curled into a ball, every muscle clenched for impact.

This was it. Really it. There'd be no coming back this time. He'd already survived two near-death experiences. He wouldn't survive a third.

At the last possible moment, the car veered sharply to the right and careened into the embankment. The crunch of metal competed with the jackhammering pound of his heart.

"Rafe!" Alex's hysterical cries penetrated Rafe's mind.

The wolfling's cold nose nudged Rafe's side. As if a reset button had been pressed, a current zipped through Rafe's body and pumped a steady stream of relief through his veins.

His stomach lurched to untangle the knots that had formed.

"I'm fine, Alex." Rafe unfurled his legs and stood, a little wobbly until his nerves settled.

"I thought you were a goner." Alex tucked his head beneath Rafe's chin and rubbed his muzzle against Rafe's neck, warming Rafe's fur with his frantic pants.

A deluge of affection greatly increased the probability of what would have been an uncharacteristic hug, if Rafe had been in his human form. *"Stop slobbering on me. I said, I'm fine."* Or he would be once his heart stopped beating against his skull and dropped into his chest where it belonged.

"What do we do now?" Wide-eyed, Alex stared at the wrecked car.

"You go home." Rafe nipped Alex's ear.

"But—"

"Go." Rafe pointed his nose in the general direction of Alex's house.

"Aw, man," Alex grumbled. Head and tail hanging low, he trudged into the woods. At the ridge, he looked over his shoulder. His eyebrows lifted in a hopeful expression.

Rafe barked a warning. Alex's nose wrinkled, pulling his upper lip over his canines. He slowly padded between the trees and disappeared from sight.

Rafe waited a few seconds and called out, *"Alex, go home."*

A disgruntled growl rumbled through the forest, followed by a rustle of leaves, then silence.

Rafe turned toward the pale green Volkswagen Beetle, the right front side pinned against the opposite embankment. His own low, frustrated growl lodged in his throat. Of all the people in the Walker's Run territory, the one woman he'd gone out of his way to avoid would have to be the one who almost killed him.

He should follow his orders to Alex and go home. The accident didn't appear to be serious enough to have injured the driver. He could howl a signal to the sentinels. They'd take care of her.

His gut pinched and something deep in his chest tugged him to move forward. Toward the disabled car. To the woman behind the wheel.

The farther he padded forward, the more intense the feeling grew. He sat on his haunches. A soft burst of electricity pulsed through his nervous system. Ignoring the ticklish current, he stood as a man. "God, I need a drink."

Chapter 2

Rafe stalked toward the disabled car. His heart beat a weird tattoo of excitement and doom. The wolf in him couldn't wait to see the human female. The man would rather be fed to a starving, angry bear.

Rafe had been sober for only twelve days when he'd met Grace Olsen at Brice's thirtieth birthday party. Encountering her once was enough to deter all future interactions. Her tantalizing scent had captivated him from across the room. So much so that he'd had a hell of a time focusing on anything but getting close to her and marking her with his scent—something he could not, or rather would not, do.

At the time, he wanted to stay focused on remaining sober and putting the pieces of his life back together. Grace presented a complication he wasn't equipped to handle and he'd gone to great lengths to avoid.

Rafe snatched open the car door. A myriad of scents—greasy fried potatoes, vanilla and sweet cream, and sickly sweet chocolate assaulted his nose.

Uck! He hated chocolate.

Snorting to clear his nose, he honed in on the more delicate musk of the woman slumped over the partially deflated air bag.

His breath knotted in the back of his throat.

"Grace?" The soft rise and fall of her shoulders were a comfort beneath his palm.

Leaning over her to shut off the engine, he breathed a deep lungful of her heady essence. A frisson that had nothing to do with the residual shift energy coursed through his body.

She squinted and a whispery moan escaped her clenched mouth.

"Grace, can you hear me?" Squatting beside her, he tucked a few wisps of blond hair behind her ear. A trickle of blood seeped from the half-dollar-sized knot forming along the hairline above her temple. "You've been in an accident."

Her eyelids opened on a sigh and the clearest, darkest green eyes he'd ever seen peered at him.

Every cell in his body froze. He couldn't breathe, couldn't blink. Damn near couldn't think. Nine months hadn't been long enough to weaken the pull he felt toward her, but he was in a better place to resist it.

"Rafe? Rafe Wyatt?"

He nodded. She recognized him and remembered his name. That shouldn't make him feel good, but it did.

"Oh, no! The wolf!" Her panicked gaze darted past him. "Did I hit him?"

Either the knock on the head had really messed her up, or she didn't know the truth about the wolves in Walker's Run.

He guessed the latter. If the pack's Alphena-in-waiting, Cassie Walker, had not confided in her best friend, then Rafe wouldn't be the one to let the wolf out of the bag.

"He's fine, Grace. I checked him before I came to you."

"What a relief." The strain on her face eased and she finally seemed to see all of him. "For Pete's sake. Why are you naked?"

He stared at the open moon roof above Grace's head, willing his body, his mind, and his wolf to behave.

"Haven't you heard the stories?" He put an edge in his voice, despite the smile scratching at the corners of his mouth as Grace covered her eyes like the see-no-evil monkey. "I run naked through the woods and howl at the full moon."

"The moon isn't full."

Rafe was thankful it wasn't. His attraction toward her was real, dangerous, and something he wanted to avoid like the mange. A full moon would only heighten his awareness of her and weaken his resistance.

He lowered his eyes to her pink tank top and pink bottoms covered with tiny cat faces.

She liked cats and the color of bubble gum. Two strikes. One more and maybe he could get her out of his head for good. "Why are you driving around in your pajamas?"

"No one was supposed to see me." She peeked through her fingers. "Hey! Don't stare." She slapped her arms over her chest, then quickly uncrossed them to grab her head. "Oh, no! I'm going to be sick."

Covering her mouth, she bumped past him. He followed her to the spot beside the road where she'd dropped to her knees. Her stomach heaved, but expelled nothing. The muscles in her back rippled beneath his touch. "Relax. Everything will be all right." He slowly stroked along her spine. As his hand warmed from the friction, something ebbed into his being. Something soft and feminine. Something that intrigued man and wolf. Something that would upend his life and he'd suffered enough upheaval. He couldn't endure any more.

Grace swayed as she stood.

"I got you." He pulled her against him. Her soft curves flush against his hard planes opened up a deep-seated yearning he needed to keep buried. But damn, it had been so long since he'd held a woman, and since he'd almost died tonight, what harm could come from a little hug?

The lightness of her feminine scent filtered through him. His ears tuned to the quiet, rapid breaths she swallowed. Her cantering heartbeat, softly thumping against his chest, slowed until the pace matched his. The synchronicity sparked an excitement that skipped along his nerves, soothing as much as it ignited him.

"I feel dizzy." Grace squeezed her eyes shut.

"Maybe you should sit down." He scooped her into his arms.

"Hey, no funny stuff," she warned meekly. "These hands are lethal weapons."

She wiggled her finely boned fingers with painted pink nails. She was so dainty and feminine, he couldn't imagine her swatting a fly.

"I'm terrified," he said mildly, although his heart raced like a hunted wolf whose only options were capture or escape. He carried her toward the disabled car. From what he could see, the front passenger side had suffered the brunt of the collision. He would know more once he got the car into his repair shop.

"You should be terrified. I was trained by the best." Grace's eyelids slowly shut.

"Who?" he asked, tucking her into the driver's seat.

"My dad. He's a former Navy Seal."

"Appreciate the warning," Rafe said to be polite. He wasn't going to give in to his attraction to Grace, so there would be no need to meet Daddy.

She nodded, then clamped her hand over her mouth.

"Try not to move. Inhale slowly, deeply. Good, now exhale."

He waited for her to complete a few deep breaths.

"I'm going to reach for your phone to call for help. No funny stuff, I promise." Holding his breath so he wouldn't indulge in her intriguing scent, he leaned over her to grab the phone from the jumbled contents of her purse on the passenger floorboard.

"What the hell is your passcode?" he asked, unable to access the keypad.

Grace scrunched her eyes and her lips stretched tight in a seal across her mouth. She clutched the hand in which he held the phone and the jolt he got from the innocent contact nearly knocked him on his ass. At least, it felt like it did. He glanced down to make sure his backside hadn't actually kissed the ground.

After she keyed in the numbers 0-2-2-7, he jerked his hand from hers and backed away. "I need to find a spot with clear reception. Don't fall asleep, got it?"

She didn't respond.

"Grace?" He didn't want to touch her.

Okay, that was a bald-faced lie. He definitely wanted to touch her again, to indulge in her softness, to see if her heat would take the chill off the soul-aching loneliness he endured.

"Grace," he said sternly. "Answer me."

With painstakingly slow movements, she gave him a thumbs-up.

"I'll be quick. Don't fall asleep." He paced about fifty feet from the car until the phone registered a signal. His thumb hesitated above the touch screen before he placed the call.

"There's a wreck on the old highway behind the Mc-Allister homestead," Rafe barked before Doc had a chance to utter a groggy, "Hello."

"Are you all right, son?" Dr. Harold Habersham's strained voice cut Rafe to the quick.

Since sobering up, Rafe tried hard not to cause his adoptive human father more grief.

Still, it lingered. Just below the surface. The old man loved his son too much for his own good.

"I'm fine." Rafe frowned at the disabled car. "But I need the Co-op responders to pick up Grace Olsen. She's got a knot on her head and dry heaves. Could be her nerves. She's coherent and her pupils aren't unequally dilated."

"If you wanted to be a doctor, you should've gone to medical school."

"I hate hospitals." Hated the smell of antiseptics, sickness and death as a child. Hated the restraints, the needles, the beep of the machines that haunted his dreams long after he recovered from the shooting.

"Yeah, yeah." The rustle of clothes muffled Doc's voice. "I'll put in the emergency call and be there in ten. Make sure Grace stays conscious."

Keeping Grace awake would be easier said than done, considering Rafe would need to nudge her whenever she started dozing off. A nudge meant touching, and he definitely needed to keep touching to a minimum.

Palms tingling, Rafe sprinted to the car. "EMS is on the way."

Grace's eyes were closed and her head had lolled to the side. Rafe's heart dropped into his stomach. "Grace!"

Her shoulders twitched and her eyelids popped opened. "Don't scare me like that."

Same here, sweetheart.

"I thought you fell asleep." He thumbed her chin, tipping her face to see her eyes. Still clear and alert. Her blush-pink lips, full and luscious, dipped in a grimace.

"Nope, I was concentrating on not getting sick. The smell in here makes me want to—"

She gagged and Rafe didn't think it was for mere effect.

"Makes me want to gag, too." He lifted her from the car, carried her up the slight embankment and sat her against an old oak log. "What is that crap smeared in your car?"

"What's left of a hot fudge sundae and French fries."

Rafe's stomach turned in a not-so-silent *blech*.

"Hey. It's my favorite midnight snack." She squinted up at him. "Don't knock it until you've tried it."

"I'll pass." Rafe was allergic to chocolate. Violently allergic. End-up-in-the-hospital allergic.

And Rafe was glad he was. It quelled his desire to kiss her. If she'd eaten one bite of the hot fudge, and his mouth and tongue touched hers, she wouldn't be the only one headed to the emergency clinic.

"Can you move out of my line of vision?" She held her hand in front of her face. "Your family jewels are quite impressive, but I don't want them dangling in my face. It's distracting."

A sharp, primal awareness pierced him. He glanced at his cock, going from semierect to fully erect in the span of a breath.

Damn.

He'd done fairly well at controlling his reaction until now.

Impressive and distracting. Her description made him proud and more than a little possessive.

He sat beside her, knee bent to cover his groin. "Better?"

Her pensive gaze dropped to his lap, then inched up his chest. "I would've preferred clothes."

His clothes were miles away in his tow truck and he wouldn't retrieve them if it meant leaving her out here alone.

After a few minutes of silence, Grace shivered. Against his better judgment, Rafe reached around her shoulders and drew her close.

"You're nice and toasty," she said, snuggling into his heat.

His body hummed from the contact and he realized he no longer wanted alcohol. What he craved was much more dangerous.

Chapter 3

What is that god-awful sound?

The incessant noise kept time with the pounding in Grace's head.

She forced open her tired, scratchy eyes and sat up in the queen-size Murphy bed. The soft glow from the muted flat screen TV hanging on the left wall cast enough light that Grace didn't feel entombed in a sarcophagus, but only barely.

Earlier, when she had woken up to use the bathroom and found the bedroom–living room area of Rafe's micro-apartment consumed in utter blackness, a blood-curdling wail had exploded from her chest. Terror scaled her throat, tightening her windpipe around the scream until she ran out of air and could no longer breathe.

From out of the void Rafe had appeared, gathered her close and calmed her with his rock-solid presence. He probably thought a nightmare about the accident had incited her panic, when really she was simply afraid of the dark.

Being locked in a windowless basement for nearly a day when she was ten had instilled a debilitating fear of the dark and she was ashamed to have never outgrown it.

Beep…beep…beep…

The grating sound kicked up her headache several notches. Searching for the alarm clock, she glanced at the long wooden dresser centered beneath the TV. All that topped it were a video game console and one controller, the wires neatly wrapped around the middle. A cell phone, the TV remote, an orange prescription bottle and an empty water bottle were scattered across the coffee table.

Asleep on the brown leather couch, Rafe lay on his side with one arm crooked awkwardly behind his back.

Ordinarily, she wouldn't have gone home with a naked man encountered on the side of the road. Rafe, however, was the best friend of her best friend's husband. If Cassie and Brice trusted Rafe, Grace would, too.

Last night, she hadn't called Cassie from the hospital because it was after midnight and Grace didn't want to worry her pregnant friend over a lousy bump on the head. Dr. Habersham would've made her stay overnight in an observation room if Rafe hadn't volunteered to keep an eye on her.

Grace hadn't known Rafe's apartment was a windowless efficiency that he'd converted from the unused storage room connected to his automotive repair business. Still, being in a concrete box with him was better than being alone in the hospital.

Her gaze traced his lightly haired legs, sleek and powerful. A bunched white sheet disrupted the graceful lines of his hips and framed his exposed lower back. The smooth, muscled planes flexed as if she'd touched him. Head tucked beneath a pillow, he sighed a deep, low, guttural rumble that echoed through her body, heating her to the core.

Of course she'd have that reaction to *him*.

Out of all the men Cassie and Brice had introduced to her, Rafe had been the only one to spark any real interest. Rafe, on the other hand, had gone out of his way to ignore her after the initial introductions.

Until last night. When he'd shown up after the accident, his hair wild, his eyes fierce, his body dangerously naked.

She wouldn't be able to unsee the vision of his perfectly sculpted form even if she used a bleach solvent on her brain. The memory had already been uploaded to every cell in her body like a rogue computer virus. The only way to get rid of the infection was to overwrite the code. Unfortunately, she sucked as a code writer.

The cold harsh truth would have to suffice in masking the easily recallable memory and her interest. For some reason, Rafe found her off-putting. She didn't know why, and when she'd shown up at his business a few months back, hoping to bridge the chasm for Cassie and Brice's sake, Rafe had flat out told Grace he wasn't interested in being her friend.

Yep, the cold harsh truth. He didn't like her.

She couldn't understand his abrupt disregard and dismissal. She always made the effort to be kind, friendly and accepting of everyone. She didn't judge, didn't discriminate, she loved the uniqueness of each person.

Whatever the reason for his dislike, Rafe had shoved it aside last night and was there when she needed someone.

Right now, she needed him to shut off the freaking alarm before her head exploded.

"Rafe, wake up!"

He didn't move, snort, or otherwise acknowledge her presence.

Grace eased off the Murphy bed, slid her feet into her pink slippers, and maneuvered between the coffee table and couch. She reached over Rafe to the alarm clock balanced on the top frame of the couch, the LED face flipped so that the time flashed into the cushion instead of into the room.

In a sudden whirl, she landed flat on her back on top of the couch seat cushions. Rafe's steely fingers clamped around her wrists, pinning them over her head. She stared into icy, cobalt blue eyes that would've stolen her breath if she hadn't lost all air when he plastered his hard, hot body onto hers.

The short crop of his auburn hair stuck out in different directions. A pillow crease cut across one high cheekbone and dipped into the reddish stubble dusting his strong jaw. His firm, full lips would look much more kissable if he smiled.

Squared shoulders rose above a sculpted chest swirled with soft tufts of hair, and a quarter-sized scar marred the taut, tan skin over his right ribs.

Her gaze slid over the ripples of his abs and the sharp indents of his hips. She couldn't follow the treasure line that arrowed down from his belly button because he was lodged intimately against her pelvis.

A giddy heat rushed her body and struck her with the acute awareness of a virile man in his prime.

"Never sneak up on me, Grace." Rafe's laser-intense eyes burned holes straight through her body. "It's dangerous."

No doubt.

From his deeply etched scowl to his silent, panther-like movements, she needed no further warnings. He was dangerous on all levels.

"Shut off the damn alarm. My head is pounding and I can barely think."

Without shifting his weight off her, he slapped the buttons of the alarm clock and silenced the wailing beep. The echo continued to throb inside Grace's head. She shut her eyes, willing the pounding to stop and wanting to break the sizzling visual contact with Rafe.

He didn't take the hint to move. Instead, his cheek grazed her jaw, his mouth forged a warm, breathy trail to the shell of her ear, and he gently nosed the dimple behind her ear. "God, you smell good."

Her own senses drowned in his scent—clean, earthy, and deliciously male. Instinctively, her hips arched against his groin. Deep inside, her muscles clenched and a slow swirl centered low in her belly. "Hey, Wyatt. This isn't what I meant when I said I wanted to get to know you at Brice's party."

Yeah? Who was she kidding?

Since her hands were still pinned above her head, her hips were plastered against his, and any perpendicular movement might've further compromised their position, Grace nipped his ear.

Rafe moved so quickly it took her a few blinks before her body registered the loss of his heat. She sat up, her arms folding across her chest to hold in the warmth.

"Get your stuff and I'll drive you to the resort." He bent over to snatch up the sheet that had fallen to the floor.

Don't look at his ass. No, don't.

Her eyes didn't listen and her body rejoiced at the vision of the tightest, most perfectly shaped butt she'd ever seen. She'd bet the house that she could bounce a quarter to the ceiling off that ass.

Rafe snapped the sheet in the air, folded it precisely in half, matched all the edges and meticulously repeated the action until he'd formed a perfect square that he tucked in a dresser drawer. He turned to Grace.

Front side, back side, all sides in between—God, he was beautiful. Not in a *GQ* cover sort of way. The rugged angles and planes of his face gave him a less cultured, rawer sexual appeal.

Frowning as he was, he looked downright lethal and sexy, and so not amused with the smile she offered.

"When a man is naked in his bedroom, there are only two things he wants." Rafe's glacial eyes would've turned Grace's breath frosty if she could actually breathe. "Sleep and sex."

"Technically," she said, finding her voice, relieved it didn't squeak. "We're in your living room. The bedroom's over there." Tipping her head toward the Murphy bed less than ten feet away, she stood. "Are you suggesting we change locations?"

Rafe's breath audibly stuck in his throat. He stared at

the rumpled bed and swallowed hard. His gaze jumped to her, his eyes wide and uncertain.

"Considering you don't like me, we won't need the bed for sex and I've had enough sleep."

"I never said I didn't like you." The low, gravelly rasp in his voice caused tiny bumps to pebble her skin.

"So, you like me but don't want to be friends?" Grace padded around the coffee table to stand directly in front of him. His silent breaths were as hard and fast as her staccato heartbeat. "Not seeing the logic there."

"You're not the type of friend I need."

"Too bad. I come with fantastic benefits." She poked him dead center in the chest. "Get dressed. I have things to do today, and you're not on the list."

Chapter 4

Testosterone and a slew of wolfan hormones stormed Rafe's veins. Burning up all his restraint, Rafe stood perfectly still as Grace moved lithely out of the room with her hips sashaying in an erotic sway that beckoned both the man and wolf.

God, she was pretty. Long, shiny hair the color of corn silk. Bright green eyes that put polished emeralds to shame. Soft golden skin and an athletic body with just the right amount of curve. None of which he should've noticed. And yet, he had, and more.

She had a ready smile and a kind heart toward people and animals. He liked her spunk, more than he should.

And she smelled really good, too.

Another time, another place. Another life. She could've been the one.

But, he'd had a true mate, bonded heart and soul, and he'd lost her.

He wasn't arrogant enough to believe it could happen twice. Besides, he wasn't compatible with a human female.

Unlike Brice, whose grandmother was human, Rafe came from a purebred line. He'd inherited no human traits. Any he had were learned from Doc.

Since childhood, Rafe wanted to do right by the man who raised him. He'd modeled Doc's manner, his style, his philosophies. He might have followed his father's career path if he could've overcome his aversion to hospitals.

He hated the gut-churning scents that permeated the air. Fear, sorrow, sickness, desperation and death.

Grace's human senses weren't developed enough for her to detect the smells as acutely as he could, but she seemed to dislike hospitals as much as he did. Last night, he couldn't, in good conscience, leave her there overnight when she clearly didn't want to be there.

When he'd brought her home, he'd expected her to drill him about his abrupt decline of her offer of friendship a few months ago. Instead, she was gracious, respectful and annoyingly considerate.

She'd even gifted him with genuine smiles as if he'd never hurt her feelings that day. He knew he had.

But, he'd done what was necessary, pushing her away. Establishing a boundary. For her safety and his well-being.

Only she still ended up hurt and he was still drawn to her in ways that defied reason.

He needed to reinforce the no-friend zone and stay the hell out of her way.

Rafe pinched his sore ear, then drew back his hand and stared at the tiny drop of blood smeared on his thumb pad.

His stomach rolled.

Ah, hell!

Grace had not claimed him.

One, she had no idea what a bite meant to a Wahya. Hell, she didn't even know what they were.

Two, they weren't having sex when the bite occurred. It wouldn't have taken much to physically tip the balance toward consummation, but close only counted with horseshoes and hand grenades, not claiming a mate.

Three, a human couldn't legitimately claim a Wahya. Only a Wahyan bite during sex could establish a mate-claim.

A mate-bond, well, that was an entirely different matter. He doubted he and Grace were compatible enough for the ethereal connection to spark, so he had no cause to worry. Whatever was between them was purely physical.

Rafe knuckled his fingers in his hair and sucked in a deep breath to clear his head. Unfortunately, Grace's scent permeated the room, overpowering his heightened senses, damn near swaying him to abandon all reason, give into primal urges and bed her hard, fast and forever.

Only forever wasn't as long as he once believed. Forever with his former mate hadn't even lasted his lifespan.

Rafe closed his eyes, willed his heart to stop racing and his body to cool. He had to get Grace out of his home and out of his system.

Without one window in the apartment, he was going to have a helluva time getting rid of her scent.

He pulled on a gray T-shirt and dark blue coveralls. Sitting on the edge of the bed, he put on his socks and work boots. He stared at the rumpled sheets, rich with Grace's intoxicating scent, then stripped the bedding. Her phone tumbled to the floor. After pocketing the device, he folded the Murphy bed into the wardrobe. Next, he grabbed a clean, white button-down shirt and the bundle of sheets, and walked down the narrow corridor to find Grace.

He hesitated at the doorway to the kitchenette. The walls were painted the same flat gray color as the concrete floor. A 1950s-style white Formica table with chrome hairpin legs and two matching chairs sat in the middle of the small room.

On her toes with her back to him, Grace leaned against the single basin sink. To her left, a tiny dish drainer on the counter held one black mug, one plate, one fork, one spoon, one knife. To her right, was his small microwave. In the space where a dishwasher would normally go, Rafe had wedged a dorm-size refrigerator. And instead of a stove, he had installed a stacking washer and dryer in the corner.

Grace muttered, opening the cupboards above the sink.

Regrettably, all Rafe's pantry had to offer were three cans of sardines, half a loaf of bread, a bag of chips and a container of beef jerky.

"I'm all out of porridge, Goldilocks."

Grace jumped. "Jeezus." She turned toward him, clutching her chest. "Wear a bell or something. My heart almost stopped."

Rafe clenched his jaw to stop himself from admitting that he knew CPR. Neither of them needed to think about mouth-to-mouth anything. Especially since her light pink tank top fit her like a second skin and she was braless.

"Put this on." He tossed her the button-down shirt.

She pressed it to her face and sniffed. A curious pride pearled in his chest at the innocent gesture of her scenting his clothes.

"Hey." Her eyes widened when she realized he was watching. "I'm making sure it's clean."

"I know how to do laundry."

"Knowing how and doing it are two different things." She shoved her arms into the sleeves.

Rafe dumped the sheets into the washer, dropped in a detergent pod and turned on the machine. He pivoted on his heels with a ta-da, but she was too busy fussing with the buttons on the shirt to notice.

"Nerves from last night?" He waved aside her trembling hands to finish the buttons for her.

"Caffeine withdrawal." She held her arms out for him to roll up the sleeves. "I usually have three cups before nine a.m. I'm a little behind schedule this morning."

"It's almost noon." He finished her sleeves.

"Explains the killer headache." She rubbed the bridge of her nose. "I couldn't find the coffee or the pot."

"Don't drink it. Don't own one." He thumbed aside the blond strands curtaining the superficial cut at her temple.

The slight wound had scabbed and a dark-purple goose egg had formed. His gut tightened.

It was only a minor concussion, but the fact that she'd sustained an injury because of him made him sick to his stomach.

"I need coffee, now! Isn't there a diner across the street?" Her ponytail swished as she wandered out of the kitchen.

He followed her down the lighted corridor. There was something about her wearing his clothes that made his insides warm and his heart kick a possessive beat.

"I don't know how you can live in this concrete bear cave."

"If I were an animal, it wouldn't be a bear, Goldilocks." He pushed open the heavy metal door.

"Let me guess. A wolf?" She ducked beneath his arm and stepped into the R&L Automotive Services side of the building.

"Yep, but he wouldn't like being closed in."

"Do you?"

"No, but I have a severe insomnia. When I converted the storage room into a living space, I decided not to cut windows into the cinder block walls. I didn't want outside light or noise to bother me when I'm trying to sleep."

"So the pills on the coffee table help you sleep?"

"Yep." Although they weren't very effective. Nothing seemed to be since he stopped drinking himself into oblivion.

Rafe led Grace through the unused customer service area. People preferred to waltz in and out of the work area to see him. He opened the glass door that was next to a large viewing window. Ushering Grace into the garage, he jabbed the panel of buttons on the wall. The bay doors squawked, retracting to allow in streams of sunlight.

"It doesn't look too bad." She stared at her car on the

rack. "It won't take long to hammer out the bumper and fix the flat, right?"

"The right front side is demolished. The bumper has to be replaced. I want to change out the brakes and check all the operating systems. It's gonna take a while before you get it back."

"Great." Her voice sounded low and flat but her stomach growled as loud as any wolfan's would when half starved. She pressed her hands to her belly. "Sorry." She flashed an embarrassed grin. "I only had a salad for supper and my midnight snack splattered all over the interior of my car." She sighed. "It's going to stink, isn't it?"

"I cleaned the interior after you fell asleep the second time." He'd needed the distraction after her hysterical scream had flooded him with adrenaline, and holding her until the effects of her nightmare faded had drowned him in hormones.

However, he'd run out of steam before he had a chance to tackle the pile of magazines and books and whatever else she'd stowed in the backseat.

"Thanks." Gratitude shimmered in Grace's big green eyes and his heart skipped a beat. "How much will the repairs cost? Wait, I don't want to know. I have a high insurance deductible. Just get it running so I can make it back to Knoxville."

"You won't pay a penny. My wolf would be dead if you hadn't swerved."

"Your wolf? You own a wolf?"

"It's a Co-op thing," Rafe said carefully. "No one actually owns the wolves, we're more like handlers. Mine caused your accident so I'm responsible for the damages. Some of the work I'll do myself, but I'll send the car to a shop in Hiawassee for the bodywork. Paint fumes make me sick."

"I don't know what to say." A grateful smile softened the worry in her eyes.

"I'm just glad you and the wolf are okay." He offered her his hand. Why? He had no idea. Because he should've been pushing her out of the R&L and out of his life instead of providing her a physical connection.

She stared at his open palm, roughened with calluses. "How did this happen?" Her fingertips traced the scar running from his thumb to his wrist.

His breathing went wonky. Too much air, too little air. It seemed his lungs had forgotten how to function.

"Stepped on a piece of glass." He swallowed a gulp.

"Most people cut their foot when stepping on glass. How did you manage doing it with your hand?" A soft breath caught in her throat. "You weren't drunk, were you?"

Well, that was like a stab to the gut. At least he covered the gasp with a sigh.

Small town, big gossip. He should've known Grace would've heard more details about his life through the grapevine than he was comfortable with her knowing.

"I was twelve." He shook his hand free of her touch. "I didn't start drinking until after my wife died."

"I'm sorry."

The second time in a matter of minutes that she'd said "sorry." He found it peculiar humans apologized for things they weren't responsible for doing and events they couldn't control.

"I tripped and fell on a piece of glass while playing in the sanctuary with my wolf." Although he had been in wolf form when he'd stepped on the shard. It was as close to the truth as he could come. Still, the tiny lie bothered him.

"You were playing with a wolf?" Grace's eyes widened. "Where was your father?"

"At the clinic." Rafe grunted. "He wasn't too happy that

night when he came home. Said I should've gotten stitches. But it healed fine."

"I hope he grounded you."

"Why?"

"Don't you think it's dangerous for children, or anyone for that matter, to play with wolves? They're wild animals and wild animals can turn vicious."

"The Co-op's wolves are different. Besides, my wolf and I are bonded. He could never hurt me."

Rafe steered Grace out of one of the open bays and to the right. She needed to learn about Wahyas sooner rather than later. As the Alphena-in-waiting's best friend, the secret could be detrimental to their relationship and it could put Grace in a dangerous predicament.

"I can't believe you were playing with a wolf when you were twelve." Grace shook her head. "Please tell me you weren't naked."

"Nudity is a natural part of my life. So is my wolf. It's the same for other Co-opers."

"So far, you're the only one I've seen naked in the middle of the road. Should I expect to see others?"

Not if the wolfan expects to keep his cock and balls attached to his groin.

"What?" Grace's pert little nose wrinkled as she looked up at him.

Every cell in Rafe's body went on alert.

She shouldn't have heard his thoughts. In human form, Wahyas didn't manifest telepathic abilities.

Except with their mates.

And Grace Olsen was definitely not his mate.

Chapter 5

The soft jingle of door chimes drowned in the sea of voices filling Mabel's Diner. The line for a table seemed endless. Headachy and jumpy, Grace needed coffee and she needed it now!

"A drive-through will be faster."

Try as she might, Grace couldn't push the six-foot man blocking the door out of the way.

"You need to eat."

"A drive-through has food. It's fast." She hiked her thumb over her shoulder. "It's going to be a long wait."

"It won't, I promise." Rafe's warm hands cupped her shoulders and he turned her around.

A shiver rolled along her spine as warmth spread through her body. Each time Rafe touched her, she felt this tingly boost, as if he was sharing his energy with her. A ridiculous notion since she barely knew the man.

The concussion must've affected her rational thinking.

"Rafe Wyatt!" A plump, seventyish woman with a bright red-dyed beehive hairdo slid off her stool behind the cash register and strolled toward them flapping her fingers in a give-me-a-hug gesture. "What brings you out this early?"

Early? It was lunchtime.

"Good to see you, Mabel." Rafe stood stoically throughout the elderly woman's demonstrative embrace.

"Who's your lady friend?" Mabel swung her head toward Grace. One of her painted-on eyebrows rose as her gaze traveled down the length of Grace and back up again. "Haven't seen you around. New in town?"

"Not exactly. I'm visiting friends." She shook Mabel's hand. "I'm Grace Olsen."

"Amazing Grace," Mabel sang. "That'll be easy to remember."

"Grace needs coffee and food," Rafe interrupted. "She was in an accident last night and hasn't eaten a decent meal since before supper yesterday."

"Gracious." Mabel's hand landed on her ample chest. "I wondered why she was dressed like that."

Grace clutched the front of the borrowed shirt she wore and looked around. Everyone's eyes were on her. "If you can't serve me in the restaurant, can I get something to go? Starting with coffee? Lots and lots of coffee?" A tank would be nice.

"Not serve you?" Mabel squawked. "I've never turned anyone away, and you're dressed just fine. We're all friends here." Mabel draped her arm over Grace's shoulders. She called to the woman wearing a Mabel's Diner T-shirt and jeans who whipped past them carrying a tray of dirty dishes and dumped them in a large gray bin. "Ronni, sit Rafe and Gracie at the table you just cleared. She's half starved. If she passes out, people will think I ran out of food."

"That would start a riot for sure," Ronni said. "Come with me."

She led them to an empty booth with a window view of the R&L's side wall and back lot.

Rafe sat opposite Grace and slid her the laminated menu tucked behind the napkin dispenser.

Ronni flipped over the coffee mug in front of Grace. "This is strong, bold and hot." She filled the mug nearly to the rim.

"Great." Grace dumped four packets of sugar into the steaming drink.

"Always said a woman likes her coffee the way she likes her men. I guess you like 'em a little on the sweet side, too."

"Sometimes." Grace took her first sip—gulp, actually—and it burned her tongue and all the way down her throat, but when it hit her stomach, her entire body sighed.

Ronni, about ten years older than Grace, had strawberry-blond hair and eyes the exact color of Rafe's cobalt blue.

"Are you two related?" Grace blurted without thinking. "Sorry. I've met people all over the world. Until Rafe, I'd never met anyone with eyes his particular shade of blue. They're quite striking and unforgettable."

Okay, she'd said way too much. She downed another mouthful of coffee before the lack of caffeine loosened her filter again.

"Ronni's my cousin," Rafe said.

"Nice to meet you." Grace extended her hand.

Ronni wiped her fingers on the half apron tied around her waist and accepted Grace's handshake. The deep lines around the waitress's eyes and mouth spoke of a hard life, or hard living. Either way, she wasn't as happy as her generous smile intimated. "Same here."

"I don't remember seeing you at Brice's party." It was at least nine months ago, but Grace never forgot a face.

"Alex and I have only been here a few weeks. My husband passed and Rafe was kind enough to give us a place to live and a new start."

"I'm so sorry for your loss." Grace's heart constricted.

"Thank you." Ronni offered her a strained smile. "Haven't seen you before, but I'm still getting to know everyone. Are you with the Co-op?"

"No. Aren't you?"

"Not yet, but we're working on it." Ronni pulled a vinyl holder from her apron pocket and flipped it open.

Grace pointed at the photo clipped inside. "Is that Alex?"

"Yep." Ronni grinned. "He's a good kid. I couldn't ask for one better."

Grace studied the photo of the tawny-haired teenager with a smile as broad as his mother's. Unfortunately, he also had the same harsh lines etched into his young face. "Handsome boy."

"Smart, too. He's my reason for living." Ronni lovingly smoothed the frayed edges of the picture. "Now, what would you like to eat?"

"Can I order the Belgian waffle even though it's lunchtime?" Grace pointed at the item on the menu.

"Breakfast is served all day."

"Great. I'll have it with the strawberries and whipped cream, and chocolate syrup on the side—if you have any."

"Chocolate?" Ronni gave her an odd look.

"I know it's weird, but I didn't get my daily dose last night."

"I'll ask Al to find ya some. Anything else?"

"Nope."

"You need something with protein," Rafe said. "You already have the shakes."

"From lack of caffeine, but I'm catching up." Grace took another gulp of coffee.

Rafe shook his head.

"Do you want the Co-op breakfast or lunch special?" Ronni asked him.

"Breakfast."

"I'll put a rush on your orders."

Rafe nodded and Ronni hurried to the kitchen.

"Is Ronni dating someone?"

"Not that I'm aware of." Rafe gave her a funny frown. "She lost her husband only a few months ago. I don't think she's looking for a new one yet."

"Ronni said she wasn't a member of the Walker's Co-op yet."

"Walker's *Run* Co-op," Rafe said. "The land and neighboring areas associated with the Co-op are called Walker's Run."

"Whatever it's called, Cassie told me the only way to join the Co-op was by birth or marriage." Grace finished her coffee, wishing she had turned over Rafe's cup and had Ronni fill it, as well. "I wasn't born here, so I thought I had to marry someone to become a member."

"Is that why you want to get to know me?"

"What?" Grace's cheeks heated. "No, not at all. I've been married and I don't want to repeat that mistake."

An unplanned pregnancy. A quickie marriage that ended in an abrupt divorce after she lost the baby.

Grace rubbed the small white infinity tattoo on her wrist.

Rafe frowned. "You were married?"

"Not relevant." She really could use another cup of coffee. "You're Brice's friend. I'm Cassie's friend. I thought it would be nice if you and I were friends. That's all."

"I don't want to be your friend, Grace."

She felt a stab of disappointment, same as before. "I appreciate your candor." She didn't really, but what else could she say?

She heard the muffled sound of her brother's ringtone. Out of habit, she checked her pockets even though she had none.

Rafe pulled her phone from his pocket.

"You're a life saver." She read the text messages. All was well and she sighed in relief. Grace replied she would call later.

"My brother," she said in response to Rafe's curious gaze. "He checks in every few hours because I worry if I don't hear from him." This time *she* had worried *him* after not responding to his last two texts.

"Why?"

"Matt was paralyzed in an IED explosion last year. When he returned to the States, I left Seattle to help him through the extensive rehabilitation process. He's fairly independent now. He's even shopping around for a suitable car that can be equipped with hand controls." She'd offered to put them in her Beetle and share the car with him, but the interior was really too small to accommodate him for an extended period.

Besides, Matt was moving on with his life and didn't need his big sister hanging around so much anymore.

"Let me know the make and model he's looking for. I know people who get cars at auction and I can install the controls for him."

"Here ya go." Ronni slid Grace a plate with a large Belgian waffle topped with strawberries and whipped cream, with a small bowl of chocolate sauce on the side.

She handed Rafe a glass of milk, a plate of scrambled eggs, grits, and two biscuits buried beneath creamy sausage gravy, a plate with a thick slice of country ham, four bacon strips, and two fat sausage links, and a plate of blueberry pancakes slathered with butter.

"You're going to eat all that?" Grace felt her arteries clog from sitting near all the saturated fats.

"If he doesn't, I'll be surprised." Ronni refilled Grace's coffee mug.

"You are a goddess." Grace lifted the steaming cup to her face, inhaling the rich, robust aroma.

"First time I've been called that. Thanks, hon." Ronni looked at Rafe. "Holler if you need me."

After doctoring her coffee, Grace drizzled chocolate sauce over her waffle. "Must be nice to have cousins. My dad is an only child. My mom is a twin, but her sister died when they were three." Grace took a bite of her waffle. The super sweetness made her empty stomach lurch.

"Ronni and I met a few weeks ago. Until then, I didn't know I had any blood relatives." Rafe continued eating.

"You took in total strangers?"

"They're family."

Rafe was turning out to be more complicated than the arrogant jerk she'd assumed him to be, which made her want to know him all the more. So what if he didn't want to be actual friends? After last night, he was officially in the league of special acquaintances. She could work with that.

Grace ate another bite of her waffle. Ordinarily, sweets didn't bother her, but the chocolate sauce might've been overkill. She pushed her plate aside.

Rafe lifted his gaze from her plate to her face. "Something wrong with the waffle?"

"Too sweet."

"I told you to order something with protein."

Rafe dumped his breakfast meats onto the platter with his pancakes. Then he scooped a portion of his eggs and grits onto the emptied plate and added two strips of bacon and half of the slice of ham.

"Eat. Every bite." He pushed the newly prepared plate toward Grace and resumed eating the remainder of his breakfast.

She shook her fork at him. "I don't find bossy men appealing at all." And if she wasn't suddenly famished again and practically drooling, she would've pushed away the plate.

"Is that so?" Rafe's hands stilled, his chewing ground to a slow halt, and he swallowed. He gave her a long, leisurely look.

Her skin warmed. "Yes."

"I am what I am, sweetheart. And you do find me appealing."

"Yeah, right."

He brandished a cocky little smile and his eyebrows twitched.

Heat flashed through Grace's body. In defiance, she casually crossed her legs. Men relegated to the league of special acquaintances were not supposed to get her hot and bothered. Maybe she needed to rethink his classification.

Chapter 6

Rafe sped toward the Walker's Run Resort. He'd gladly pay any fine as long as he delivered Grace before he did something stupid.

The conglomeration of smells in the diner had masked her true scent, giving him a chance to breathe and relax.

Closed inside the tow truck, though, her soft, feminine musk engulfed his senses. His skin prickled with awareness and his thoughts turned to long, luscious kisses and dangerously indulgent caresses.

He lowered the windows, hoping the rush of cool air would clear his head. A slight shiver shook Grace's shoulders but she didn't complain. Humming softly to herself, she continued staring out the window.

Hands clamped on the steering wheel, he steeled himself against the urge to pull off the road, haul her against him and warm her with his heat while his hands roamed her curves, preferably while they were both naked.

She'd slept in his bed, worn his clothes and shared his food. To a Wahyan male, she was practically his.

Only she wasn't. She couldn't be.

He was merely horny.

Ever since his mate died, he'd been celibate.

Moon-fucks didn't count. Wahyas needed sex during the full moon to keep their hormones in balance.

Out of necessity, he and Loretta Presley, a widow with three kids, had become exclusive moon-fuck partners. Their encounters were always in wolf form and they avoided each other socially, as agreed, to ensure no emotional entanglements.

Almost two weeks past the last full moon, Rafe shouldn't feel the urge for sex. Yet Grace's scent bombarded him with such tantalizing force he could think of little else.

Different from the animalistic drive the full moon unleashed, the pull toward Grace was tangled in pure, unadulterated desire.

He punched the buttons on the console to turn on the heater and sliced the vents to blow in her direction. A blast of heat blew back the loose strands of her hair, revealing the discolored Ping-Pong-ball-sized lump at her temple.

She gave him a side glance, then adjusted the vent so that the warm air hit her arms.

His stiffly curled fingers made it difficult to turn the wheel. The sooner he and Grace parted company, the better off he'd be. The last thing he wanted was her scent mucking up his life.

He parked in front of the Walker's Run Resort and hopped out of the vehicle. A pack sentinel, working as a valet, reached for the passenger door. An instinctual warning growl rolled from Rafe's throat. The barely twenty-something wolfan backed away.

Grace's warm fingers clutched Rafe's outstretched hand as she stepped down from the vehicle. The energy sparked from the touch buzzed up his arm, down his spine and spread into every nerve.

It wasn't the kind of electrical surge that could drop a man to the ground in convulsions. This was a gentle quiver of warmth, the kind that slowly saturated the skin, seeped into every cell, thawed the deepest, darkest, most frozen places within and, therefore, was the most dangerous vibration of all.

Fidgeting with the bag slung across her body, Grace

strolled past the valet. "Hi, Jimmy. No more drive-through runs for me. The Beetle is out of commission for a while."

"Anytime you want something, give me a holler. Twenty-four seven. I'll be at your beck and call." Jimmy grinned with far too much interest.

Rafe Gibbs-smacked him as he passed. "Not necessary or recommended."

As his and Grace's steps synchronized, Rafe's hand gravitated to her lower back as if touching her was as natural as breathing.

The scent of cinnamon and cloves greeted them inside the resort. A few people with luggage in tow stood at the guest services counter. An older man lounged in a seating area reading the paper. The amicable chatter from the dining room didn't mask the subtle hum of the descending elevator.

The doors parted with a swish.

"Grace!" Cassie Walker, a petite, abundantly pregnant woman with curly red hair, stepped out. "I've been looking for you. Where have you been?"

Her gaze traveled up and down Grace and cut to him. "Rafe? Why is she wearing pajama pants and your shirt?"

"Long story," Grace said. "Before I begin, trust me when I say I'm okay."

"Why doesn't that make me feel better?" Cassie's brow creased.

"Doc said Grace needs to rest. Would you make sure she gets it?"

"Doc?" Cassie's eyes widened. "What happened?"

"A small fender bender, nothing serious." Grace's gaze lingered on Rafe and he suddenly didn't want to leave.

"Call me if you need anything. My number is in your phone." An impulsive act last night that might bite him in the ass sooner rather than later.

Walking away, he consciously forced his muscles to

relax instead of conspiring against him to make him look over his shoulder.

"Rafe, wait!"

Not the voice he would've expected.

He turned and waited for Cassie to catch up.

"What's up, Red?"

"I won't ask about what happened between you and Grace last night. She'll tell me all about it."

Rafe hoped she wouldn't mention his state of undress. The fewer who knew that tidbit, the better. It was bad enough Tristan Durrance, the responding sheriff deputy, and a pack sentinel, had arrived before Doc got there with an old pair of sweats for Rafe to wear. He expected it would be a long time before Tristan would let him forget getting caught bare-ass by a human female.

"I hope you used the opportunity to get to know her a little better," Cassie continued. "Grace is like a sister to me and she's become an important part of mine and Brice's lives. Just as you are."

"What are you getting at, Red?"

Laughter rose above the soft chatter of guests in the lobby. Rafe's gaze slid to Grace, directing a family into silly poses as she took their picture next to an indoor totem pole with several wolf heads carved into the wood.

"It's okay to let people into your life again," Cassie said. "People like Grace. She's fun, and kind, and never meets a stranger."

"I'm managing fine with the way things are."

"Managing isn't the same as living." She touched his arm. "Trust me, I know."

"Here you go, little mama." Grinning, Grace held out a cup of hot tea she'd made in the microwave. Her posh suite at the Walker's Run Resort was nothing short of a small apartment equipped with a kitchenette, a cozy living room, and a luxury bedroom with a balcony view of the forested mountainside. All compliments of Cassie's in-laws, Gavin and Abigail Walker, the resort's owners.

"Thank you." Cassie, her best childhood friend, accepted the drink. They'd reconnected through social media after Cassie had married.

The internet was Grace's lifeline. Not only was the internet vital to her web design business, it helped her stay connected with friends all over the world. She needed it as much as she needed coffee.

But, moving to Knoxville last year to help her brother had put Grace within driving distance of Cassie. She and Brice had visited while Matt was at the rehabilitation center. After Matt's discharge, and once he was comfortable staying a few days by himself, Grace had accepted Cassie's father-in-law's open invitation to stay at the resort.

Since Cassie had no family after her mom's passing, Gavin said Cassie needed a "sister."

How could Grace say no?

Now she had her own room—dubbed the Grace Olsen Suite, available anytime she visited.

"Want anything else?"

"I'm good." Cassie tucked a loose red ringlet behind her ear. "I hate that you're doting on me. You have a concussion."

"It's only a bump and I have a hard head." Grace sat on the couch, drawing her bare feet beneath her.

"I can't believe you saw Rafe naked." Cassie stretched her legs and propped her tiny, swollen feet on the coffee table. "Funny, Brice was naked when we met, too."

Cassie rubbed her pregnant belly. "See where that led me?"

"Don't jinx me. I will adore the little girl right there," she pointed at Cassie's belly, "but I don't do serious relationships and I don't want to be a single mom." Grace had seen how hard it was on her mother, single parenting every time her father was deployed.

"I never planned on this, either. Yet here I am and I couldn't be happier."

"It's different for you. You're planted here." Grace fluffed her pillow. "I've never lived in a place longer than a few years."

Cassie sipped her tea. "Maico was no different from any other of the half-dozen towns my mom dragged me to. I expected we'd be here for eighteen months tops before we moved on. Then, she died, I had nowhere to go and Maico became home."

"Because you got stuck here. Once Matt gets on his feet again—figuratively speaking, I'll be free to live anywhere."

"What about here? Maico is a great place." A hopeful smile lit Cassie's face, just like the one she'd given Grace when they were seven and Cassie had asked her to be friends. "Give it a chance to become your home, too."

Growing up in military housing, Grace had always craved a real home. A place where she could put nails in walls to hang her pictures and posters. But, every time she started getting comfortable, her family would move again. Eventually, Grace stopped unpacking her suitcases and boxes. Why bother if she was going to repack them anyway?

Cassie tucked an errant red curl behind her ear. "I want you around for Brenna's sake, when she finally gets here."

"No matter where I am, I'll only be a text away."

"You can't hold her over the internet."

Grace clenched her jaw. Many of her childhood milestones had had to be video relayed to her father overseas or emailed. She thought it sucked then. It would suck if she did the same to Cassie's baby.

"I'm only a few hours away."

"For now. How long until you move away?" Cassie's

red brows angled over her eyes and Grace hoped it wasn't bad luck to make a pregnant woman frown. "I remember you used to complain about moving so often. When you grew up, you wanted a big two-story house, a husband and six kids."

"I got used to moving. Now it's in my blood and I get antsy if I stay too long in one place." Grace shook her head. "I must've been crazy to want six kids. I have a hard enough time keeping up with myself. As for a husband, I'll stick to friends with benefits for now."

"How's that working for you?"

"I'm in a slump." More of a Sahara dry spell, actually. She'd left her sex buddy in Seattle and hadn't had much opportunity to meet anyone in Knoxville.

"Any sparks with Rafe last night?"

"If we were beakers in a chemistry lab we would've blown up the building."

"He's a great guy. Good-looking. Dependable." An impish grin broke on Cassie's face and she rubbed her palms.

"Sometimes the packaging doesn't match what's inside."

"Rafe's does." Cassie's face pinked. "Not that I've actually seen his package."

"He has a mighty fine ass." Grace laughed.

"You should explore that." Cassie's flush deepened. "I mean, your attraction to him. He really is one of the good ones."

"So was Derek, or so I thought."

"Rafe isn't Derek." Cassie set her cup aside. "Trust me. You've never dated someone like Rafe."

"Uh, no." Grace shook her head and a heavy weight settled in the pit of her stomach. "I prefer sex with men who actually like me."

"Why do you think he doesn't like you?"

"'I don't want to be your friend, Grace.'" She mimicked Rafe's deadpan delivery.

"I told Brice the same thing." Cassie giggled, pointing her index fingers at her belly.

"Not funny."

"Don't analyze Rafe. He says exactly what he means and only what he means. Simple, concise, no hidden context. So, he doesn't want to be friends. He left the door wide open to be something else."

"Not interested." A smidgen of a fib she'd stand by.

"I wish you would put Derek behind you and move forward with your life."

"I have, and I'm a pro at moving."

"You sound like my mother." The corners of Cassie's mouth sagged. "Imogene died never finding her happiness. She ran from life instead of making it her own."

"My life is my own. I have a comfortable, portable web design business and I've traveled the world. What more could I want?"

"Someone meaningful to join you on those travels." Cassie rubbed slow circles across her abdomen. "Someone you love to the moon, someone who loves you beyond it."

"I'm happy you've found that with Brice." Grace swallowed to soothe the burn in her throat. "Be happy that I'm happy with the life I live."

Most days. Sometimes the loneliness ate at her.

"Still have your old dream book?"

"Yes." A school project from their days in Mrs. Haverty's art class. "I'm surprised you remember it."

Grace had carted the old scrapbook with her on every move. The opening pages displayed pictures of the perfect house, a two-story stone and log-plank house with floor to ceiling windows. Clippings of an antique apothecary, a Queen Anne couch, Tiffany lamps, and everything else she thought would make a perfect home filled the rest.

"It's filled with the dreams of a seven-year old," Cassie said.

It was much more. Grace had added to it over the years, up until she'd lost the baby and Derek asked for a divorce.

"Burn it." Cassie's pointed look meant business.

"I'm not burning it."

The tattered scrapbook served as a reminder. Broken hearts, broken dreams and broken trust were all she got from the men in her past. No way would she trust one with her future.

Chapter 7

"I expected you in my office yesterday." Gavin Walker's voice scraped down Rafe's spine.

The screwdriver slipped and stabbed Rafe's right hand. He dropped the rail glide he was trying to fasten to the end panel of the changing table. Cursing, he shoved the bloody knuckle into his mouth. A strong, iron taste pricked his tongue.

At sixty, the Alpha wolf still had a keen nose, agile steps and a paw in everything happening within his territory.

Apparently Rafe's senses were skewed since he hadn't heard or scented Gavin's approach. He blamed Grace for mucking up his nose and filling his head with distracting thoughts.

He'd hoped the nursery project would keep him too busy to think about how yesterday, he'd almost drowned in the rich green depth of her eyes, or dwell on the rush of excitement he felt whenever she gifted him with a smile.

"Are you all right?" Gavin's gaze narrowed on him.

"Peachy." Rafe shook out his injured hand and picked up the wood screw that had fallen out of the precut hole.

"You were supposed to see me after safely delivering Grace to the resort. Maybe it slipped your mind."

It hadn't. Rafe simply didn't want to hear another lecture on being reckless and putting the past behind him. The pack needed to mind their own damn business and leave him the hell alone.

"I heard Grace went home with you after her accident. How did that go?"

Rafe fumbled the screw again.

Gavin was baiting him and Rafe wasn't interested in playing the Alpha's games, particularly if it involved Grace. "Your experience must've been pleasant, considering your butterfingers at my mention of her."

Gavin entered the room and sat in the rocker. He rested his hands across his waist and laced his fingers over his belt buckle. "Grace. A lovely woman, don't you think?"

Awareness flared in Rafe's body. He recalled the sweet musk of her true scent, the dimples produced by a real smile and the golden sheen of her shoulder-length hair.

Suddenly, he sensed the inexplicable gentleness of her presence and knew at that exact moment she was happy and safe.

Gavin's laughter disrupted the fragile connection that Rafe discounted as a figment of imagination. After all, how could he possibly know what Grace was feeling?

"With all due respect—"

"I doubt that." After all these years, the old wolf still had a burr in his paw about the time Rafe and Brice had painted Gavin's entire office in silly string. As boys, they'd faced a grueling inquisition. Neither of them had confessed culpability. Likely, they never would.

Rafe smiled, remembering the abject horror on Gavin's face when he saw their handiwork. A few remnants still remained on the exposed wood beams in the ceiling above his desk.

"Ask your question or make your point," Rafe said. "You wouldn't want your granddaughter's crib to fall apart because you distracted me while putting it together."

Gavin's thumb tapped his buckle in an aggravated cadence. "The sheriff's office is involved with Grace's accident."

"Tristan said he would file a clean report." Most notably, he promised to omit the detail of Rafe's nudity at the scene.

"The new sheriff isn't Co-op friendly. Tristan mediates Co-op issues when he can, but it's putting him in an uncomfortable position with his employer. He thinks the sheriff is looking for a reason to investigate us."

"The pack has been good to the people of Maico."

"Humans are fickle. They can be swayed by bad press, especially when it preys on primal fears." Gavin's dark brows, a contrast to his snowy-white hair and short-cropped beard, slashed over his eyes. "I imposed the curfew to reduce friction between us and the sheriff's department. I will not allow rule breakers to jeopardize the safety of my pack."

"Alex wasn't the only wolfling to break curfew."

"I'm not only talking about the wolflings, Rafe. You shouldn't have been out as a wolf. The curfew also applies to you."

"Running the woods keeps me from drinking."

"Find another distraction." Gavin rocked forward, resting his elbows on his knees. "Better yet, find a mate."

"We're not having this discussion again."

"You need a mate, Rafe. A woman you can hold in your arms and make love to. A real woman. Not a memory. Let go of the past. Grab onto your future. If you don't—"

"Stop." Rafe held up his hand. The shattering of the mate-bond that he'd shared with Lexi had unleashed a maelstrom within him. She had been a balm to his restless nature. Now, he had to learn to manage without her. "I have let go, Gavin. I'll decide if or when I take another mate, not you."

Gavin gave a slight nod. "In the meantime, here's what I do expect from you. Stop working around the clock. You don't need the money."

True. After the demise of his birth pack, Rafe inherited everything belonging to his former pack mates. It wasn't a lot in the beginning, but Doc had wisely invested the funds for him. Now Rafe had enough money that he could retire, three or four times over.

"Establish reasonable business hours," Gavin continued, "and stick to them."

"I have a lot of work." Rafe liked to stay busy. Idle hands reached for bottles.

"Hire help, or refer customers to some of your trusted competitors."

Rafe wasn't inclined to do either. He'd turned a lot of business away during his drinking days. When he got sober most of his customers returned. He didn't want to reward their loyalty by handing them over to someone else.

"I'll let the pack know I've ordered you to cut back. If you don't, I'll shut you down. Understood?"

Rafe reluctantly nodded. Technically, the Co-op owned his business and every pack member's business.

Members tithed thirty percent of their income to the Co-op. In return, they received free housing, paid college expenses, free health care, and if they wanted to open their own business the Co-op paid to have it built and provided the start-up income.

"Good. With your workload reduced you'll have more time to devote to Alex. Start by picking him up before and after school. He's been truant. I want it stopped. He's also struggling with his schoolwork. Find him a tutor. Ronni's working toward her GED and I don't want Alex's shenanigans to derail her efforts."

Stunned, Rafe ran his hand across his chin, feeling the stubble he'd forgotten to shave. Other than Alex breaking curfew, Rafe had thought the boy was doing well. And, Ronni had never mentioned not having a high school diploma or working toward her GED.

As Alpha, Gavin knew everyone's business, but Rafe didn't like being caught unaware of his family's situation.

"I'll take care of Alex and help Ronni with whatever she needs."

"Now that's settled, let's talk about Grace."

"I'd rather not."

"She presents us with a delicate dilemma," Gavin began, as if Rafe had no objection to the topic. "She and Cassie have become close over the last year. Close enough that it's inevitable for Grace to discover what we are."

"Tell her before it becomes a problem. She seems trustworthy." A woman who would give up her life to move cross-country to care for her disabled brother knew a thing or two about loyalty.

"I would prefer Grace to bond with one of our pack's eligible males. A mateship is the easiest and most expedient way to introduce her into our world, but she's proven quite difficult—"

Good for you, sweetheart.

"—in the matchmaking arena."

Rafe chuckled.

"Did you say something?"

Rafe stayed silent, his ears tuning into the soft, limping footsteps coming down the hallway.

"Regardless of whether or not she accepts a mate," Gavin continued, "I will ask Grace to join the pack after my granddaughter is born."

Rafe wasn't surprised. This wasn't the first time Gavin had played hard, fast and loose with the pack's initiation rule. Doc was neither Wahya nor married to one. He'd been inducted into the pack simply because he was Gavin's best friend since their college days.

"After all, Grace will be my granddaughter's godmother. It's imperative to keep her close. To keep her safe."

"Why are you telling me this?" Although Rafe was close to the Alpha's son, he wasn't usually taken into the Alpha's confidence.

"Because you're the baby's godfather." Brice leaned in the doorway, all smiles and smugness.

"Like hell I am." Rafe was still putting his life back together. How could Brice think he'd make a suitable godparent?

"You're my best friend and Grace is Cassie's best friend." Brice flashed a very unwolfan-like smile.

"Find a new best friend," Rafe half-heartedly told Brice. Though, he was deeply touched by his friend's faith in him.

"How about Shane?" A gleam lit Gavin's eyes.

Rafe had to be careful not to over-tighten the screw and strip the threads. Shane MacQuarrie followed Tristan's wham-bam-thanks-for-the-good-time-ma'am creed. Grace deserved better and like it or not, Rafe felt a degree of protectiveness toward her.

"Personally, I think Shane has a better temperament than Rafe," Gavin continued smugly. "Since Shane and Grace already have a friendly rapport, a nudge or two in the right direction could turn their relationship into something more."

"Hell, no!" An unpleasant heat erupted from Rafe's core.

"Need some water to cool that temper?" Smiling, Brice shook his water bottle at him.

Rafe swallowed and held a breath deep in his chest until the echo of Brice's laughter subsided.

"Shane's too young and cocky," Rafe said more evenly. "He's all wrong for her."

"Perhaps." Gavin's gaze seemed to bore into Rafe's skin, making him more irritable. "I want Grace to get to know the pack. I'll arrange for her to enjoy a few select pack events. I'd prefer for her to attend with someone other than Cassie to avoid the appearance of nepotism."

"It is, isn't it?" Rafe returned to assembling the crib.

Gavin issued a warning growl.

Rafe bit back a smile and Brice covered his grin by

taking a drink of water. It was a nice feeling to ruffle the Alpha's fur.

"Considering you're indebted to Grace because she didn't kill you with her car," Gavin snapped, "no one will think twice about her showing up with you."

Rafe fumbled the screwdriver. "You want me to be her date?"

"Date, escort, guardian. The terms are fairly interchangeable." Gavin kept a steady gaze on Rafe.

"Not in my dictionary."

"Perhaps you prefer *friend*."

Brice mouthed, "With benefits." He held up his thumb.

Rafe had an urge to knock the goddamn twinkle out of his best friend's eyes.

"I want Grace to trust us, not fear us. Making friends among us will ease her anxiety when she finally learns what we are."

"Want her trust to us? Tell her the truth. The sooner the better," Rafe said. "Or else this entire scheme will blow up in your face."

Chapter 8

"Tighten 'em up, Pops." Rafe handed Brice a Phillips screwdriver so the father-to-be could fasten the last four screws into the crib.

Though miffed at his friend for involving him, Rafe understood the reason. The Alpha family was protecting their own. Cassie.

Cassie wanted Grace close. So, the Alpha family would move heaven and earth, and probably a little bit of hell, to see Grace safely settled in their midst. In a twisted, deranged way, the Alpha family had paid him a huge compliment.

He'd rather have free-range runs.

"Thanks, man." Brice beamed and tackled his token assignment.

After they inserted the mattress, Brice pulled a package out of the closet. "How about this?"

"What is it?" Rafe packed up his tools.

"Stuff the sales clerk said we had to have." Brice read the package description. "Crib sheet, coverlet, bumpers."

"Sorry, Walker. Bows and frills aren't my department." Rafe shook his head.

Brice frowned, placing the package on the crib Rafe had put together.

They broke down the boxes and stuffed the trash into a garbage bag. "Mom and Dad are out with friends tonight. I'm firing the grill to toss on some burgers for supper. We'll have plenty if you're hungry."

A wolfan was always ready to eat.

"Grace is joining us."

Dread and excitement competed in racing Rafe's heart. Part of him, the stupid part, wanted to see her again. The smart half wanted to get the hell out before she showed up.

"I've got work to catch up on. Maybe next time."

"There might not be a next time with Grace. You know what my dad is planning."

"It won't work."

"Cassie said there's a spark between you and Grace."

Rafe gave him an eat-shit look.

"My mistake." Brice's lopsided grin said he didn't think he was wrong at all. He grabbed an armful of trash.

Rafe snatched up the remaining garbage and followed him to the side entrance of Gavin and Abby Walker's home, their family quarters adjacent to the resort.

Brice stayed outside to light the grill. Rafe ducked inside to retrieve his toolbox.

"Rafe? What are you doing here?" Cassie met him in the corridor connecting the Alpha family's residence to the resort.

"Helping Brice with a project." Rafe's gaze skimmed the top of Cassie's head to his real target. Grace.

"Does he still have all his fingers and toes?" Cassie's eyes widened against her pale skin.

"He did, but he's outside lighting the grill." Rafe's gaze jumped back to Grace.

Her hair looked professionally sleek. He liked it better in a mussed ponytail. She wore denim shorts with a tiny bit of lace at the hem and a pale pink top with little bows on the capped sleeves. Her nails, painted a dark pink with a black swirly pattern at the tips, matched the toes peeking through the openings of her low-heeled sandals.

"Hey, Sunshine." Brice strode toward them.

Cassie beamed as he wrapped her in his arms for a big, juicy kiss.

Brice urgently hiked his thumb behind Cassie's back and gave Rafe the bug eye.

"Come with me." Rafe clasped Grace's hand and led her inside the small nursery the Walkers wanted set up for their daughter.

Grace's lightly glossed lips parted in a soft sigh. She trailed her hand over the newly assembled furniture. "This was your project?"

Rafe nodded, swallowing the lump in his throat at the longing he saw in Grace's eyes.

Grace gripped the crib's cherrywood rails, and for a second, Rafe thought tears shimmered in her eyes. "She'll love it."

"Do you know what to do with this?" He handed her the packaged bedding set.

Grace's rich, full-bodied laugh did something funny to Rafe's stomach. "Two grown men couldn't figure out how to put sheets on a baby mattress?"

"I sleep on a couch."

Grace's cheeks pinked and her tongue peeked between her soft lips. "How could I forget?"

Her heated gaze licked his body, inch by tortuous inch, just as it had when he stood in front of her, naked. His body reacted the same as it had yesterday. His muscles clenched, his breath quickened, and his blood felt too hot for his veins. Trapped behind the zipper, his cock strained against its confines.

He spun her toward the crib. "Hurry."

Grace quickly tucked the corners, smoothed the fabric and tied perfect little bows.

Grace's eyes watered and Cassie burst into tears when she entered the room. Rafe thought it peculiar human females cried when happy, particularly when Cassie did it. She had never been overly emotional. Pregnancy had changed her.

"It's beautiful." She moved from Brice's arms to squeeze Rafe's hands. "Thank you."

Sorrow simmered behind the joy in her eyes. "You will come more often to see us? To see the baby?"

Rafe tipped his head. The loss of his child didn't mean he couldn't be happy for theirs.

"Well, then." Brice clapped his hands together. "You can start by joining us for supper."

"Oh goody," Grace whispered in Rafe's ear. "I won't be a third wheel tonight, after all."

She playfully bumped against him and the jolt of her touch unleashed a flood of wolfan hormones into his bloodstream. The sudden rush deafened his ears and he had the sense of tumbling down a waterfall. His lungs tightened, his heart pounded, his skin dampened.

He locked gazes with Brice. Instead of offering a lifeline, the damn wolf smiled.

Riotous laughter and curses rose above the roar of racing street cars. Hand drying a plate, Grace peeked out of the kitchen at the two formidable men perched on the edge of the couch, hunkered over the game controllers gripped in their tight-fisted hands.

The big-screen TV anchored to the wall in the Walkers' den flashed images of a high-speed street race. One car tapped the other, knocking it into a tailspin.

"What the fuck?" Brice's arm swung out, punching Rafe's shoulder with enough force to knock an ordinary man clean off the couch. Rafe's body absorbed the shock with barely a ripple. However, his virtual car careened off course, crashed into a building and exploded.

"Keep your paws in the game, Walker, and off me," Rafe

snapped, although Grace saw no true menace in the narrowed gaze he speared at his friend.

"All's fair in love and war and my toys," Brice chuckled.

Grace returned to the sink. "Do men ever grow up?"

"Depends on the man. A good one knows how and when to step up, and will." Cassie absently rubbed her belly. "It's good to see Rafe having fun."

"At least, he is now." Grace placed the freshly dried plate in the cabinet and laid the damp towel across the empty dish drainer. "He was so tense during supper."

Sitting beside him at the table, Grace had felt his tension in palpable waves. His muscles had been primed and pumped, as if he'd been waiting for the chance to dart out the door.

"He's never accepted a dinner invitation from us until tonight. Maybe he wasn't sure what to expect." Cassie waddled to the kitchen archway. Her head tilted as she watched the men play their game.

When she turned to Grace, a smile twitched her lips. "Maybe Rafe is here because he wants to get to know you."

"That's ridiculous." Grace grabbed her glass of iced tea from the counter and chugged a big gulp.

"You batted your eyes to get him to stay for supper." Cassie made a sympathy face, dramatically exaggerating the opening and closing of her eyes.

Grace tossed the dish towel at her. "I did not."

They both laughed.

Cassie carried the nearly forgotten condiments to the refrigerator. "I think he liked your travel stories."

Grace had more than a few about the Swiss Alps, Mt. Fuji, Pompeii, Madrid, the rain forest, the Luxor—the real one, not the one in Vegas. Other places such as Beaufort, San Diego, Arlington, Jacksonville, Okinawa, Guam and Germany had been "home" during her father's military career.

Brice and Cassie had peppered her with curious questions during dinner. Rafe had remained silent.

"He seemed bored to me."

Cassie wiggled in her seat to get comfortable. "If Rafe was bored, he would've left once he finished eating."

"He kept his head down and his eyes on his plate." Grace eased into the chair across the table from Cassie. "Not a great endorsement for interest."

"Eating is serious business for men like Rafe, but it doesn't mean he wasn't paying attention," Cassie said. "Remember when your napkin fell off the table? Rafe caught it midair, folded it, and placed it next to your plate."

"He has quick reflexes."

"The point is that he noticed." Cassie's face lit up with a wide grin. "He's probably observed more about you than you realize."

Come to think of it, Rafe had handed Grace the mustard before Grace asked for it. It didn't seem out of the ordinary at the time because they were eating burgers. But, he'd only passed her the mustard. Not the ketchup. Not the mayo. Neither of which she liked.

"And if he's tuned into you it's possible you've piqued his interest." Cassie held up her hands to show Grace her crossed fingers.

"I hope it's just a casual interest. You know I'm not looking for anything more."

"Not all men are jerks. Some can be trusted not to break your heart, Grace."

In her experience, they always did.

Her dad had been the first. Strict, unemotional and mostly absent, he'd broken promise after promise. Birthdays, holidays, award presentations, he'd sworn to attend them all. She only needed one hand to count the number of times he had attended anything.

Derek, her college sweetheart turned ex-husband, swore

he loved her, but after the miscarriage he couldn't get out of their marriage fast enough.

Even Matt had crushed her heart, joining the military after he promised he wouldn't. Now he was paralyzed.

"Hey, Goldilocks." Rafe strolled into the kitchen. "If you're ready to go, I'll walk you to your room."

Grace regarded his outstretched palm.

Though his voice had sounded indifferent, his eyes dared her to take his steady, open hand.

So she did.

As he pulled her to her feet, electricity sparked in his fingertips and zipped through her neural pathways. The jolt flushed her skin, a flutter disrupted the rhythm of her heart. Her eyes, mouth and throat immediately turned dry as all the moisture in her body pooled between her legs.

Something dark and primal flickered in Rafe's eyes.

She jerked back her hand.

They said their goodbyes to Cassie and Brice, then walked down the corridor to the hidden entrance to the resort lobby.

"How did you know I was ready to leave, or was it a lucky guess?"

"When I came into the kitchen for another bottle of water, I saw you rub the tattoo on your wrist." Rafe reached around her to open the heavy mahogany doors.

"Lucky guess it is."

"You touch it when you're anxious."

"I do not."

"You rubbed it while we waited for the emergency responders after the accident, again at the hospital, before you fell asleep, at the diner when we ate breakfast."

"Oh," Grace said softly.

So Cassie hadn't been off the mark about Rafe's observation skills.

Strange that he would watch Grace so carefully after he

confessed no interest in becoming friends. She bit back a smile. Maybe he was warming to the idea.

Music filtered over the chatter of people spilling from the lounge into the lobby. Rafe cupped the back of her arm, navigating them through the masses.

He stabbed his finger at the elevator call button and mumbled something about the damned crowd.

"There's a singles convention going on."

"Is that why you came down this weekend?" Raw surprise registered before he blanked his expression.

"Um, no. I don't hook up with strangers."

"You prefer friends."

"That would be the benefit I mentioned." She poked the button as if that would help the elevator to appear faster. "You're not eligible, you know. Since we aren't friends."

Rafe's face tilted up.

"Did you hear that?" Grace looked around for the source of a growl. Not a service or therapy dog in sight.

Maybe she'd imagined the sound.

The elevator dinged.

Ushering her inside, Rafe's hand slipped down her back and skimmed her bottom.

Her body, having just cooled from his last touch, ignited again. She couldn't remember a man revving her up as fast as Rafe could, and he wasn't trying.

"Thanks for the escort. I know the way from here."

Rafe studied her for a moment, then stepped forward. The doors closed before she could push him out.

Mercifully, the stone-silent ride to the fifth floor was quick. She shoved the card-key into the electronic lock. The device blinked red to taunt her. She tried again.

Still red.

No matter how she jammed the card into the reader, the light blazed red.

Rafe's fingers closed around her wrist. The gentleness

of his touch scrambled her brain and jellied her knees. He drew back her hand and eased the key from her death grip. Turning it over, he drew the key through the slot.

The result?

A perky, green glow.

Grace wanted to slap him.

Rafe pushed opened the door.

Her breath caught in her throat. The maids had turned off all the lights after they'd cleaned the suite.

"Wait here." Rafe entered the room.

Grace lingered in the doorway, watching his muscles bunch and flex as he moved silently through the cozy living area to turn on the lights. He stepped into the bedroom. Thankfully, housekeeping had straightened the rumpled queen-sized bed and picked up the towels she had dropped on the floor.

He turned on the television and turned down the sound. "Better?"

Nodding, she nearly choked on emotion.

Rafe, a man who barely knew her, showed more concern for her deep-seated fear of the dark than her own family.

He crossed the room as she stepped inside. Lifting his hand to her face, he grazed his thumb against her temple. He frowned, gingerly fingering the residual bump at her hairline. Then, he drew his hand down the side of her face and brushed her hair behind her ear.

She stood still, not daring to breathe.

His soft-whiskered jaw skimmed her cheek and he nosed the shell of her ear before nuzzling the sweet spot behind it.

Her heart seemed to flutter into her throat. Her breaths quickened and her body hummed.

"Sleep tight, Goldilocks," he murmured.

Grace didn't remember closing her eyes. By the time she opened them, Rafe had vanished.

Chapter 9

Rafe cut off the lights on the truck and stared at the simple little A-frame house, the personal touches he remembered screamingly absent.

A fragile, feminine she-wolf, his mate, Lexi, had loved soft, frilly, pretty things. She had transformed a plain, wooden box house into something akin to a fairy-tale cottage filled with flowers and pillows, candles and gnomes.

She'd loved garden gnomes.

Now the wildflower patch in front of the house had withered away and the gnomes had been relocated to Maico's Botanical Conservatory where she had worked. He always thought the gnomes would be happy there because she certainly had been.

Although he'd given the box Ronni packed to the director, Rafe had not actually visited the public gardens since the shooting. He couldn't.

Same with this place.

The counselors at rehab had said his ability to face his former home would be a ruthless challenge to his sobriety, but one he needed to overcome.

Instead, he'd given the house and small parcel of land to Ronni and Alex upon their arrival. He'd never visited them here, preferring to meet them at the diner or talk briefly on the phone.

He wasn't giving them the brush-off. He simply wasn't much of a talker. Most people found his silence awkward and thought he wasn't paying attention. If he didn't have anything pertinent to add to the conversation, he didn't join in. Didn't mean he wasn't listening.

The porch light came on and the front door opened.

He climbed out of the truck.

"Rafe? Are you here for more boxes?" Ronni stood in the entryway. Since moving in, she had slowly packed away the remnants of his former life. Box by box he distributed everything to where he thought Lexi would want her things to go.

Clothes went to the charity thrift store. So did the dishes and housewares. Ronni had brought her own.

More personal items he planned give to his former mother-in-law.

"I'll take what you have." He stepped on the first porch step.

"Are you all right? You look a little peaked."

"Rough day." Being surrounded by baby stuff, and Grace.

I should've kissed her.

No, his lips needed to stay far away from hers.

He had a bad feeling about the situation. One of those gut-twisting "no matter what you do it's gonna get fucked up" type of feelings.

"Do you want to come inside?" Ronni squinted at him with a worried-mom look.

"Maybe next time." He'd had too much upheaval today. "I want to talk with Alex."

"I grounded him for being out after curfew on Friday night. He won't do it again, I promise." Ronni rolled her lips together.

"He's a good kid and hasn't done anything the other wolflings haven't tried."

Ronni breathed a sigh of relief.

"We need to make some changes so he doesn't get into any more trouble. Would you call him out?"

"Alex, come here," she yelled over her shoulder. "Bring the boxes on the kitchen table with you."

Loud thuds fell on the stairs inside. Seconds later, Alex appeared and helped Rafe load the boxes in the tow truck.

"Later."

Ronni hooked Alex before he disappeared into the house. "Rafe wants to talk to us." Tension hardened Ronni's body.

"I heard you skipped school a few times."

Ronni gripped Alex's shoulders and shook him. "What have I told you about missing school?"

"I hate school!" Alex's mouth twisted. "It won't do me any good."

"It won't if you keep missing classes," Rafe said. "Starting tomorrow, I'll take you to school and bring you home after I close up."

"I don't need a friggin' babysitter."

"If you aren't responsible enough to do what you ought, then, mister, you certainly do need one." Ronni crossed her arms. "And watch your language."

"This ain't fair!" Alex stormed inside.

"Be ready at seven," Rafe called after him. "Or I will hog-tie you and drop you off dressed the way I found you."

Ronni snickered. "He's at the age where he thinks he's too old for pajamas."

"That's why I said it." Rafe noticed the tired droop around Ronni's eyes and the slight hunch in her back. "How are the GED classes coming?"

"I'm holding my own." Ronni straightened. "Alex comes by his dislike for school honestly. His dad and I weren't the best students."

"You have a fresh start here," Rafe said.

"You do, too." Ronni eyed him curiously. "The woman with you at the diner, her scent is still all over you. Who is she to you?"

"A friend of a friend."

"Not your friend?"

He shook his head.

"Well, why not?"

Rafe thought for a moment.

"She talks a lot." When Grace wasn't talking, she hummed. Her voice had a nice, soft melody that stayed on his mind after they parted.

That's what really bothered him. She shouldn't be on his mind at all.

"You must be kiddin' because you ain't that dumb. Unless this docile pack has sucked the wolf right out of you." Ronni, two steps up from him, leaned forward with her hands still tucked beneath the arms crossed over her chest.

She was only ten years older, but the one cocked eyebrow and the side-scrunched mouth were a perfect imitation of his mother. He still had memories of his life before coming to Walker's Run and she wore that look in a lot of them.

"Don't get me wrong," Ronni said. "I've met some fine people here, but they're outta touch with their nature. You're getting yours back. I see it in your eyes. Don't be afraid of it. Be proud of who you are. Proud of where you come from, because you come from good stock."

Silence hung between them but neither felt any urgency to fill it. They were family by blood, still getting to know each other. Still testing the boundaries of trust and confidence.

"So, blondie talks too much. That's it?"

"It's a lot of words to absorb. She doesn't stop until she's asleep."

"Huh. You know this how?"

Somehow he was digging himself a deeper hole in a conversation he didn't want to be in.

"I see." Ronni pressed her lips. "Does she get your heart racing and your blood pumping straight down to your cock?"

He did not want to have this discussion with a woman who favored his mother way too much.

"I can see by your face, she does. Well then, don't worry too much about her talking. Find something better to do with her mouth."

Not the advice he was hoping for.

"One thing she can do is eat," Ronni called after him. "Bring her to supper. Thursday is good. I'll have the rest of your things packed by then."

Chapter 10

"Thanks for the ride." Grace unbuckled her seat belt.

"I do what I can for my friends." Humor and interest danced in Shane MacQuarrie's steely gray eyes. Twentyish, he had sandy hair and a young, handsome face, yet an edgy aura warned he wasn't as carefree as he should be at this age.

They'd met the first time Grace checked into the Walker's Run Resort and became fast friends.

Not of the benefits variety, but he kept trying.

A few years her junior, she considered him more of a little brother.

His gaze drifted past Grace's shoulder. "The R&L looks closed. Wanna grab a late lunch at Mabel's?"

"I had lunch with Cassie."

"I don't want to leave you stranded."

"I've backpacked across Europe, Shane. I can handle myself in Maico." Grace stepped down from the truck.

His stare made her feel as if he were assessing her ability to do so.

She closed the door and waved goodbye. She didn't drop her practiced smile or let her shoulders drop until Shane's truck disappeared down the road. The mechanical hum of cars from the nearby highway sounded more like a lullaby than the racket of city traffic.

She glanced at the large, Colonial-design building on the far side of the town square. According to Brice, the top floor housed the town's small municipal court while the first floor was home to the Maico Historical Society, the

Merchant and Tourism Advocacy, and a few other public interest businesses she'd researched on Google. Most had poorly developed websites and social media accounts, some had none at all. This morning she'd called to inquire if they were interested in updating their online presence and she had received informal invitations to drop by tomorrow to discuss services.

Might as well drum up some new clients for her web design business since she was going to be in town for a while.

Cars dotted the parallel parking spaces of the mom-and-pop shops framing the pretty little park of bright green grass, huge shade trees and wooden benches. The quiet, picturesque scene looked and felt homey.

She snapped a few pictures using her phone. A pinch of longing seeped into her heart. Because of her father's military career, Grace didn't have a childhood hometown. She envied people who committed not only to someone, but also to some place.

When she got married, Grace believed she'd finally settle down in a real home. They'd started with a small apartment, but had had plans to grow.

She'd hoped the restlessness within her would fade. Pretended that it had. Truthfully, she'd felt trapped. Until Derek had asked for a divorce after the miscarriage, she hadn't known he felt the same.

Grace thought a new beginning in a new place would help. Derek refused. He wanted out, wanted to pretend the marriage and the baby had never happened. It was difficult to understand because they'd never fought during their brief marriage. She thought he'd loved her. She had loved him.

When it was over Grace had realized she wasn't cut out for permanency. How could she be when she'd never known what it was?

Some dreams were better kept in a scrapbook.

A horn tooted and she turned around to face the old

converted service station. R&L Auto Repair was painted in black across the glass front window.

Two side streets flanked the building. An abandoned store stood on the right corner, the paint peeling in long curls. Spider-webs and hornets' nests decorated the dirty front window and a metal sign dangled above the door. At one time, it might've read Bait-N-Tackle, but the rust had eaten holes in the lettering, so only "Bai" and "ckle" remained.

Anchoring the left corner, Mabel's Diner, painted bright yellow with white trim windows, bustled with patrons, even in the midafternoon.

The R&L storefront was dark and the bays were closed, so Grace followed the sidewalk around to the back and sat on the ground. The tow truck was gone from the lot and the gate was locked. Either Rafe was out on a roadside call, or he'd played hooky from work to go fishing or hunting. Or run with the wolves, naked.

No, no, no. She didn't want to think of him naked, again.

Okay, she did. But she really, really shouldn't.

A ticklish current ebbed through her body as a white double-cab tow truck turned the corner.

Waving, she flashed her best smile, then stood to brush the gravel off her backside with the borrowed shirt she was returning.

The gate behind her clicked and slowly opened. Rafe motioned her inside the lot and waited until she reached a safe distance before he drove in behind her.

"Why are you here?" Rafe shut the truck door.

"Hello to you, too." She held up his wrinkled shirt. "I forgot to give this to you last night."

Rafe caught it in his left hand when she tossed it.

Grace turned to the sulky teenager cautiously studying her. "You must be Alex."

"Yeah." He approached, squinting at her with the same cobalt blue eyes as Rafe had, and his were just as intense.

"I'm Grace. I met your mom at the diner Saturday."

The teenager stared at her outstretched hand.

Walking past, Rafe thumped the boy on the back of the head. "Mind your manners."

Alex adjusted the backpack slung across his shoulder. "Um, hi." He squeezed her hand for a half second and bolted after Rafe.

Grace followed them inside the garage. The faint odor of motor oil and citrus greeted her.

Automotive supplies stacked in precise order filled the large metal shelves along the wall and all the tools in the work area looked clean. Immaculately, obsessively clean. Even the gray, concrete floor shone like it had been polished.

When she was here before, her focus had been on getting her coffee fix, not the pristine order in which Rafe kept everything.

Her mother ran a tight ship when it came to cleaning, her father even tighter. Rafe's fastidiousness surpassed them, which kinda freaked her out.

"Go to the kitchen and get started on your homework," Rafe said to Alex.

"I hate math. I hate school." Alex lowered his head but his eyes lifted toward Rafe, hard and angry. "I hate you."

"Homework." Rafe hit a series of buttons on the wall and the service bay doors rumbled to life. He held open the metal door to the customer service area. "Now."

Alex didn't budge.

Tension leavened the air like sweltering humidity.

Rafe's eyes narrowed and a low menacing, guttural noise rose from his throat.

"I hate this friggin' place." Alex huffed, squared his shoulders and stomped past Rafe.

Rafe shut the door and strode toward the large metal toolbox. Grace intercepted.

"Did you growl at him?" It sounded a lot like the one she'd heard at the elevator.

"I have a lot of work, Grace." Rafe gently bumped her aside. "Stay out of the way."

She noticed he didn't tell her to leave.

"You could've handled Alex better. Maybe offered to help. Make him cookies. Given him some of your time, rather than issuing orders." She bumped Rafe back.

He glared down at her, rumbling.

She poked his chest, hard. "You're doing it again." Only the sound turned less menacing. Becoming softer, sexier. "Are you purring?"

"There's nothing soft, cuddly or feline about me, *sweetheart*."

"I am not your, or anyone else's, sweetheart." She jabbed him center-chest again.

Rafe's stony expression could've been set in granite, but a twinge of humor warmed his eyes. He captured her hand, stroking his calloused thumb over her tattoo.

An explosion of tiny bumps erupted across her skin. Her body alternately flushed hot and hotter until she shivered and Rafe released her.

"I gave Alex and Ronni a home and a car, and I'll give them whatever else they need."

Her dad's military check had paid for all their necessities and more than a few nonessentials, but his career had meant far more to him than his family. During the brief times he had come home on leave or between deployments, he'd ordered her and Matt around like mini-soldiers rather than treating them as children.

"Invest time. Share an experience. Teach him something you love to do. Participate in something because he asks."

"I will once I get caught up on my work." Rafe side-stepped her and rolled the large, wheeled tool chest to the car in the first bay. He turned on the antique radio on one of the metal supply shelves. Not once as he set up his work area did he glance at Grace.

She sauntered behind him as he leaned over the engine of the car. "What if I make you an offer you can't refuse?"

Chapter 11

Rafe banged his head on the open hood.

"Goddamn it." He grabbed the sore spot and slowly turned, his muscles rigid, his brow frowning, his mouth pulled flat.

"If you have a computer and internet service, I'll help Alex with his homework."

"That's the offer I can't refuse?" Rafe leaned against the car grille, arms crossed high on his chest and a very grumpy look on his face. "I nearly knocked myself out when you snuck up behind me and whispered in my ear."

"I didn't sneak or whisper." She lowered and softened her voice. "If you want to compare boo-boos, mine is far worse." She lifted the hair covering the goose egg at her temple.

The hardness in his demeanor cracked. His gaze warmed the ugly bruised spot even after her hair fell back into place. "Come with me."

Shielding her grin, she followed him from the garage, through the customer service area. He opened the heavy metal door to the apartment and ushered her inside.

The door clanged shut, cloaking them in blackness.

Her lungs constricted inside her chest and refused to accept any air. A half gurgle, half gasp was all she could force from her cottony mouth.

She spun around, smacking into a solid wall of muscle. Rafe's warm hand pressing against her back slowed her panic.

She wasn't ten, she wasn't alone and she wasn't trapped.

Overhead, a soft incandescent glow appeared and pushed back the void. Rafe peered down at her.

Heart tripping over its own beat, Grace could only stare up at him. And wait.

Wait for the ridicule because only small children and wusses were afraid of the dark.

"I won't let anything hurt you, Grace. Not even the dark." His hand glided slowly up and down her spine, the heat spreading through her muscles and easing the spasm in her chest. "Better?"

She nodded.

He took her hand. Warm, steady, strong.

Her heart still pounded, but for a different reason.

He guided her down the hallway and paused at the dark kitchen. Rafe flipped on the light. No Alex.

A few steps farther, they reached the bedroom-living area. Rafe opened the door. Light from the flat-screen TV mounted on the wall filled the room. Alex sat on the couch, a video game controller in his hand, his attention glued to the race car exploding on the screen.

Still holding her hand, Rafe turned on the overhead light. "This is not where I told you to go or what I told you to do." Annoyance sharpened his tone.

Surprise and irritation flashed across Alex's face.

"Go to the kitchen. Grace is going to help with your homework," Rafe said. "Be mindful and do what she says. I won't take kindly to you disrespecting her."

Alex tossed the controller on the coffee table, snatched his backpack and trudged past them with glaring eyes.

Rafe left Grace standing in the doorway, walked to the dresser and pulled a laptop from the top left drawer.

"The Wi-Fi password is rlauto." He handed her the device.

"Your password is ripe for hacking. You should include

an upper- and lowercase letter, a number and a special character."

"I have a secondary password for my files."

"You aren't doing yourself any favors if it's as easy as your first."

"It isn't."

She followed him out of the room. "Would you mind if I did a video chat with a friend? He's a math whiz and I think he can help with Alex's attitude."

"As long as Alex gets his homework done, do whatever you think is best." Rafe continued down the hallway.

Grace walked into the kitchen and sat the laptop on the table.

"Nothing to eat or drink." Alex slammed the small refrigerator door. "This sucks."

Grace reached into the cabinet above the sink, pulled down the plastic container of beef jerky she remembered seeing and tossed it to Alex.

"Thanks." Alex ripped open a package and chomped the first bite.

"Math gives you trouble, huh?" Grace booted the laptop. Several business-related folders appeared on the desktop, and one labeled family history.

Knowing Rafe was adopted, she assumed he was researching his biological family. She would ask him later if he wanted help. She had a friend who was an expert genealogist.

"Math is boring." Alex unloaded two books from his backpack. "And I'm never going to use it."

"What career are you planning?"

Alex shrugged. "Don't know yet."

"Then you can't be sure you won't need math." Grace clicked on the internet icon and accessed a video chat app.

"What do you do?"

"I design websites and manage social media accounts, so

I need to understand the analytics data on social networks to target appropriate audiences for my clients."

Alex gave her a cautious look.

She laughed. "I call my friend, Raj, when I need help. He's a math geek and works for NASA."

Alex's eyes widened. "You know someone at NASA?"

"Sure do." She directed Rafe's computer to dial Raj's number. "He taught me how to play a decent game of chess and I taught him how not to suck at baseball."

"For that you have my lasting gratitude." Rajesh Patel's dark-haired, dark-eyed, bronze-skinned image burst onto the computer screen. "Are you okay? I saw the TouchBase post about your accident."

TouchBase was a social network that Grace and two friends had created in high school, specifically to help her military-brat friends stay connected with each other in a secure online environment.

"I'm good. Can't let a little bump on the head get the best of me." She turned the laptop so Alex could see the screen. "Raj, this is my new friend Alex. He's having math troubles. I'm hoping you have a few minutes to give him pointers."

Raj's face lit up the way a parent's did when talking about their beloved child. He seemed to forget about Grace and jumped right in to help Alex with his calculus homework.

Her skin began to tingle. She glanced at the kitchen entryway and saw Rafe lingering in the hallway. He turned to leave. Grace eased away from the table to follow.

"Hey," she said, before Rafe reached the heavy door at the end of the hallway. "I thought you'd gone back to work."

He turned, his brow creased. "I wanted to make sure Alex wasn't giving you a hard time."

"He was a little grumpy about your lack of snack foods, but we're getting along fine."

"The NASA guy," Rafe said. "He's just a friend?"

"Yeah. We attended the same junior high school in Oki-nawa. I kept in touch with him and most of the military kids I knew growing up." Spread all over the world and in varied professions, they were her virtual family.

They shared screen time, traded snippets of their lives in the form of posts and photos, but they weren't actually part of each other's lives. Grateful as she was for their continued camaraderie, Grace longed for more tangible relationships, especially since Matt returned home from the service.

There was an awkward pause between them.

"I should get back to Alex."

"Ronni invited you to supper Thursday. What should I tell her?"

"Are you going?"

"Yeah."

"Then tell her we'll see her Thursday."

A large, black truck bearing the Walker's Run Resort's wolf logo rolled to a stop in front of the R&L's open bays. Brice climbed out of the passenger side. Rafe pushed aside an irrational flash of jealousy to nod at Shane behind the wheel before he drove off.

Earlier, Rafe had noticed Shane's scent on Grace. Gavin has said the two were friends and Rafe didn't like the pos-sibility of Shane moving from friend to one with benefits.

Brice walked into the service area with a slight limp.

"I thought Shane worked the resort's registration desk. What's he doing playing chauffeur?"

"He's a full-time sentinel now." Which meant the young wolf was at the Alpha family's immediate beck and call.

Rafe shut the hood of his friend's Maserati and wiped down the front end with a clean shop towel. "Let me know when you're ready to sell this baby. I know an interested buyer."

"Never." Brice patted the top of the vehicle. "Drives like

a dream. As often as I go back and forth to Atlanta, I need something that handles well."

"And flies like the wind?"

Brice grinned.

"I don't see room for a baby seat and stroller and play-pen and diaper bag." Rafe paused. "I can go on."

"Don't." Brice paled. "Some moments I'm over the moon about having a baby. The next I'm terrified."

"You'll be fine." And if Brice wasn't, Cassie had a level head, a quick mind, and she planned for every possible scenario.

Rafe liked that about her.

He liked order. Chaos, not so much.

He didn't know how Grace did it. Bouncing from one place to the next. No sense of balance or stability.

She was brave in ways he never could've imagined.

"Dad asked me to run a security drill this week. I need your speed." Brice leaned against his car, easing the weight of his bad leg.

"What about curfew? He'll chomp my ass if I cause another *incident*." Rafe began cleaning his work tools. "It's not like I ran in front of Grace's car on purpose. She damn near killed me. It was close." Way too close.

"We'll do it early. Can't have the Alpha's son publicly thumbing his nose at the Alpha's idiotic rules." Brice snorted.

Faint laughter pulled Rafe to the front of the garage. Grace and Alex had relocated from the kitchen to sit in the shade of one of the old oak trees in the park.

The kid gobbled up her attention. Rafe understood why. Grace had a vivacious presence that wrapped you in a big, warm hug. Something about her called to him.

He was attracted to her six ways from Sunday and hoped that was all the pull toward her meant.

"Grace is under your skin, isn't she?" Brice asked.

"She's like a bad penny, showing up when I'm not look-ing." Rafe folded his arms. "Since your dad made me her guardian, I can't get rid of her, either."

"She's a godsend for Cassie, especially since the preg-nancy. She misses her mom and my grandmother. Grace fills that void. Maybe she'll do the same for you." Brice stepped beside him. "It's okay to like her. And it's okay to fall in love again. Time does heal, if we let it."

It had taken a long time for the wound in Rafe's heart to close. Now that he was moving forward, or trying to, people needed to leave him alone while he was still figur-ing out who he was without Lexi.

Everything he'd wanted in life, he'd planned with her. He didn't want to pick up the pieces of the dreams they'd shared and jigsaw them together with a substitute, as if the partner didn't matter.

He wanted to forge a new life, new dreams. To do so, he would need to start from scratch, build a different future with new materials. To make his life his own.

And he would.

As soon as he figured it out for himself.

In his own time.

Brice squeezed Rafe's shoulder. A silent show of under-standing and support. "Mom signed me up as a team cap-tain for the baseball tournament at the Co-op's spring festival again. She said I might be slower at running the bases because of my leg but there's nothing wrong with my pitching arm. I'm assembling my team." He walked around the car. "Tristan will play first base, Shane's covering cen-ter field. I want you to catch for me."

Brice never commanded or demanded the way his father did. He simply expressed his wishes. The natural weight of authority carried in his tone and stance, and secured compliance.

"I haven't played in years. Don't blame me if I drop the ball and lose the game."

"You won't." Brice opened the car door. "Oh, we're having dinner at Taylor's tonight. Cas needs to get out for a while."

"Not getting along with your parents?" Rafe couldn't imagine living under the same roof as the Alpha.

"Their relationship is good, but Cassie was on her own for a long time. Living with my parents, even though it's temporary, is getting on her nerves, especially because they want to dote on her and she isn't having any of it." Brice tapped the roof of the car. "Grace is coming with us, so show up and do your guardian thing or some other wolfan might do who-knows-what with her."

"Screw you."

Grinning, Brice slid into the driver's seat and started the engine.

"Grace said she was catching a ride back to the resort with you."

"She looks busy. See that she gets back in time to go to supper. Or better yet, bring her yourself." He gave Rafe a thumbs-up.

Rafe gave him the finger.

Laughing, Brice closed the car door and peeled out of the garage.

Chapter 12

A gorgeous blond man with an easy stride and killer smile sauntered into Taylor's Roadhouse. The googly eyes of every single woman in the building followed his every move. More than a few mouths dropped.

Ordinarily, Grace might be among them because, yes, he was that good-looking. But tonight she was looking for someone else. Someone with a short crop of deep auburn hair and piercing blue eyes.

"Hey, pretty lady." Tristan Durrance, the fair-headed sheriff's deputy who'd investigated her car accident, sauntered toward Grace to the dismay of a dozen women.

Sitting beneath the dim house lights on the opposite side of the restaurant from the bar, she shifted her legs beneath the table of the circular booth she shared with Cassie and Brice. Both of whom had momentarily deserted her for a slow dance to the soft ballad played by the country-rock band.

"Hello," she said coolly, then sipped her glass of white wine, allowing the light, sweet flavor to sit on her tongue.

"Aah, still mad about Friday night?" He slid into the booth and winged his arms over the back of the seat.

"You accused me of drunk driving."

"I merely asked if you had been drinking. It's a standard question when investigating a car accident."

"You know me. I don't drink and drive."

"I know everyone in this town, and would've asked any

one of them the same question. It's my job, doll." He flashed a blinding smile. "Cut me some slack."

"Stop calling me doll and I'll consider it." She ended the sentence with a smile.

Cassie and Brice started back toward the booth. Brice's hand rested on the small of Cassie's back. She looked up at Brice and said something. His face brightened and love rolled off him in palpable waves. No one could've doubted she hung the moon in Brice's world.

When they reached the table, Tristan scooted out of the booth. "Cassie, lovely as always. I would give you a kiss, but your ol' dog would pound me into the table." He hiked his thumb toward Brice.

"I'd keep pounding until you were six feet into the ground." Brice gave Cassie a light kiss. His hand rested on her belly, guarding her from the edge of the table as she sat down.

Brice nodded for Tristan to sit. "Glad you could join us."

"The pleasure is all mine." Tristan winked at Grace.

She smiled, but her gaze drifted to the people entering the restaurant.

Still no sign of Rafe.

When he had dropped her off at the resort, she'd invited him to Taylor's, saying he would be doing her a huge favor by rescuing her from Cassie and Brice's matchmaking endeavors at Singles Night. He didn't say he would come, but nodded when she said, "I'll see you later."

"One dance and I'm pooped." Cassie's cheeks were rosy from exertion and tiny beads of perspiration dotted her hairline. She picked up a menu and furiously fanned herself.

Brice waved to a nearby server who scurried over with a water pitcher to fill Cassie's glass.

"Iced tea, please," Cassie said nicely.

"Mom said you drank an entire pitcher today, Sunshine."

Brice draped his arm around Cassie's shoulders. "Doc said to slow down on the caffeine."

"He told me the same thing. What's his beef with caffeine?" Grace teased.

"He wanted me to wean off it when I started my third trimester because caffeine could contribute to low birth weight." Cassie patted her belly. "At this point, I don't think I need to worry about that possibility."

"Well, I'm not pregnant so I'll happily stick to my daily pot of double-leaded coffee. It's the best part of waking up."

"Oh, I wouldn't say that." Brice aimed a mischievous grin at Cassie and rubbed her belly.

"How about we let the lovebirds have some quiet time?" Tristan held out his open palm. "Let's dance."

She checked the front of the restaurant. If Rafe was coming, he would've shown up by now.

Taking Tristan's hand, she noticed a definite absence of the zip of energy that coincided with Rafe's calloused touch. "I have to warn you. It's been a while since I've danced."

"No worries. It's like riding a bike. I'll be your training wheels." Tristan whirled her onto the dance floor.

The country-rock beat thumped through her body and her feet followed. Tristan spun her, dipped her and held her hips as they gyrated to the music.

"He isn't coming." His husky voice scraped her cheek.

"Who?" She turned in Tristan's arms to face him and he pulled her closer.

"Rafe." The playfulness in his expression faded. "He never comes."

She twirled around and Tristan turned her right back.

"Readjust your sights. Rafe is damaged. You might think you can fix him, but he doesn't want to be fixed."

"We're all damaged. Most of us hide it behind a smile, a laugh or a thousand other things."

"You're setting yourself up for a world of hurt, Grace.

I see your disappointment every time you check the table and he isn't there."

"I'm not looking for him." Grace laughed. "I'm starving. I'm scoping the table for our food."

On cue, her stomach howled.

The seriousness in Tristan's face broke and he burst into laughter. Their dance steps realigned and a moment later he said, "Doll, if I were the settling-down type you'd be the perfect woman for me."

Doubting she would, Grace checked the table for Rafe, again.

Atop the high peak on Walker's Pointe, the noise of human life faded. Rafe basked in the silence.

He loved this place. Not only Walker's Pointe, he loved all of the Walker's Run territory.

Barely seven when he lost his parents and pack to a virulent strain of wolfan influenza, Rafe had been close to death when Doc saved him and brought him here, to his new home. Alone, scared and near-feral, Rafe didn't trust anyone in his adoptive pack at first. Not even Doc.

Recovered from the illness but traumatized by all the changes, Rafe had refused to willingly take his human form. He fought against sleep until his body simply gave up and he passed out from exhaustion. Of course, the moment he lost consciousness, his body shifted from wolf pup to small boy. Then Doc would pick him up and tuck him into bed.

One night, Rafe woke up during a severe thunderstorm. The wind whipped through the trees, limbs banged the windows, the house shook and the power went out. Terrified, he ran as fast as he could down the hallway. Doc met him halfway, knelt on one knee, opened his arms wide, then gathered Rafe in his arms and hugged him tight. He kept whispering, "I've got you, son."

That night Doc became a true father in Rafe's heart.

In defiance of the whisperings among the pack that a human could not raise a wild wolfling, Rafe had done his damnedest to prove them wrong. So he dressed like Doc, wore his hair like Doc. He wanted to be everything Doc was. Kind, respected. Civilized.

Eventually the pack and the Woelfesenat accepted the arrangement, believing Rafe had truly been tamed.

Rafe had believed it, too.

Now he was somewhere in between. Limbo.

Half in the dark, half in the light. He wasn't sure which side he wanted, or if he had to choose.

Sobriety was drawing something from him. He could feel the ripple of movement in his soul. What he couldn't feel was what it all meant.

He sat on a soft patch of moss, closed his eyes, listened to the sound of quiet.

Thoughts of Grace floated into his head.

Her essence, so full of life. Bouncy and brimming with wonder.

A smile stretched his mouth. She was like a present he couldn't wait to open. He couldn't of course. Shouldn't.

Wouldn't.

Still, he couldn't stop smiling.

He was an idiot. A smiling idiot who couldn't wait to see her again.

She'd agreed to tutor Alex for his upcoming exams. Two birds with one stone.

May not be exactly what Gavin meant when he instructed Rafe to mentor Alex and watch over Grace, but it made things simpler for him.

Rafe liked simple. The less complicated, the better.

The engine purr of an F150 climbed the mountain.

A few minutes later, a truck door closed and heavy footsteps fell against the ground.

"You all right?" Tristan sat next to Rafe.

"Why wouldn't I be?"

"Got a call you blew past the security gate."

"Gate was wide open, no need to stop. Can't blow past anything on the road to this place unless you want to pop an axel."

"Guess you went a little faster than Sam thought you should." Tristan scratched his jaw.

"I wasn't. People need to mind their own business and stop supposing something's wrong with me. There's not."

"People are worried. You were in a bad place for a long time. No one wants to see you get lost there again."

"Neither do I."

"What are you doing here?"

"Gavin slammed the curfew on me. No more night runs." Rafe was counting on the tranquility of Walker's Pointe to settle his thoughts and ease the craving for a drink.

"So, you're good?"

"Peachy."

They stared out over the territory in silence.

"How do you do it?"

"Do what?" Tristan cocked his head.

"Date so many women without getting attached." Rafe met Tristan's gaze.

A smile stretched across his smug face. "Women are like roller coasters."

"I shouldn't have asked." Rafe shook his head.

"I like riding roller coasters," Tristan continued. "But I don't want to live in a carnival."

"Be helpful or leave."

"Truth? You're not the polyamorous type."

Not exactly where Rafe was going with his question.

"Grace mentioned she prefers sex buddies to relationships."

"Damn. Wish I knew that earlier."

"Stay the hell away from her." Rafe caught a whiff of Grace's perfume on Tristan's clothes. "Were you with her? Tonight? Before you came here?"

"And there it is." Tristan flicked him on the shoulder. "The reason why no-strings bump-and-grinds won't work for you. You're overprotective and jealous. Your wolf isn't going to stay out of the way, no matter how hard you try to leash him."

"He doesn't need a leash. I can manage him."

"Really? You got awfully snarly at the scene of Grace's accident. You shoved me, remember?"

"You made her cry."

"You reacted instinctively." Tristan jabbed his finger at Rafe. "Any other deputy would've arrested you for assault on an officer."

"I didn't assault you. If I had, you'd be missing teeth in that stupid grin of yours."

"Probably so." Tristan laughed.

Rafe plucked a ladybug off his leg and placed her on a blade of grass an arm's length away.

He never should've asked Tristan for advice. And asking Brice would be like dousing a match with kerosene. Already he had ideas of Rafe and Grace becoming an actual couple.

Maybe he should talk to Doc. His bachelor father had had lady friends over the years. Not as many as Tristan, but a few.

"Are you seriously considering starting something with Grace?" Tristan's nonchalant gaze roamed their surroundings.

"Considering the *idea* of sex buddies. Not a *particular* one."

"Isn't Loretta your steady moon-fuck partner? She might be up for experimenting."

"I'm not bedding Loretta." Other than meeting for their

monthly encounter, he wasn't interested in her. He couldn't quite pinpoint why. Rafe simply didn't feel a connection.

"She's got kids. It would get complicated. I want simple. I'm lonely, but I can't do forever again."

There was a pregnant pause.

"In your head, you have to believe bedding the woman is only about the sex. No emotion can be involved." Tristan's tone sounded flat, resigned. It bore none of the light-heartedness that usually filled his voice. "Whatever you say, whatever you do, do it with one goal in mind. Fucking her. Once you're done, leave. Don't see her, talk to her, message her. Stay zipped on the communication. Treat this exactly like your moon-fucks."

Didn't sound like much fun to Rafe. Moon-fucks were a biological necessity. He wanted sex with a soft, warm-bodied female because he was so damn tired of being lonely.

Maybe he could figure a way to combine the two without overcomplicating things.

"Be sure of the road you take. There might not be any exits when you need to change direction." Tristan stood. "And the final destination could be a tundra you can't escape."

Rafe nodded his thanks.

"Do me a favor," Tristan said. "Stay under the speed limit and don't run any traffic signs. You're on Sheriff Locke's shit list. He thinks the former sheriff was too lenient on you after the DUI accident last year."

"I pleaded no contest." Rafe rubbed the tight muscles behind his neck. "Served the judge's sentence of twenty-eight days in rehab. No one else was involved and I haven't taken another drink."

"Locke came into office with a grudge and an agenda. From his perspective, you're Co-op. Grace is a friend of the Co-op. I worked the scene and I'm Co-op. He sees a

Co-op cover-up." Tristan grinned. "Which was something you should've done. I didn't need to see your junk."

"Impressive jewels, according to Grace."

"She has strange taste in accessories." Tristan laughed. "Seriously, though, the sheriff is fishing for something. He's asked for a meeting with Gavin."

"About me or my wolf?"

"Both."

Chapter 13

Grace closed her eyes and tilted her head back to catch the warm sunshine on her face. Breathing the crisp spring air, she exhaled the nervous energy welling inside her body. No matter how many times she met with potential customers, the jitters always knotted her stomach.

Today she'd added four businesses to her client list. One requested a standard start-up website design, the other three chose customized annual service packages.

She was more than grateful. Her contract with a microbrewery in Knoxville was about to expire. The owner was a difficult client with whom she'd rather not work again. Without new clients to bridge the income gap, she wouldn't have the financial option of not renewing his contract.

An enormous weight lifted from her shoulders. She stepped out of her heels and tucked them into her shoulder bag, then took out her sandals and slipped them onto her feet. "Aahh. Much better."

She practically skipped down the contemporary concrete steps of the old Colonial-style building.

"Miss Olsen?" An older man dressed in a blue, short-sleeved uniform shirt with a silver badge pinned over his heart stopped her. "Grace Olsen?"

The weathered crags in his face, the cold gleam in his eyes, the flat pinch of his lips—he looked to be a man on a mission.

"Yes." Grace adjusted her bag, which was beginning

to slip off her shoulder. "Is there something I can do for you, Officer?"

"Sheriff. Sheriff Carl Locke." He smiled, but it wasn't very friendly. "How are you faring since your accident?"

"Fine, thank you."

"No problems with the Co-op? They aren't harassing you in any way?"

"Why would they?" An uneasy feeling knocked at her recently unknotted stomach.

"Let's say the Co-op's wolves have been involved in several incidences over the last several years. Several *fatal* incidences. You were fortunate, *this time*."

"I don't expect a *next* time. Once Rafe completes my car repairs I'll be more cognizant of wolves crossing the roads at night."

"Ah, Rafe Wyatt."

Grace didn't like the sinister way he said Rafe's name.

The sheriff's sharp, dark, beady eyes narrowed on her. "Some friendly advice. Stay away from Wyatt before you end up dead."

"Why would Rafe hurt me?"

"I wouldn't," Rafe said, bounding up the steps. His voice was hard and icy, but still the sound warmed her skin.

The sheriff's glare lifted from Grace to Rafe and then to the pockets of people exiting the building on their lunch breaks. Some gathered at the food trucks stationed around the town square. Others strolled into the fresh foods market and other businesses framing the park.

None seemed to pay attention to the awkward situation on the steps.

"What are you doing here?" Grace asked Rafe.

"I was getting lunch in the park. Saw you come out and thought you might want to join me."

Grace grinned. For a man who said he didn't want to be her friend, he seemed to like her being around.

The sheriff grunted. "We'll talk again, Miss Olsen."

"Contact her lawyer first." Rafe climbed one step higher, to the one below where Grace stood, putting them at the same height. Although they didn't physically touch, she liked the comfort of his nearness.

"Who might that be?" The sheriff's gaze targeted Rafe.

"Brice Walker," Grace answered. Brice was the only local lawyer she knew and she didn't think he would mind if she asked him for legal advice.

"Of course he is." The sheriff's reptilian smile made Grace shiver. He restarted his journey up the steps into the building.

"Weirdos shouldn't wear badges." Grace shook off the creepy vibe. "He thinks something's up with the Co-op's wolves."

Rafe didn't speak as his gaze moved over their surroundings.

"Everything is on the level, right? Nothing illegal or immoral?"

"The Co-op's focus is to provide for and protect our wolf pack and community. The wolves are a part of who and what we are. So far, there aren't laws prohibiting our lifestyle."

Rafe's assurance eased her mind.

He looked at her, studying her face with a slow, sweeping intensity that left her a little breathy.

"Let's eat." Rafe laced his fingers through hers.

The nerve endings in her hand took notice of the spark the contact generated. Her body shook off the ickiness from the encounter with the sheriff as the crisp tingle of awareness invaded.

He led her across the street to a food truck.

"Hey, Rafe. Your order is ready." The wiry vendor wearing a red Wieners-and-Chicks T-shirt waved his tongs at the blue plastic tray loaded with four hot dogs smothered with chili and cheese. "He didn't know what you wanted, Grace."

"Have we met?" Grace's mouth watered at the sweet smell of teriyaki sauce coating the chicken skewers on the grill.

"Nope." He wiped his hand on a towel and offered her a handshake. "I'm Frank. Heard Rafe's been seen with a pretty blonde named Grace."

"Wow. Word travels fast around here." She smiled. "I'll take the chicken, please."

He slathered more sauce on the meat and turned the skewers. "You might make it into the *Maico Monitor* again. Your ruckus with the sheriff on the steps is the most excitement we've had since your accident, which make you and him—" he pointed at Rafe "—the darlings of page two."

"What's on page two?"

"The gossip column," Rafe said, tight-lipped.

"Oh." The heat fanned across Grace's cheeks. "Sorry."

"Now, now. Opal insists it's the society and special interest page." Frank flashed a toothy grin. "A wolf, a damsel in distress and—I quote Opal here—'a handsome rescuer' is hot news."

"I'm not a damsel in distress and I didn't need to be rescued."

"Opal is a busybody," Rafe said. "She should mind her own business and stop making up shit."

"There's a betting pool on how long it takes you and Grace to get together." Frank wrapped two chicken skewers in a small sheet of wax paper, laid them on the tray alongside the chili dogs and took two bottles of water out of the cooler. "Can I get any insider tips before I join in?"

"Don't waste your money." Rafe and Grace said in unison.

"Sooner rather than later." Frank laughed. "Got it, thanks!"

Chapter 14

Rafe rapped his knuckles against the ornately decorated front door of the Reinhardt residence.

Today had been a good day.

Most days were just days. But on the ones he encountered Grace, her lively energy stayed with him, even in her absence.

When he'd dropped her off at the resort, he'd almost kissed her. Again.

Gavin expected him to be Grace's friend, confidant, protector, and all Rafe could think about in her presence was touching her, kissing her, bedding her.

He heard the light footsteps coming to answer his knock.

"Rafe?" Cynthia Reinhardt's soft voice sounded so much like her daughter, Lexi, that Rafe's heart paused.

"It's good to see you, Cynthia." Her dark brunette hair glittered with a few silver threads. Her delicate features and golden skin showed minimal signs of age.

Cynthia's daughter had been her mirror image in appearance and temperament. Looking at Cynthia, he didn't have to imagine what Lexi would've looked like had they grown old together.

"What a surprise." Cynthia grabbed him in a motherly hug. "I've missed you."

He missed her, too. In the beginning, his emotions had been too raw and painful to reach out to her. After a while, it became habit to keep his distance. Especially since her mate, Clayton Reinhardt, blamed him for his daughter's death.

"I visited Lexi's grave on her birthday last week. The spot where you watch over her was still warm." Concern shimmered in her eyes.

"It wasn't me." Rafe would've expected Cynthia to have detected a residual scent and identified to whom it belonged. However, if she was crying at the time, her scenting ability could've been compromised. "Did you ask Clay?"

"No." She shook her head. "I assumed it was you."

"I made my peace with Lexi when I stopped drinking. I haven't been back to her grave since. She's gone, and I had to let her go. I hope you understand."

"I do."

"I, um…" He paused. "I gave the house to my cousins."

"I heard." She patted his cheek. "It's okay, Rafe. Lexi wouldn't mind your kin living there."

"Ronni's been packing stuff away for me. I gave the clothes and housewares to the thrift store. The conservatory got the gnomes, books went to the library." He tipped his head at the dolly loaded with boxes. "Thought you might like to have the personal stuff."

"Bring them inside. I'll go through everything later."

Rafe followed her to the den and stacked eight boxes, two by two. Hard to believe that was all he had left of his former life.

"Anything you want to keep?" Cynthia asked.

"It's best if I don't."

Rafe left, feeling a little sad but otherwise okay, which was a hell of an improvement from feeling like a shitty failure.

A male was supposed to provide for his mate and protect her from all threats.

If he had said no to the impromptu picnic…

If he had scented the poacher's presence…

If he'd been a half step slower, maybe the bullet would've killed him instead of her.

If, if, if—

As he reached the tow truck parked on the side of the road, a car turned into the driveway. Purposely taking his time, Rafe secured the dolly in the backseat, closed the door, leaned against the vehicle, his arms crossed high on his chest and greeted his former father-in-law. "Evenin', Clay."

Chest puffed and shoulders broadened, Clayton Reinhardt stalked toward him. He had a permanent look of smelling something bad chiseled into his craggy face and his cropped, spiky hair reminded Rafe of a hedgehog.

"What the hell are you doing here?"

A dozen or so inflammatory responses danced on Rafe's tongue. Although Lexi had loved her father dearly, he was a pretentious, egotistical ass.

Out of respect, Rafe kept his tone civil. "I've given the house to my cousin. She packed away Lexi's stuff and I gave the boxes to Cynthia."

Clay's nostrils flared and stuck. He had really big nostrils. The kind a bloodhound would envy.

"The house belongs to my daughter!"

"Not anymore."

"You have no right to give away her home." Clay's ears turned a shade darker than the red in his face.

"Get a handle on your grief, Clay. Or your beast will get the best of you."

Unreasonable, uncontrollable and without conscience, the primitive monster lurked inside every Wahya. A hormone unique to their species kept the beast at bay with sex. Most critically during the full-moon phase.

Extreme distress could also produce a flood of wolfan hormones, triggering the monstrous transformation. Rafe used to wonder if his beast would've emerged if Lexi hadn't died instantly. If he'd watched her suffer as her life bled out in a dark red flow, knowing the child they'd struggled to conceive would also die.

Deep within, the darkness rippled.

Rafe held back a shudder.

He shouldn't dwell too long on "ifs" anymore.

"My daughter is dead because of you." Clay slammed his fingers into the center of Rafe's chest.

When Grace poked him, Rafe found her amusing and adorable. He dominated her in size, yet she wasn't afraid to command his attention and show him her grit.

There was nothing amusing or adorable about Clay. Malice gleamed in his black eyes and Rafe knew the man wished his fingers were claws, able to slice through Rafe's chest to rip out his heart.

"Lexi died because a hunter shot her." Rafe bore his thumb into Clay's palm, bending the wrist backward, almost to the point of fracture. "Not because I loved her."

Rafe shoved his former father-in-law aside and climbed into the tow truck.

"Her name is Alexis!" The muscles in Clay's neck strained and the veins on either side of his throat bulged. *"Alexis Maria Reinhardt."*

All the other times he and Clay argued, Rafe had always added *Wyatt* with a resounding growl.

"My little girl died because you failed to protect her." Clay grabbed the door before Rafe closed it. "And I'll never let you forget it."

During his drinking days, Rafe dutifully bore the piles of guilt Clay shoveled onto his back and shoulders without complaint.

Not anymore.

As Rafe told Cynthia, he'd made his peace with the one who mattered.

"Goodbye, Clay." Rafe pulled the door closed with a little more force than necessary, cranked the engine and drove off.

Chapter 15

Damn it, Rafe! Answer the text.

Five minutes without a response and the wait was gnawing at Grace's insides.

Ordinarily, she wouldn't have messaged him at midnight, but it really was an emergency. Although the hotel had a wonderful dessert menu, not one item contained chocolate. And she really needed chocolate.

Matt had called. He and his partner had decided to move in together. She was happy her brother had found such a wonderful guy, but it kinda left her out in the cold.

Matt hadn't asked her to move out, and she didn't think he would, but being a third wheel in her own apartment was not how she wanted to live. Yeah, she had expected to move out at some point. This sped up the timetable during the worst possible time.

Laying the phone next to her laptop, she scooted off the bed. Did a few stretches. Padded to the bathroom for a potty break.

Checked her phone.

Zero new messages.

"Ugh!" She tossed the phone on the bed and walked onto the small balcony that faced the dark forest.

Her ears adjusted to the blended sounds of insects and the flowing river she couldn't quite see beyond the rise.

A zillion diamond points winked in the black velvet sky. The flowery scent of the fresh night air held onto a tiny bite of winter. Hugging herself, she rubbed her hands up and down the exposed expanse of her arms.

She missed the howls from the wolf sanctuary several miles downriver. The last few times she'd visited, the woods had been strangely quiet.

She wondered if Rafe was out there, somewhere, prowling with his wolf. *Naked.*

Now she'd done it.

Made her current dilemma worse.

Not only was she chocolate-less, now she was horny.

She sat cross-legged on the balcony floor. Closing her eyes, Grace sucked in a deep, cleansing breath. Held it a few seconds, then released it, little by little, until her lungs ached for more air. She repeated the process, immersing into a meditative calm to conquer her cravings.

Or, at least, to abate them. And her worries.

Matt and Aaron had been together for almost six months. A firefighter, Aaron had met Matt at a veteran's breakfast hosted by the city. As far as she could tell, Aaron was a kind, considerate, generous man.

None of which meant he was dependable for the long haul. She hoped for Matt's sake he was.

"Grace."

Her eyelids popped open. Alone on the balcony, she looked over the railing.

No one on the ground.

No one in her suite.

A pound at the door caused her to jump.

Heart racing, she peeked through the peephole.

A dangerously decadent hot fudge sundae stared back at her.

There was a god of chocolate, after all.

Grace squealed and did a little happy dance as she opened the door. Rafe handed her the ice-cream treat.

"Thank you, thank you." She locked the door behind him. "I was jonesing for this. How did you know?"

"Your message said 'Midnight snack emergency.' The night of the accident, you said an ice-cream sundae was your favorite midnight snack." He followed her into the living room. "I knocked twice. Were you asleep?"

"Meditating on the balcony. I wasn't expecting you because you didn't respond to my text."

"Didn't realize it was a conversation." He sat on the couch in the living area of the suite, opened the fast-food bag and methodically set three wrapped sandwiches, an extra-large order of fries, napkins and a plastic spoon on the small round table.

"How can you eat like that and not have an ounce of fat?" She knew he didn't because she'd seen every inch of him.

"I run almost every night." Rafe unwrapped the first sandwich, wadded the paper and dropped it in the bag.

"You don't look like a runner. They're usually lean and lanky." Grace pulled a bottle of water from the small in-room refrigerator and placed it on the table for Rafe. "You're thicker, more solid."

Elbows on his knees, holding the sandwich in front of his face, he took a giant bite, chewed slowly and swallowed. "You think I'm dense and slow?" His gaze lifted to her with a challenge in his eyes.

"No." She joined him on the couch. "Think of greyhounds and rottweilers. Greyhounds are sleek, elegant and fast. Rottweilers are—"

"Blocky and stout?"

Neither of which described Rafe.

"I was going for strong and durable." She picked up the spoon and shoveled a big scoop of delicious, soft, vanilla ice cream drowning in hot fudge into her mouth.

Her entire body cheered.

"I could give a greyhound a run for its life."

"Keep eating junk and you won't."

Eying the sundae in her hand, he halted before taking another bite of his sandwich. "Who's the pot and who's the kettle in this conversation?"

"Hey. This is my only vice." She savored another bite. "Mmmmm."

"What about coffee?"

"Isn't a vice. Coffee is as essential as oxygen."

"If you stopped breathing, which would you rather have, mouth-to-mouth resuscitation or a cup of coffee poured down your throat?" Rafe's gaze lingered on her mouth.

Her lips tingled. She gave her spoon a slow, sensual lick. "Depends on who's providing the rescue breathing."

Rafe snorted softly and resumed eating.

"Mind if I have some fries?"

"They're yours."

"Thanks." She drew one long fry from the holder, dragged it through the fudge and devoured it.

Rafe's mouth twisted in disgust.

"Weird, I know, but it's delicious." She dipped another fry and held it toward him. "Try one."

"It might kill me." He polished off his second sandwich and unwrapped the third.

"Those greasy, sauce-slathered burgers will give you a heart attack before this little delicacy will."

Mouth full, Rafe shook his head.

"Oh, come on." She jiggled the chocolate-coated fry. "Be adventurous."

"I'm allergic to chocolate."

Aaack!

All Grace could do was stare, openmouthed. A life without chocolate? She wouldn't last a week.

"My first Halloween with Doc I got into my candy bag before he checked it." Done with his third sandwich, Rafe opened a bottle of water and chugged it down. "Ended up in the emergency clinic. My lips and tongue were swollen, my throat closed, I couldn't breathe and had a horrible case of hives."

"That sucks." Not only for him, but for her, too. No way would she get the kiss he teased her with earlier.

"No kidding. I hate goddamn hospitals." He spoke with such vehemence that Grace simply stared at him.

"But, you came to see me after the accident." And he'd brought her home with him.

"I know what it's like to be alone in a hospital. Thought you'd appreciate the company." He guzzled a bottle of water.

"I did." Much more than she was willing to admit.

Kicking off his shoes, he dropped the empty water bottle into the drive-through bag, picked up the French fry holder and plopped his feet on the coffee table.

"Hey." She playfully smacked his arm as he shoved several plain fries into his mouth. "Those are mine."

He didn't look apologetic.

"Thanks for overcoming your fear of hospitals so I wouldn't have to go through all that alone." She bumped her shoulder against his.

"I'm not afraid of hospitals, just don't like 'em."

He offered her some fries, which she accepted, dipped into her ice cream and thoroughly enjoyed.

"What are you afraid of?"

He gave her an imposing look. "You."

Rafe bounced his knee slightly and twitched his hip, but the vibration against his thigh wouldn't stop.

Finally, he slapped his hand against his leg, his palm patting the pocket of his shorts for his phone. Opening one eye, he fumbled to shut off the silent alarm.

He had an hour before he picked up Alex for school.

Grace wiggled against his ribs, snuggling into him like

a pillow. Her warmth seeped through him, pleasing and ir-ritating him all at the same time.

He shouldn't have fallen asleep on the couch in her room.

He shouldn't have responded to her midnight text.

He shouldn't have given her his number in the first place.

Because now he couldn't figure out how their limbs managed to get so tangled. Painstakingly, he twisted and turned until he slipped from her clutches.

Her face scrunched and she moaned a cute little protest as he picked her up. Her scent, already imprinted in his nose, wrapped around him. She intrigued him on a primal level and his wolf was all too aware of her.

He wanted to come out and play. After all, Grace's scent was all over him. And his was all over her.

As far as the wolf was concerned, she was his.

Rafe carried her to the bed. He stood still, transfixed by the angelic halo of her hair settled on the pillow.

God, she was beautiful.

Every masculine molecule in his body charged.

He pulled the comforter over her, resisting the urge to kiss her. To climb in beside her. To get naked and sweaty with her.

She probably wouldn't be too thrilled if he tried.

The clock on the nightstand flashed the time. Fifty-five minutes to go. Great.

From the resort, it was only a ten-minute drive to pick up Alex and another ten to the school.

He had thirty-five minutes to kill.

Strolling into the bathroom, he saw several towels on the floor. He picked them up. Big mistake. One smelled like the fragrance in her hair. The other held her true scent, not the perfumed one that masked it. Sweet, musky, full-bodied female.

He held the towel to his face and his body caught fire.

At least, it felt like it did. Heat flashed through him from head to toe. Lust clouded his mind like thick billowing smoke.

His cock grew hard. Too hard to ignore.

He turned on the shower, cold water only, and stripped. The icy spray bounced off his skin like water chips. The body wash on the shelf smelled like pears and cucumbers.

He dumped it on his body anyway. It made a nice lather that tickled his skin. He tried to clear his mind, only he couldn't stop hearing Grace's giggles when she'd told him about a convoluted shower contraption at an Irish B and B. He couldn't really remember the details of the actual story because visions of her naked, in a hot, steamy shower, her skin slick, her face flushed, and oh, so ready for the taking, had bombarded his brain in a hailstorm of lust.

He focused on that fantasy, knowing how soft her body was pressed against his. They hadn't kissed, but he could imagine her soft mouth nibbling his lips, her tongue sliding into his mouth.

He pumped his cock, envisioning every inch of her bare skin. She'd seen him naked, twice. He wondered if she had touched herself thinking of him and what she'd imagined him doing to her.

His hand fisted tighter around his shaft, sliding up and down and back up. His thumb swirled against his slit. With his other hand, he massaged his sack.

Wet, hot, tight. He knew she'd be all three.

Tension pooled and weighted his groin. His strokes grew shorter, faster, less rhythmic until he spurted in orgasmic release.

It took a while for his breathing to even out, his heart to stop racing and his ears to stop ringing.

He felt the cold water now. He showered quickly, making sure to rinse away any evidence of his morning hand job.

Usually whatever fantasy he indulged in while showering faded the moment he stepped out of the stall. Grace's presence with him had seemed far too real. The touches he'd imagined lingered despite the vigorous rub of a towel against his skin.

No more midnight snack deliveries and no more spending the night on the couch with her twisted around him like a pretzel.

He wiped the condensation from the mirror.

Who was he kidding? The moment he'd put his number into her phone he knew he'd come whenever she called.

Chapter 16

"When a man shows up at your door after midnight, with or without ice cream, it's a booty call," Matt teased. "I can't believe you simply fell asleep on him. Poor guy."

Grace finished tying her ponytail and frowned at her brother's grin on her phone's video chat. "For Pete's sake. He's just a friend of a friend. Nothing more."

"Yet you've spent the night with him, twice."

"It won't happen again."

"Like hell it won't." Matt laughed. "Admit it. You like him."

"I admit nothing." She lifted her bangs to show him the bruise on her temple. "Concussion. It could be affecting my judgment."

"Nightingale effect. Take advantage of it, sis." Matt leaned closer to the webcam. "You deserve a chance to let loose and enjoy yourself."

"Um, I am. That's why I stayed at the resort instead of renting a car to drive back to Knoxville."

"And how have you spent your vacation?"

"I went to the spa, a barbecue, went dancing." Had a picnic with Rafe in the park, but Matt didn't need to know that, or the tidbit about seeing Rafe naked.

"What are your plans for the rest of the week?"

"The resort has excursions to the local sights and attractions." She'd need to be back before three, though. To meet with Alex.

And see Rafe.

This morning after his phone alarm went off, she'd pretended to stay asleep in case he wanted a quick departure. Instead, he'd picked her up and tucked her into bed.

She dozed on and off through his shower, it seemed like a long one.

He also started the coffee, making him a god in her estimation since she hadn't been able to figure out the darn contraption posing as a gourmet coffeemaker. A part of her wished he would come by every morning to make the coffee so she wouldn't have to schlep out of bed and drag herself down to the restaurant for a carafe.

Room service was much too slow for the caffeine deprived.

The stolen kiss goodbye that she'd held her breath for turned out to be a warm nuzzle against her cheek. The cozy feeling it gave her remained with her, even though he'd left over an hour ago.

"Boring." Matt yawned. "Group tour to see yet another mountaintop that looks like a dozen others you've seen, instead of getting it on with a sexy mechanic." Matt scratched his bed-head hair. "Hmm, you've got the wrong idea of entertainment."

A rap sounded at the door.

"Hold on. Someone's here." Grace moved across the room, phone in hand.

"Maid service and room service. Some people have it so good," Matt teased.

"Suck it up. You're the one who didn't want me to come home, remember?"

"Because I want you to have a life."

"There better not be a week's worth of dishes in the sink when I get back." Grace swung open the door and nearly dropped the phone.

"Mornin'."

Every cell in Grace's body went berserk.

Rafe leaned against the door frame. He'd changed into cargo shorts that hung low on his hips and a dark green polo stretched tight over his chest.

His mussed hair looked like he'd combed it with his fingers. Short whiskers, a shade darker than his auburn hair, covered his jaw and framed his mouth, making his lips look oh-so-kissable.

How dare he show up looking so sexy?

"Grace?" Matt's voice interrupted. "Everything okay?"

"Matt, this is Rafe." She flipped the phone so her brother and Rafe could see each other.

Rafe simply nodded at the device.

She switched the video chat to audio and held the phone to her ear. "Gotta go."

She ended the call.

"I cleaned out your car yesterday before I towed it to the body shop for the framework and paint. I didn't think to bring this last night." He handed her a bag filled with paperbacks, magazines and a pair of socks she'd been missing. He also gave her a large, tattered scrapbook.

"You found it!"

He followed her into the suite, stopping at the archway to the bedroom. She dropped the bag on the floor and plopped onto the edge of the mattress.

"What is it?" His curious gaze fell on her, not the book.

"It's the dream book I started when I was a kid. Pictures of the house I wanted to live in and all the things I wanted to go in it." It had been a constant in her ever-changing homes.

"We weren't allowed to nail anything to the walls." She opened to one of the pages filled with pictures of artwork. "So in here, I stapled everything wherever I wanted it."

A protest for permanency that never materialized.

Her finger traced the staples and the fraying edges of the magazine paper beneath. There'd been a time when she'd truly believed she would have all these things, if she kept the faith.

After so many disappointments, her faith cracked and eventually disintegrated.

"Thanks for bringing this to me."

"Wanna go for a ride?" Rafe's dark blue gaze smoldered with inscrutable emotions. Whatever was going on in those turbulent depths, Grace was definitely game.

Yep, he was an idiot.

After dropping Alex at school, Rafe had found himself right back at the resort knocking on Grace's door when he should've been headed to Franklin.

He didn't consciously decide to go back to the resort. He simply wound up there as if his internal autopilot was drawn to Grace by a magnet.

Because she was still dressed in her pink pajamas when he'd arrived, he waited in the suite's living area while she dressed in the bathroom. Hearing the rustle of her clothes as she got ready tormented him with visions of her soft, golden skin.

Sitting next to her as he drove, Rafe kept his hands gripped around the steering wheel so he wouldn't reach over to touch her. He needed to stay focused on the road.

There were automotive supply retailers closer. However, he preferred one over the state line in Franklin. The errand got him out of Maico every couple of weeks and the drive was usually peaceful.

The radio screeched off the country station Rafe hadn't changed since the day he had bought the tow truck.

"How can you listen to this stuff and not want to hang yourself? Someone's always leaving, cheating or dying." Grace fiddled with the buttons set to no particular frequency.

"It's the only station I can pick up around Maico." He

punched the scan button. "Press this again when you want to stop on a song."

The speakers crackled throughout the search cycle until the country station popped up again.

"Oh, for Pete's sake." Grace sighed dramatically. "Sorry I'm so antsy. I think the server gave me decaf at breakfast."

With all the sugar she'd poured into her cup, Rafe was surprised she could taste the difference.

"Addiction is a bitch," Rafe said mildly. "Even when it's coffee. Maybe you should cut back, slowly."

He'd quit drinking cold-turkey, but he was also in the hospital after driving off the road so his tremors and vomiting and migraines were medically managed. The cravings he learned to handle in rehab. His counselor had told him to focus on a positive activity as a means of distraction.

He couldn't get out of the facility to run, so he channeled his love of history into a genealogical project. What started as an attempt to preserve his family legacy eventually led him to Alex and Ronni. At least the maternal line would continue. Sadly, what he'd been able to reconstruct of his paternal lineage suggested Rafe was actually the only surviving descendant of the once-noble Wyatt clan.

The interest in his family history lead eventually to him investigating the origins of Wahyas. Of course there were no official records earlier than the last two hundred years, when the Woelfesenat had formed, but Rafe studied myths, legends and actual historical events in an attempt to piece together wolfan evolution. He found the research fascinating, but had not uncovered any verifiable data.

The speakers crackled and hissed.

"The reception will clear when we get closer to Franklin," he said.

Grace turned off the radio. Within a minute or two, she began humming. It didn't sound like any particular tune to him but she didn't miss a note, her head gently swaying with the soft, sweet melody.

"Oh, there's the overlook." Not quite plastered to the window, Grace pressed her face close enough to the glass that Rafe saw her animated expression in the reflection.

"We're stopping, right?"

Rafe would rather make up for lost time. Instead of going to a drive-through as usual, he'd eaten at the breakfast buffet with Grace at the resort restaurant which put him behind schedule. He liked schedules. Schedules kept things running smoothly. Schedules ensured that he always knew what to expect. And when.

Grace turned to him. Her golden skin shimmered in the sunlight that filtered through the glass. Her eyes sparkled. And that smile, full of warmth and expectation—there was no way in hell he'd say anything to dampen that brilliance.

"Whatever you want." He wiped away the beads of sweat dotting his upper lip.

"Are you all right?" Her hand on his arm caused the heat building inside him to flare.

"I'm fine." He flicked the air vent to blow on him and cranked up the AC.

"Oh, no." She sucked in her breath. "It's not where you had your accident?"

"What?"

"Cassie said you ran off the road last year. Are we getting close to the spot where it happened?"

"Different road."

"Good." Grace returned to the window. "I wouldn't enjoy the view if you almost died there."

He eased the tow truck onto the wide shoulder and parked. Grace jumped out before Rafe pulled the key out of the ignition. He tucked her phone into the pocket of his shorts.

"It's beautiful," she said when he caught up with her.

The rapturous glow on her face was worth any time lost on his schedule.

He stood close behind her, reveling in her heat and the beautiful scenery. He loved living in the midst of the Smoky Mountains. Something about them harmonized with his soul. He had no doubts this was where he truly belonged.

"Why is it hazy over there?" Grace pointed to the mountain range in the distance.

"It's a natural fog that clings to the mountaintops."

The trees below them rustled. No particular scent drifted upward, so Rafe focused his vision on the movement. His body automatically made subtle changes from relaxed to heightened awareness, ready to whisk Grace to safety if danger presented itself.

His senses rose, then ebbed. He reached over her shoulder and whispered, "Look."

"What is it?" She leaned forward and Rafe's other arm curled around her to prevent her from leaning on the rickety rails.

"Watch and see."

She hugged her waist, trapping his arm between hers. "Gosh, you're nice and toasty." She cozied into him. "I wouldn't have worn a skirt and sandals if I'd know it would be this cool."

Rafe smirked at what she called a skirt, not much longer than the shorts he'd seen her wear. Not that he minded. She had nice legs. Legs he shouldn't imagine tangled with his.

He refocused on the movement below them. "Here he comes."

"It's a bear!" Grace's ponytail flounced against Rafe's chest. "It's a bear!"

Rafe couldn't resist. "Yes, Goldilocks. It's a bear."

"Oh, darn. I left my phone in the truck."

Rafe reached into his pocket and withdrew the device.

"Thanks." She gifted him with a delightful grin and turned to record the animal.

The bear ambled a ways, swung its head, stood on his hind legs. His nose twitched to scent the air, obviously detecting Rafe's wolfan scent.

"That's so cute." Grace's giggles echoed around them.

The animal yowled and slapped his paw in their direction.

"Oh, look. He's waving." Grace returned the greeting.

The bear waited for Rafe's, a test to determine friend or foe.

Rafe howled a friendly acknowledgement. Satisfied there was no threat, the bear grunted and ambled off.

"For Pete's sake." Grace stared at him with glittering green eyes. "You growl, you howl. Aren't you taking your wolf obsession too far?"

"Grace, Co-opers have a special affinity to the wolves in the sanctuary. It may seem strange to you. But to me, they're family."

Chapter 17

A perfect day. Rafe hadn't thought those existed anymore. Today had proved him wrong. He pushed back his empty plate, satisfied with the meal and the company.

"Your meat loaf is delicious." Grace devoured the last bite.

"Thank you. It's my specialty." Doc gave an easy grin.

Rafe balled his napkin and dropped it on his empty plate. "It's the only thing you ever learned to cook."

"That's why it's a specialty." Doc winked. His phone buzzed and he excused himself from the table.

"Thanks for inviting me." Grace picked up the plates.

"Figured you could use a home-cooked meal." Rafe certainly appreciated it. Mostly eating fast food and takeout, Rafe looked forward to his weekly meal with his father. Even the nights when they exchanged no words.

There'd been no lack of conversation tonight.

Grace talked about everything she'd seen today. She spotted things Rafe never cared to notice and he liked the way she saw the world—bright, colored, teeming with vitality and wonder. Rather than the drab, barren landscape he was used to seeing.

He gathered the glasses and followed her into the kitchen. "Thanks for helping Alex with his homework."

"He's a smart kid. Eager to please." Grace rinsed off the plates and put them in the dishwasher.

"Only when you're around." Rafe didn't fail to notice how cozy the kitchen felt with her in it.

How cozy he felt with her.

"Alex misses his dad." She moved aside. "You should take him fishing or something."

"I'll see what I can do." Rafe emptied the glasses in the sink and placed them on the top rack of the dishwasher. Then he rearranged the haphazard way Grace had set the plates in the bottom rack.

"They'll get clean no matter which way they're turned." She dried her hands on a dish towel and turned around.

Rafe stood so close she bumped him.

"Oops, sorry." Her clear green eyes glittered as she looked up at him.

All day, he'd contemplated kissing her and had resisted.

He cupped her face. Her lips parted with a soft breath as he leaned closer.

"Don't mind me." Doc came into the kitchen.

Disappointed by the interruption, Rafe grazed Grace's cheek instead of finding her mouth.

"I'm needed at the hospital. I've got to change and head over there."

"Thank you for supper. I'm sorry you have to rush off." Grace gave Doc a hug.

A flash of jealousy whipped through Rafe. Absolutely irrational, but he was jealous all the same.

"Come anytime. The door's always open." Doc patted Rafe's shoulder before heading upstairs to change.

Rafe walked Grace to the tow truck. His hand gravitated to the small of her back as if it was the most natural thing in the world to do. He reached around her for the passenger door and she turned to face him.

"I had fun today." She tugged the front of his shirt.

Rafe moved closer, blocking her against the vehicle. His lips found her mouth in the soft, unhurried kiss he'd wanted to give her in the kitchen.

He'd had fun with her today, too. Something that went

beyond a good time. He'd enjoyed every single moment with her because he'd felt no pressure to be something he wasn't.

After coming to Walker's Run as a child, Rafe was taught how to dress, how to eat, and how to function in society more like a human, less like a wolf. And he always felt slightly out of sync because of it.

In rehab he learned if he wanted to stay sober, he had to come to terms with his true self. Each day since, Rafe had dropped a little more of his facade and allowed a little more of himself to come through.

But with Grace, he was simply and totally himself.

At her soft whimper, all pretense of restraint evaporated. His tongue swept inside her mouth with unbridled urgency. He cradled the back of her neck and tilted her head for the right angle to deepen the kiss, slowing down only to rev up to a maddening frenzy. Their tongues danced and mated, devoured and conquered.

His hand trailed down her back, gently molding her against him. Soft in all the right places, she fit him perfectly, like a piece of the same puzzle.

A silvery light flashed in his conscience with one imperative thought, *Mine*!

He broke this kiss. He wasn't ready to accept another mate. Hell, he didn't know if he'd ever be ready for one, but he'd definitely warmed to Grace's idea of being a friend with benefits.

"Wow." Dreamy-eyed, she smiled.

"Yeah, wow."

Rafe heard the race of an engine before a Mercedes swung into the driveway and slammed to a stop.

Rafe yanked open the tow truck passenger door. "Stay inside and lock the doors," he warned and slammed the door shut.

Rafe didn't ask how Clay had found him. Everyone knew where to find him on Wednesday nights.

Small town, few secrets. The pack had been more than fortunate to keep theirs for so long.

"What the hell are you doing?" The ugliness in Clay's voice matched the sneer on his face.

Rafe clucked his tongue over his teeth. "In general? Or right this second?"

"Don't be flippant, you son of a bitch. Do you think I'm stupid?"

Stupid, no. Pretentious. Arrogant. Oppressive. Reactionary. The list could go on for a quarter mile, at least.

"Who is that woman?" Clay jabbed his finger toward the tow truck.

"Not your business." Rafe kept his voice level. "Why are you here?"

"I want *all* of my daughter's things returned. The jewelry box, the stuffed animals, her gardening books. Everything."

"That might be a problem." The jewelry box broke years ago and Lexi had tossed it in the garbage. The stuffed animals she gave to the hospital pediatrics department after Rafe claimed her.

"I gave it away." Rafe rubbed the muscles bunching at the base of his neck. He really hoped this would be the last time he encountered Clay.

"You bastard! How dare you treat Alexis's possessions like garbage." Clay grabbed Rafe's shirt.

Rafe shoved him back a few steps. "I gave her stuff to the people and places she would've wanted to have her things go." It was the last act of kindness he could ever do for her.

"I want it all back!"

"Collect it yourself. Cynthia knows where it all went."

"What's left at the house?"

"Nothing that belonged to Lexi. Ronni packed up everything for me. The house is hers now."

"Your blood-kin have no right to be in my daughter's house. If you don't get them out, I will."

Rafe kept his hands fisted at his sides so his fingers wouldn't latch around Clay's throat. "Stay away from my family, Clay."

"Like you stayed away from mine?" His cold, harsh laugh scraped Rafe's auditory senses.

"Get your blood-kin out of my daughter's house." Clay's gaze cut to the tow truck. "Keep your paws and your cock to yourself. I won't allow you to desecrate my daughter's memory by whoring with other women."

Purple-faced, Clay barreled past Rafe.

Rafe spun around and sank his fingers into Clay's shoulder. "She is under my protection and if you go near her, it won't end well for you."

"You promised to protect my daughter. Now she's dead."

The truthful words punched Rafe in the solar plexus.

He had failed to protect his mate. He'd grown too docile, too tame, too oblivious to the dangers of predators.

It didn't matter that they were in a protected sanctuary. He should've scented the intruder and stopped him before he focused his sights and pulled the goddamn trigger.

He let go of Clay's shoulder and took a deep breath.

"I warned you to stay away from her. You didn't listen." Clay stepped so close Rafe had to tilt his face to lift his gaze to see something other than the bulging veins in Clay's neck. "Stay away from her." Clay jerked his head toward Grace inside the vehicle. "Or she may end up dead, too."

"Get away from my son!" Doc stormed down the porch steps and shoved Clay away from Rafe. "Keep licking that old wound if you want, but come near Rafe again and I'll end this feud. Permanently."

Rafe's father might appear harmless and gentle, but a

human male couldn't run with the Alpha wolf if he didn't have the balls and fortitude to keep up.

"So be it." Clay spat and walked away.

"Everything okay?" Grace twisted in her seat to buckle the seat belt. Her lips still tingled from the kiss they'd shared, but she no longer had hopes of anything more developing tonight.

"Peachy," Rafe practically snarled. He jammed the key into the ignition and gripped the steering wheel until his knuckles turned white.

Tires squealed as the Mercedes spun out of the driveway. She wished for a flock of birds to shit all over his shiny expensive car. Karma for spoiling Rafe's good mood.

"Who is he?"

"Clay Reinhardt, my former father-in-law," Rafe said, tight-lipped as turbulent emotions stormed in his eyes.

Rafe snapped on his seat belt and eased onto the road. Grace waved goodbye to Doc, who stood by his car watching them leave. Such a nice man.

Grace didn't press Rafe further about the incident. She sat quietly, sliding through the day's pictures on her phone. She smiled at the one of Rafe at breakfast. Head down, eyes focused on his plate, his intense expression left no doubt eating was serious business.

Her favorite photo, of the dozens she'd clicked, was at the scenic overview. They'd huddled together for the selfie. Rafe's chin rested on her shoulder, his cheek sealed against hers, his mouth firmly set, the shadow of a smile dancing in his bright, blue, devastating eyes.

Before they arrived at the resort, Grace touched his arm, the muscle hard and warm beneath her fingers. "I'm sorry that jerk ruined the day."

"Why do you do that?" His hardened gaze fixed on her.

"Do what?"

"You say I'm sorry as if you actually have something to apologize for."

"Old habit," Grace said. "When my dad was home on leave, sometimes the simplest thing would set him off. Somehow I was always to blame." When the cat clawed the curtains, it was her fault because she wanted a pet. When her dad stepped on one of Matt's Legos it was her fault because she hadn't checked to make sure he'd put them all away. When her mom burnt dinner it was because Grace forgot to remind her to set the timer.

"Grace." Rafe interrupted her thoughts. "You aren't responsible for the bad blood between me and Clay." He glanced at her. "What you are responsible for is making today perfect."

Her insides melted. "Thank you."

He smiled a real, honest-to-goodness smile.

It was merely a flash, but whoa! He should wear a label. Caution: Smiles can provoke heart palpitations, shortness of breath, and the sudden urge to get naked and sweaty.

She adjusted the air vent before she acted on the impulse.

Chapter 18

A gentle wind sifted through Rafe's fur. He lay on a bed of new spring moss with a clear view of the first quarter moon hooked high in the heavens. Lower in the sky, a few storm clouds drifted north. By the time they were swollen enough to drop rain, they'd be hanging over Gatlinburg.

Three feet away, Brice tipped his snout upward to watch a moth fluttering above his head, though his eyes kept flickering over to Rafe. Brice had never been as comfortable as Rafe was with silence.

They were breaking curfew. Not that Brice cared about his father's edict not to shift into their wolves after 10:00 p.m. He'd vocally opposed his father in private, and when Rafe said he wanted to talk, Brice had suggested a night run in the sanctuary, knowing Rafe was closer to his wolf nature than most in Walker's Run.

Tonight, Rafe had a hard time putting words to his thoughts. He struggled to make sense of the enigmatic pull toward Grace.

All wrong for him, she was impulsive, scattered and human.

All wrong for her, he was scheduled, organized and wolfan.

But the sexual energy between them was damn near combustible. Coupling was inevitable. It was only a matter of time.

Rafe didn't agree with Gavin's wait-and-see plan for Grace. She needed to know the truth and if the Alpha family remained silent, he needed to be the one to tell her.

"How did you explain being Wahya to Red?"

"She saw me shift on the night we met." Brice's blue eye glittered and his green eye seemed to glow. *"Why?"*

"Grace deserves to know the truth. I don't want her hurt, and the longer we keep her in the dark, the harder it will be for her to trust any of us." Especially him.

"Are you planning to tell her?"

Rafe ignored the question and stretched out on his side.

"You know the rules, man."

Wahyan law strictly forbade exposing one's wolf to a human unless the human was in mortal danger, or if the human was the wolfan's mate.

"So do you, and yet you shifted in front of Red the first time you met her."

"Cybil had her pinned."

"Cybil?" Rafe snorted. *"The old sow was probably sniffing her for a candy bar. Hardly constitutes mortal danger."*

"No, but Cas and I are mates."

"Did you know that at the time?"

Silence.

"I didn't think so."

"Cas freaked when it happened and when a mate-bond began forming between us, she completely resisted it." Brice lifted his muzzle toward the sky. *"Sometimes I wonder if she'd known me as a man first, would she have had an easier time bonding with my wolf?"*

So much for Rafe following Brice's lead. Terrifying and alienating Grace wasn't how Rafe wanted to introduce her to wolfan life.

"We all want Grace to know the truth," Brice continued. *"But we need to be careful. Truth can bring people together or tear them apart."*

"So do lies."

"Not divulging something is not necessarily a lie."

"Spoken like a true lawyer."

"Since the accident, I've teased you about Grace be-

cause you're so damn easy to rile. But, is there something going on between you and her? Is it possible she could be your new mate?"

Anything was possible.

Technically, if Grace were commitment minded, Rafe could easily establish a mate-claim by biting her during sex. The mate-claim could be established without thought, consideration or credence given to forming a mate-bond.

The problem was, Rafe wasn't the type of man to claim a female without experiencing a mate-bond.

Not all wolfans developed the mystical ties to their mates. Those who did experienced a merging of heart and soul that surpassed the mere telepathy the mate-claim produced. Even at great distances, a mate-bonded couple could sense each other's emotions and share dreams.

From the beginning, Rafe's wolf had wanted Grace. Now, the man wanted her, too.

But, he wanted Grace to have an honest understanding of him. Revealing his wolf would make an affair more personal for him, but it didn't have to lead to a mate-claim.

He'd barely survived the loss of his first mate and it took a long time for him to get to a better place. Since his sobriety, he'd started figuring out who he wanted to be as an individual, not half of a couple. He wasn't ready to lose himself again. Not even to Grace.

"I can't do another mateship," Rafe finally responded to Brice's query. *"And Grace is only interested in a sex buddy."*

"There's a fine line between lust and love." Brice's gaze seemed to burn through Rafe. *"If your heart decides to cross that boundary, you won't be able to stop it."*

For Grace's sake and his own, Rafe needed to make sure his heart didn't get involved.

Chapter 19

It's too early for Cassie's baby. Way too early.

Arms hugging her chest, Grace paced the hospital's emergency clinic waiting room.

She'd had a lot of nice thoughts about Rafe today.

Ten minutes ago, all those nice thoughts dissipated like wisps of smoke. She unhooked her arms and glared at the cell phone in her hand. "Why haven't you answered?"

The better question was why she had texted Rafe in the first place. He hated hospitals.

She could rationalize until cows started producing chocolate milk that she asked Rafe to come because he was Brice's best friend, and Rafe should be here to support him. Truthfully, Grace was scared and Rafe made her feel safe.

Brice was in the treatment bay with Cassie, even though he'd been told to stay in the waiting area. Good thing no one actually protested when he ignored the order. He might've torn down the place to be with her.

Grace actually felt good about his reaction. He wasn't going to allow his wife to face a terrifying unknown alone.

Grace, of course, didn't have the commanding presence Brice did. She'd been relegated to the waiting room. Facing a crisis alone made her stomach roll.

It would've been nice to have someone sit with her. Rafe's presence wouldn't change the outcome of what would be, but she would've been grateful to not hear the news by herself.

Sitting in a plastic, straight-backed chair, Grace waved

her fingers at the little boy being rocked against his mother's chest. He squinted tired, weepy eyes to hide from her, then peeked one eye open. She waved again and he giggled.

"I'm Grace. What's your name?"

He squealed and hid his face.

"Connor, you're not being nice," his mother said. "I'm Loretta."

"Grace." She didn't extend her automatic handshake because Loretta's arms were full with her son.

"I saw you come in with Cassie and Brice. Is she in labor?"

"I hope not." Considering Cassie was only six-and-a-half months pregnant.

"Gray-see." The little boy lifted his head and grinned, even though his big, brown eyes shimmered with unshed tears.

"Nice to meet you, Connor."

He stared at her outstretched hand, grabbed her fingers and pulled them to his pert little nose. "You smell funny."

"Connor," Loretta said sharply. "That's not polite."

"It's all right." Grace laughed. "What do I smell like?"

"I dunno." He crinkled his nose. "Lots of things."

"It's her perfume." Rafe's strong, quiet voice slipped over Grace's shoulder. "Some women like to change their scent. Grace is wearing a combination of strawberry, violets, gardenia, jasmine, vanilla and grapefruit."

"Are you making that up?" Grace looked at Rafe.

"My wife worked at the botanical gardens," he said simply. "I learned to identify a lot of floral scents."

"Rafe, it's good to see you." A radiant smile lit up Loretta's face and her dark brown eyes warmed to the color of hot fudge. Even the contours of her face softened. From the highly-charged vibe Loretta cast, she definitely had a thing for Rafe.

"What brings you here?" She adjusted Connor on her lap, exposing her low-cut T-shirt and ample cleavage.

"Grace asked me to come." Rafe's hand squeezed Grace's shoulder, yet he gazed at her with an absolutely blank expression.

Nothing reflected his perception, reception or assessment of Loretta's interest, how he felt about the text from Grace or if he wanted to kiss her again.

"Any news?"

Grace shook her head as the heat from his touch seeped into her muscles and eased some of her tension. Regardless of whether or not he wanted to be there, Grace appreciated his presence.

"You're getting a little shaggy," Loretta said to him.

"I like it," Grace blurted at Rafe. "You look more laid-back, comfortable." Sexy, but she didn't dare say it out loud.

Rafe cut his eyes at her, the tease of a smile in his gaze.

"He prefers a clean-cut style," Loretta huffed, then turned to Rafe. "I can come by the R&L to give you a trim if you're too busy to stop by the barbershop."

"I'm trying something different." Rafe rubbed Loretta's son on the back. "Got an earache, Connor?"

"Yeah." The boy pushed out his bottom lip in an exaggerated pout.

Loretta kissed Connor's head. "I know Doc came in for Cassie, but if he's done before we see the on-call pediatrician, would you ask him to examine Connor?"

Rafe nodded and slouched in the chair next to Grace, lacing his fingers behind his head and stretching out his legs. His knee grazed hers, sending goose bumps scurrying up her spine to high-dive into her belly.

His eyes slid shut.

So much for conversation to keep her distracted.

She glanced at Loretta. Her friendly demeanor had cooled. Though no true malice was reflected in the narrow-eyed look Loretta gave her, continuing their chitchat didn't seem likely.

Grace closed her eyes in another silent prayer for Cassie, then opened a social media app on her phone. Her message board was filled with notes from friends all across the globe. Reading them, it struck her how everyone talked at her and not really to her. Posts were generic updates on what they did or where they were going. No one actually said anything in an attempt to go beyond the surface to delve into a deeper, more meaningful relationship. For the first time, the lack of depth in their communication bothered her.

Rafe shut his eyes. He'd taken a sleeping pill and was almost asleep when he got Grace's text. The adrenaline rush of seeing her urgent message had dampened the sedative's effects.

Though no longer tired, he pretended to sleep to avoid talking to Loretta. His efforts to deter unwanted attachments with her hadn't been as successful as he'd hoped.

Loretta's snippiness toward Grace and the flash of jealousy in her eyes when he'd touched Grace's shoulder signaled it was time to find a new moon-fuck partner.

He heard Grace lean forward in her seat, her feet tapping the floor in an agitated beat. Her breathing sounded shallow and harsh. In the half hour he'd been with her, she'd barely relaxed, except when he touched her. He wished he could say it had been accidental. It wasn't, although after the shoulder touch he'd tried to make the occasional bumps and grazes appear accidental in an attempt to thwart Loretta's jealousy.

A hairstylist and manicurist with three kids, she wasn't violent. Then again, she'd never been jealous of him, either.

When she disappeared into a bay with Connor, Rafe lightly trailed his fingers down Grace's spine. She gave a startled jump beneath his touch. He sensed her turn to him, but he kept his eyes closed, trying to imagine anything other than her big, green eyes staring at him.

He strummed the muscles in her back methodically. Slowly, she began to relax, and so did he. Her tension had been so high he'd felt the weight of it on his own body.

She was much too intense for her own good.

He knew some horizontal activities that would help her relax. A few vertical ones, too.

Footsteps sounded in the corridor behind the closed double doors. From the stride, he knew his father was coming.

Rafe stood and Grace's worried gaze caused his gut to clench. He wanted to ease her mind, tell her everything was fine, but without knowing that all was well, he wouldn't promise her it was.

He offered his hand, signaling with a curling finger for her to stand. Without hesitation, she gripped his fingers and walked with him to the doors.

Doc stepped through, Gavin and Abby a few steps behind. All looked relieved.

"Cassie's fine," Doc said with a smile.

Grace seemed frozen, unable to process the news.

"Can Grace see her?" Rafe slipped his arm around her waist and gave a gentle squeeze, despite Gavin's frown.

"Come with me." Doc rubbed Grace's shoulder. "She really is doing well."

With Grace pressed against his hip, Rafe walked into the east wing triage ward. If Doc had been at the hospital when Cassie had arrived, he would've directed them to the Co-op's west wing, where Wahyas and their families were treated.

But Cassie was human and likely wanted Grace to be with her once the emergency passed, and humans not affiliated with the Co-op weren't allowed into the west wing—in case they saw something they shouldn't.

"Cassie and the baby are really okay?" Grace asked softly.

Deep inside, Rafe felt the depths of her concern and her fear. Without thinking, he leaned into her, nuzzling her cheek.

"See for yourself." Doc pulled back the bay curtains.

"Cassie!"

"Grace!"

Instant relief was mirrored on their faces.

Rafe glanced at Brice, standing bedside. His features were tired, but relaxed. He stepped aside so Grace could wedge in next to Cassie.

Grace crawled right into the bed and the women hugged.

"I had some false labor pains and my blood pressure got too high," Cassie said. "It's down now."

The women's animated chatter turned into a whirring noise inside Rafe's head.

He leaned toward Doc. "Loretta brought in Connor. He's pulling at his ears and looks fevered. They're with the on-call pediatrician but she wanted you to check him."

"I'll pop over to see them."

Brice walked over as Doc left.

"You all right, Walker?" Rafe asked.

"Yes." Brice released a heavy breath. "Cassie will need to take it easy. She's not going to like it much."

Rafe stuffed his hands into his pockets.

"Thanks for coming, man." Brice cuffed Rafe's shoulder. "It means a lot to me that you're here."

"Glad Red's okay." Rafe glanced at Grace, her head bent toward Cassie as they laughed at something on Grace's phone.

"Grace has a way of putting people at ease," Brice said. "Cassie wants her to be in the delivery room. Apparently, I don't have a very good bedside manner when my mate is scared and in pain."

Rafe really didn't want to discuss labor and delivery plans. "Since Red's okay, I'm gonna head home."

"Do you mind taking Grace back to the resort? She rode with us but Doc wants Cassie to stay overnight and I'm not leaving her."

With fatigue beginning to catch up with him, driving all the way to the resort and back into town might be pushing his limits. "I'll take her home with me." His apartment was only a few minutes away from the hospital. "Grace will want to be close by in case Cassie needs her."

"Careful now." An irritating grin lifted the tension and worry etched on Brice's face. "Keep spending the night with Grace and you'll ended up mated."

"Screw you."

The humor in his friend's eyes as he painstakingly turned his gaze in slow-motion toward Grace told Rafe exactly who Brice thought he should screw.

Chapter 20

5:47 a.m. flashed on the digital clock.

Rafe flipped the clock face down into the top of the couch back.

A few hours ago, Grace had fallen asleep within minutes of crawling into the Murphy bed.

Stretched out on the couch, one arm draped behind his head, Rafe stared at the ceiling. Grace's soft, even breaths were like a lullaby. More than anything he wanted to crawl next to her. Feel her heat. Smell her skin. Sink deep inside her until he came undone.

She had no idea what she did to him.

Her presence ate the silence. Even in the quiet of the early morning, she filled the void.

Hell. He had a hard enough time keeping his mind off her. Her scent permeating his home wasn't helping.

Willing his mind and body to settle, he rolled to his side, burying his face in his pillow. It didn't stop him from breathing in Grace's scent. He tried holding his breath, but somehow her essence filled the room with a warmth that seeped into his skin. His nerves danced with awareness. Everything in him, except his common sense, wanted to crawl next to her, press against her heat and give into her softness.

His groin, tight with arousal, showed no signs of easing, Unable to fall back to sleep, Rafe tossed aside the white sheet and slipped quietly out of the room. He padded into the bathroom and turned on the shower, adjusting the temperature just enough to take the bite out of the cold water.

Standing in the cool spray, he soaped his chest and stomach. His thoughts kept drifting to Grace. He could disappear in those vast green eyes of hers and a mere glimpse of her genuine smile could warm him for days.

Her scent, her skin, even the timbre of her voice called to him in ways he never imagined would ever be possible for him again.

He wanted her.

No surprise there. He'd been drawn to her the moment his wolf had first detected her scent. What he'd dismissed as a fleeting interest hadn't dissipated in the following months when he'd actively avoided her. He'd been right to keep his distance.

Grace's hadn't merely wrecked her car; she'd crashed into his life.

Nothing would ever be the same again.

Something inside him had known this at Brice's party and Rafe had been wise enough to remove himself from her path. He'd been too new to sobriety, his grip on rebuilding a new life too fragile, and his heart not nearly mended enough.

Now, Rafe had reached the point where he wanted companionship but not commitment. Still, he didn't want to live like Tristan, a different woman every night.

Well, to be fair, Tristan had said he really didn't bed a woman nightly, or even weekly anymore. Still, that was his reputation and Rafe didn't want it to be his.

Rafe had hesitations, but he was ready for more intimacy than his moon-fuck partnership provided.

He doubted Grace would seriously consider putting down roots in such a small, unsophisticated town. He hoped that would work in his favor. A down-home kind of guy, he couldn't imagine living anywhere else. The differences in their very natures would prevent any serious pursuit. This could work.

Rafe's soapy hands slid down his abdomen. His erection, not diminished by the spray of cool water, begged for attention.

This time, he refused to give it. Grace was in his home, under his protection. If he kept jerking off to fantasies about her, it would cloud his judgment.

If she wanted to initiate something, so be it. He'd let it be on her terms.

Rafe shut off the water, climbed out of the shower and grabbed a towel, rubbing it roughly over his body. The friction warmed his skin, but didn't take the edge off the chill inside him.

He stared at his reflection in the mirror. The dark circles that had once ringed his eyes were barely visible now. He had allowed his hair to grow a little longer than he usually wore it, but it was not nearly as shaggy as it had been when he was drinking.

The shadow along his jaw and chin felt more natural than a clean-shaven face so he put the razor back in the cabinet over the sink.

Instead of combing his hair, he ran his fingers through the damp strands, spiking it instead of slicking it into place. A little wild, but not unkempt.

He liked it.

The tiny changes he'd started making were more freeing than he imagined. He didn't feel quite so constrained. Until he'd stopped drinking, he hadn't realized how confined he'd always felt. The first seven years of his life, he'd been raised on the outskirts of civilization. More wolf than boy, he'd loved running free in the forest, tracking rabbits, pouncing on fish in the streams.

He still liked those things.

He wondered if Grace would mind that he did.

* * *

"Rafe?" Grace knocked on the door. "Are you almost done?"

She shifted on the balls of her feet. How long did a man need in the bathroom, anyway?

She'd been waiting over twenty minutes and she had to pee so badly her eyeballs were starting to water.

"If you don't come out soon, I'm gonna—"

The door opened. "Gonna what?"

Rafe peered at her with sharp, intense eyes. His damp hair was tousled but not messy and he hadn't shaved. Bare chested with a white towel draped around his hips, he leaned against the door frame.

Her heart stumbled over itself. No man should look that sexy in the morning when she had bed hair, crust in her eyes and a really bad taste in her mouth.

His dark blue gaze took its sweet-ass time assessing her. "You've seen me naked. You could've come in at any time." A smile played on his lips. "I have nothing to hide."

She ducked past him, closing him out of the bathroom. "Some matters deserve a little privacy."

He chuckled beyond the door, but in case he was close enough to hear, she turned on the water spigot to mask any noise she made emptying her bladder.

When she was through, Grace grabbed a clean washcloth from the small wall cabinet fastened above the toilet. Every cloth and towel was meticulously folded and lined up perfectly on the two shelves. Everything in Rafe's apartment was crisp, clean and symmetrical. Nothing out of place, nothing out of line.

Her father had demanded military orderliness with white-glove cleanliness. As soon as she left home for college, she thumbed her nose at his regimented compulsion.

She didn't rebel so far as to turn into a slothful slob, but she did messy very well.

At least Rafe didn't yell at her for leaving a hand towel on the sink rather than hanging it on the bar with the edges perfectly lined up, or leaving a glass on the coffee table without a coaster or dropping cookie crumbs on the counter, the couch, the bed.

She dampened the cloth and scrubbed the sleep from her face. Rummaging through the medicine cabinet, she found the hair tie she'd dropped last night and Rafe's comb.

After untangling the knots in her hair, she did a quick, loose braid and fastened the ends with the tie. She rinsed her mouth and wrinkled her nose at her reflection.

Certainly not the face of a runway model, but at least she was presentable.

"I smell coffee." She walked into the kitchen.

Dressed for work, wearing a white T-shirt beneath his coveralls, Rafe lifted a cup from the Keurig and offered it to her. The delicate aroma wasn't the usual rich, bold fragrance of the brew that brought her up to speed in the mornings. Still, she gratefully accepted his offering. Weak coffee was better than none. "I thought you didn't own a coffeemaker."

"Saw it on sale." He turned, putting the half-decaf, half-regular K-cup box in the cabinet over the sink.

Wish I had known, I would've had a cup or two while I tutored Alex.

Grace blew over the rim of the cup before taking a sip.

"That's why I didn't tell you."

Grace choked on the sip of coffee she'd just swallowed.

"Ya all right?" One reddish eyebrow inched up.

"Went down the wrong pipe." She coughed again. "How did you do that?"

"What?"

"Respond to something I thought but didn't actually say."

He stared at her for a long moment. "I think you didn't

realize you said it out loud. I can't read your thoughts, Grace. That would be…crazy, right?"

"Yeah." Except she was pretty sure she hadn't said it. Maybe her reduced caffeine intact yesterday had messed with her brain.

She took another drink of coffee, noticing he kept his hair in the same sexy, wind-blown, tousled style he'd worn stepping out of the bathroom, and the stubbled shadow on his chin and jaw made her want to test if it was soft or prickly. "I like the new look."

She'd thought him sexy before, all straight-laced and whatnot, but the looseness in his limbs and posture, and the touch of wildness called to her in a way no man ever had.

"You mentioned that last night." He leaned against the counter, his legs stretched in front of him, his arms loosely folded across his chest.

She inched toward him.

Interest flared in his eyes and suddenly the kitchen filled with high-octane energy. One spark and *kaboom!*

She needed some kaboom.

Sitting the cup on the counter, she sidled right up into his personal space. He stood straighter, pulling his legs back so she could get close. Closer.

Closer still.

His breathing remained calm, steady. Hers, she held.

He leaned in, nudged along her jaw, drawing a deep sigh as she was finally forced to breathe.

He lightly kissed her lips, and his hands slid beneath her shirt, skimming her ribs until he found her breasts.

Her hands roamed his chest down to his groin. Her palm ground against the hardening bulge.

The alarm on Rafe's phone went off.

Grace nibbled his bottom lip. "Sorry, sweetie. Time to pick Alex up for school." She peppered the hollow of his throat with kisses. "How about a rain check?"

"Are you seriously going to leave me like this?" Rafe's gaze panned to the erection tenting his coveralls.

Grace gave him her best smile and she strolled out of the kitchen.

Chapter 21

"Keep spending the night with Rafe and this could be your future." Cassie pointed to her belly. Her eyes smiled as much as her mouth did. Settled in a recliner in her in-laws' family room, she appeared rested and alert after her overnight in the hospital.

Brice, Cassie reported, hadn't slept all night, so he was passed out in their bedroom, snoring to the rafters.

"So not funny." Grace grimaced. Cassie didn't know about the miscarriage so her friend had no idea how much the idea of pregnancy scared her. "It was all very innocent. I slept in the bed, he crashed on the couch."

"What about this morning?"

"What about it?" Guilt made Grace's voice a little squeaky. "We got up. He made coffee and dropped me off here on his way to pick up Alex."

"Nothing spicy happened?"

"Uh, no."

"Why are your cheeks red?" Cassie giggled.

"They aren't." Grace touched her face, and her skin felt warm against her fingers. "Okay, we shared a little touchy-feely time. Nothing serious."

"So? You're both single, have lots of sexual chemistry. There's nothing wrong with you having fun."

"Things could get complicated. Rafe is a down-home, let's make a commitment guy. I'm looking to have fun."

"With a steady partner, right?" Cassie sipped her hot tea. "You won't find anyone steadier than Rafe."

"How are my girls today?" Gavin entered the room, stopping at Cassie's chair to give her a fatherly hug, then gingerly rubbed her belly.

"I'm fine," Cassie said, reaching behind her to adjust her back pillow. "Your granddaughter must be dreaming of chasing rabbits. She's moving a lot."

"Maybe she's burning off the nervous energy from last night. Should I call Doc?"

"No. It's nothing out of the ordinary for her."

Gavin kissed the top of Cassie's head. "Do let me or Abby know if there is anything we can do for you."

"When Brice wakes up, keep him occupied. He gets panicky over every little thing."

"Abby will tell you, I acted the same way." Gavin smiled and turned to Grace. "We're grateful you're here. I know Cassie feels better having you so close. If you need anything, don't hesitate to ask."

"You've been very generous, Mr. Walker, but I don't want to wear out my welcome. I've already asked my brother and his partner to pick me up on Saturday."

"I was hoping you would change your mind." The disappointment in Cassie's voice squeezed Grace's heart.

"You'll miss Co-op spring festival." Gavin sounded surprised. "Didn't Rafe invite you?"

"Um, no. He hasn't mentioned it." Grace noticed a flicker of irritation in Gavin's eyes. "Besides, I'm not a Co-op member. Wouldn't it break the rules for me to attend?"

"Nonsense. You're practically family." Nothing sinister registered in his smile but it gave Grace the uncanny impression he wasn't as straightforward as he seemed.

"Oh, please come." Cassie's face lit up.

"It will be an excellent opportunity to meet Co-op members other than those who work for the resort." Gavin paused, with a crafty smile in place. "I'll tell Abby to add one more to the count."

Grace didn't appreciate Gavin seemingly making the decision for her, but there wasn't any pressing reason she couldn't extend her visit. She was keeping up her client's work orders and Matt was doing fine without her.

"I'd love to attend the festival." Grace enjoyed meeting new people. Besides, something explosive was happening between her and Rafe and she didn't want to miss the kaboom.

Rafe rubbed the back of his hand across his itchy nose for what seemed like the hundredth time. The sickly sweet odor from the pan of drained antifreeze dominated his sense of smell.

He poured the yellow-green liquid from the drip pan into a can, capped it with a tight lid and placed the container in the corner where he stored automotive waste until his monthly trip to the county's hazardous waste disposal center.

The old radio on the shelf provided company in a steady stream of country songs. A soft spring breeze provided just enough cool wind that he didn't need the oscillating fan sitting quietly, out of the way.

Returning to the vehicle in the second bay, Rafe double-checked that the drain valve was closed before he opened the radiator pressure cap to fill the reservoir with water. Next, he cranked the engine, turned the heater on high and let it run for about ten minutes while he made notes in his logbook.

Someone drove into the back lot. He reached inside the car to shut off the ignition for the engine to cool. Heels clicked across the concrete floor.

Rafe cleaned his hands, tossed the towel into a small laundry basket and turned to face his customer.

"Hey, sugar." The tall ebony-haired she-wolf sauntered toward him, wearing tight-fitting jeans, a low-cut red blouse and a sensual smile that caused an uneasy prickle in Rafe's gut.

Ah, hell.

This visit wasn't going to be about a routine oil change.

Loretta sauntered so close Rafe had to step back and bumped against the grille of the car behind him. Crossing his arms over his chest only prompted her to curl her long fingers around his biceps.

"Got a minute?" she asked, her voice light and teasing.

"No." Since he'd closed up shop yesterday, he had a lot of catching up to do today.

"Instead of meeting at our usual spot on the next full moon, come to my place for dinner. Afterward, we'll run the woods, make our way upriver to the falls. Let the moonlight bathe our bare skin." Her voiced trailed. Tenderness pooled in her brown eyes. She caressed his cheek and leaned in to nuzzle him.

From any other she-wolf the unwanted intimate touch would've sparked a harsh, immediate response. However, Rafe owed Loretta kindness for the sake of their moonfuck partnership.

"No." He gently removed her hand from his face.

"I know your needs have changed." She tipped her chin down and looked up at him through a veil of thick, dark lashes. "I can give you what you need."

Loretta's red-painted lips pressed against his mouth and her fingers clutched his hips.

Nothing in her kiss set him on fire the way Grace did. And Grace didn't have to touch him for sparks to flame.

From her, a simple look, a laugh, a soul-warming smile could light up every cell in his body.

He turned his head to break the kiss and used the back

of his hand to wipe away the wetness. "My needs have changed, because I have."

Rafe straightened to his full height and peered down at Loretta. "What do you see when you look at me?"

Her mouth curved into a coy smile. She began describing his physical characteristics. Her words, her voice became a hissing noise in his head as her hands slithered up his chest.

"Not what I look like." Rafe captured her fingers. "What do you see inside me? The real me?"

Confusion flashed across her features. She searched his face, her gaze settling on his.

Rafe dropped the practiced pretenses, the ingrained idiosyncrasies, the cultured lies.

Fear rose in Loretta's eyes, a dawning discovery of his true feral nature.

"You're afraid." He released her with a laugh.

"No." She stepped back, clearing her voice. "Surprised. I shouldn't be, considering all you've gone through. You just need someone with the patience to help you find your way back."

"Back to what?"

"Back to yourself."

"I've never been more myself than when I'm with Grace."

"She's human, Rafe. She can't tame the wildness in you like I can."

"I don't want to be tamed." His wolf prowled in his conscience, irritable and restless, until a sudden rush of Grace's essence filled him.

She was coming.

Visions of picking up where they'd left off this morning danced in his mind.

"I think it's best if you find a new moon-fuck partner." Rafe picked up a shop towel and cleaned the red lipstick smear from the back of his hand.

Loretta tossed her hair, jutted her breasts and cocked an eyebrow at him. "We've been together three years. I'm not walking out now."

She stalked over to him, shoved her hand against his chest hard enough for him to stumble back against the car behind him and perch on the edge of the hood.

The distinctive sound of a truck engine hummed through the open bays. His nerves snapped with anticipation and his heart kicked up a few notches.

"Loretta, stop," he said, wanting to dispatch her gently and quickly.

She grabbed the front of his coveralls, sealed her body against his and planted her lips on his mouth, swallowing his protest.

"Oh!" Grace's gasp echoed in the bays. "I…um…" She spun around and hurried out of the building.

Rafe scrambled to push Loretta aside. Unfortunately, she seemed to have grown octopus tentacles. As soon as he freed her hand from one spot she latched onto another, including squeezing and pumping his cock.

"Enough!" He shoved her only hard enough to break free.

"When your fascination with Grace passes, call me." Loretta thumbed the corners of her smiling mouth. Her gaze dropped to his erection evident through his coveralls. "And I'll finish what I've started."

Loretta sashayed out the back bay to her car. Rafe dashed out the front, searching for Grace.

His heart drummed in his chest. His wolf howled. His erection grew more persistent.

Loretta had gotten it wrong. She hadn't made him hard.

Grace had.

Chapter 22

Grace sat on a park bench, swinging her feet. Her ears rang, her vision remained tunneled and sweat broke out on her skin even as a hard chill rocked her body.

Rafe wasn't supposed to have a current lover. If he did, it made her "the other woman." She despised cheaters and didn't want to be involved with one.

"Grace!" Rafe's husky voice penetrated the chatter in her head.

He came into focus. Of course his erection would be the first thing she saw.

"Your girlfriend has time to take care of your hard-on." Grace looked away. The park was empty except for them. "Alex has another forty-five minutes before school is out."

"Loretta isn't my girlfriend."

"Could've fooled me." Grace swung her head toward him.

His lips and chin were smeared with scarlet lipstick. The buttons of his coveralls were undone past his waist. One more button and the fleshy tip of his cock would be visible. "You should probably clean up." She pointed at his face and groin.

"Damn."

Yeah, damn. She'd caught a ride into town because she wanted that rain check before Alex got out of school.

He buttoned the coveralls to midchest, used his sleeve to wipe off most of the lipstick, then he sat so close to her that their hips touched.

She ground her teeth, resisting the tingle spreading through her body.

"You're rubbing your tattoo again." His hand gently closed over her fingers massaging her wrist. "What does it mean?"

Swallowing the burn rising in her throat, she slowly traced the loops of the design. "I had it done after I lost my baby."

"Ah, hell," Rafe whispered, rubbing his fingers against his jaw.

"It reminds me that no matter what I'm going through, it will never be as bad as that day."

"Grace." He dropped his arm across her shoulders and tucked her against him.

"I'm okay," she said without making any effort to move. "Just a little confused. I didn't realize you were involved with someone."

His chest heaved with a deep sigh. "The thing with Loretta—"

"I know," Grace interrupted. She inched away from him. "It's complicated."

"Actually, it's pretty straightforward." He leaned back, stretching out his legs and folding his hands over his waist. "Loretta lost her husband a few months before my wife died. We were both grieving." His voice trailed.

"You've been together all this time?"

"Not actually together. We'd meet briefly once a month, that's it."

"Is it that time of the month?"

Rafe gave her a puzzled look.

"All the kissing and groping I interrupted. Was it because today is your monthly meet-up?"

"No." He scratched the back of his head. "She's ready for a relationship with a real commitment. She was hoping to convince me of the same."

"Did she?"

"Considering I'm sitting here with you," he gently elbowed Grace, "I'd say no."

"To be clear, it's over between you and Loretta."

"There's nothing to get over. Like I said, it was a very brief once-a-month thing. It's not like we ate supper together, or fell asleep on the couch watching TV." He hmmphed. "She never texted me in the middle of the night for ice cream."

Rafe looked sidelong at Grace, a crooked smile hitching up the corner of his mouth.

"I liked doing those things with you. I was wrong when I said I didn't want to be your friend. Now that we are, I can't imagine not doing more of those things with you."

There was no guile in his eyes, no flicker from her gaze, no hesitation in his voice, and Grace knew in her heart he spoke the truth.

"Well, that's because I'm a fun person to be with," She grinned as a certain restlessness within her lifted. "With or without the extra benefits."

Rafe laughed. "Yes, you are."

"But you'd prefer with benefits, right?"

"Hell, yeah."

"Me, too." Grace wouldn't have imagined him to be the type who could maintain a no-strings relationship for an extended period. Now she knew that he was, she wouldn't worry about things getting too serious.

"Come on." She stood. "I'll race you to the garage."

Grace didn't give Rafe time to react, she simply started running.

It took about ten seconds before she heard him gaining.

"Hey, Goldilocks." Rafe spun her around, tossed her over his shoulder and started walking. "The only way you'll get to the finish line ahead of me is if I carry you."

"I'm not a sack of potatoes."

"I can tell by your weight."

"Hey!" She balled her fist and playfully punched him above the kidney. He didn't seem to notice.

"It'll serve you right if I throw up," she said, jostling upside down.

"Won't be the first time I've seen you puke." He squeezed her leg. "Be still before I drop you."

He crossed the street and strolled into the R&L.

Rafe's fingers danced over her hips and gripped her waist. Her feet finally touched solid ground inside the repair shop. She stood with her eyes closed until the dizzy sensation subsided.

"Here." Rafe handed her a half-empty bottle of water he snatched off the top of a large upright tool cabinet. "Drink sips, not gulps."

He sauntered across the garage and punched a panel of buttons next to the door leading inside the customer service area. The front bay doors creaked and screeched, sliding slowly down to cut off the view of the park.

Grace swallowed a tiny splash of cool water and propped herself against the back end of the car behind her.

Brow creased in concern, Rafe joined her. "Feeling better?" He cradled her jaw, his thumb lightly stroking her cheek.

"Peachy," she said.

Rafe frowned.

"When I say 'peachy,' I mean it. I'm not being sarcastic like you are."

"You think I'm sarcastic?" he whispered against her ear, then he nipped and licked the lobe.

"Sometimes." Her voice sounded breathy. "Maybe a little. You should work on that."

She loved the rough feel of his palms kneading the curves of her hips.

"I'd rather work on this." Rafe nibbled a trail down the column of her throat.

Her entire body tingled.

Beneath her shirt, his hand trailed down her abdomen. Her stomach quivered the lower he went. He unzipped her shorts, his palm cupping her mound, his fingers moving aside a thin piece of lace to glide between her folds.

"Oh, God." Her eyes closed.

Each long, luxurious stroke was as reverent as a prayer and brought her closer and closer and closer to heaven.

And then it stopped.

"What's wrong?" She panted, hovering on the cusp of ecstasy.

"Time to pick up Alex." A twisted, mischievous tease glinted in his eyes.

"Are you seriously gonna leave? Now?"

As soon as she said it, he chuckled.

"Turnabout is fair play, sweetheart." He zipped her shorts and kissed her on the nose, then waved behind him as he strolled out of the building.

Chapter 23

Passing the crooked tree beside a stump that looked like a knotty troll, Rafe slowed down for the hidden turn. Alex and Grace's easy banter filled the tow truck's double cab. An improvement over the frustrated tension he'd sensed from Grace earlier, when he'd left her to pick up Alex.

He'd argued with himself as to whether or not the empathic sensation was real or imagined. After all, she'd put him in the same predicament this morning, so of course he knew how she felt.

What he hadn't expected on the drive alone to the school was the sensory bombardment of Grace's orgasm when she finished what Rafe had started with her at the R&L. The disruption in his perception had been sudden, intense, and damn near made him drive off the road.

The only explanation for the phenomenon was that a mate-bond was forming and had linked their emotions.

He didn't know whether to laugh, cry, hurl curses at the moon or blow kisses. Although he leaned more toward hurling curses. He didn't like irony or complications of being linked body and mind, heart and soul to Grace. It could make it harder to resist the urge to claim her, but not impossible.

He eased into the pebbled driveway, came to a full stop and jammed the gearshift into Park.

"Cute place," Grace said, leaning close to the windshield, her gaze seeming to take in every nuance of the little homestead.

Ronni stepped outside, arms crossed over her chest, but she offered a small finger wave and a smile.

Alex bailed out of the backseat and shuffled to his mother. She wrapped him in a hug before sending him inside.

"Are you sure it's okay for me to come to supper?" Grace unbuckled her seat belt.

"Ronni invited you." Rafe's voice sounded hollow and distant in his ears.

"What's wrong?" Grace's fingers curled around his arm. Warm, calming, kind, her essence ebbed into him.

"I used to live here. I haven't been inside the house since my wife died."

"Oh." She squeezed his biceps. "We don't have to stay."

Damn good idea, he almost told her.

"Do you want me to tell Ronni we'll need a rain check?"

In his heart, Rafe knew if he didn't do this now, he never would.

"No." He scrubbed his hands over his whiskered jaw and climbed out of the truck.

Grace met him in front of the vehicle with a smile, wordlessly took his hand and walked beside him.

"Y'all come in." Ronni stepped back into the house.

Hand on the small of her back, Rafe ushered Grace over the threshold and followed closely, holding his breath.

"Hope you don't mind how I redecorated," Ronni said, watching him with uneasy eyes.

"It's fine, Ronni." Rafe wanted to reassure her, but his words came out clipped and tight.

"I love the drapes." Grace walked to the front room windows. "Where did you get them?"

"Made 'em myself." Ronni smiled. The first authentic smile he'd seen from her since they met.

"Wow." The dimples Rafe loved to see framed Grace's mouth. "What else can you sew?"

"Clothes, quilts. I even made the tablecloth on the dining room table. Come look."

Grace cast him a questioning look. He nodded for her to follow Ronni.

Rafe sat on the couch, freshly cleaned and decorated with a pale yellow afghan. Looking around, he saw his former home stripped of his former life and stamped with Ronni's personal style.

He appreciated her waiting to ask him in until she'd sanitized the house of his memories. It would be easier to see the house as hers now.

Laughing, Ronni and Grace returned to the living room.

Rafe liked how Grace never seemed to meet a stranger, how she had a gift for making people comfortable and how simply adorable her dimples were when she was happy.

His heart kicked an extra beat as she walked toward him, all smiles and twinkles.

"Your cousin has mad sewing skills, Rafe. She could do it professionally."

"It's sweet of you to say so, Grace. But I don't have any formal training. I make up stuff as I go along."

"A true artist." Grace beamed and so did Ronni.

"Mom!" Alex galloped down the stairs leading up to a bedroom loft. "When is supper?"

"Right now. Wash up and set the table for four," Ronni told him.

"Four?" Alex stared at Grace. "You're eatin' with us?"

"I am." Grace's genuine smile lit the room.

Alex's eyes went glassy and his tongue nearly lolled out of his mouth.

Rafe needed to plan a day to take him fishing and explain wolfan puberty. Ronni probably did a fine job with the basics, but some things were passed down male to male.

"Go on." Ronni pushed Alex toward the kitchen. "Set the table proper."

Alex tackled his task with gusto.

Grace sat beside Rafe, her leg a fraction of an inch from his.

"Thanks for helping Alex with his homework." Ronni sat in a straight-back rocker. "His attitude toward school is better."

"No problem at all. He's a fast learner."

"Did he really talk to someone at NASA?"

"He did." Grace relaxed into the couch, but with her shoulders angled slightly so that she leaned against him.

Rafe cozied into the couch, as well.

"Raj," Grace continued, "is a mathematician on one of their projects."

Rafe wondered what, if any, benefits Raj had shared with Grace.

A silent growl rolled through Rafe's mind.

This is what Tristan had warned him about, and it had only been a few days.

"Alex told me his birthday is tomorrow. His sweet sixteen, right?"

"He'll be sixteen, all right. Don't know how sweet it will be." Ronni snickered.

"I'd like to make him cupcakes."

"He'd love them as long as they don't have chocolate."

"Is he allergic, too?"

"We all are. Didn't Rafe tell you?"

"No, it never came up." Grace glanced at Rafe.

"Well, strawberry is Alex's favorite," Ronni said. "He'll be in hog's heaven if you make those. He wanted a party, but the Co-op's spring festival is this weekend, so most people will be out there."

"The festival is this weekend?" Rafe had completely forgotten about the pack's annual event. Gavin would string him up if he didn't show up with Grace.

"Yeah. We were looking forward to it, but Alex said you were working."

"I'm going." Grace smiled. "I'll ask Gavin if you and Alex can come with me."

Ah, hell. Gavin knew he'd screwed up. But, he cared less about the Alpha's displeasure and more about Grace being paraded around to the pack's single males—which is exactly what Gavin would do if she showed up without Rafe.

"Not necessary," he said. "I'll take the weekend off. Ronni, you and Alex can be my guests." He looked at Grace, his heart racing unexpectantly. "I know you've already been invited, but I wouldn't mind if you came as my guest, too."

"I'd love to. But first we need to give Alex a birthday party." Grace looked at him with those big, beautiful green eyes. Full of hope and expectation.

A man would be fool a to disappoint her. Rafe was many things, but a fool was not one them.

Chapter 24

"Are you going to pick one or stand there all night?"

Rafe tore his attention from the variety of condom boxes lined on the shelves to glare at Tristan, dressed in the dark standard uniform of the Maico Sheriff's Department.

"Maybe you need a little help." Tristan's arrogant smile deepened Rafe's bad mood, frustrated by the simple task of buying a box of condoms. He had no idea of the multitude of brands or types. Or colors. Neon? Really?

As an adolescent he'd listened to Doc's lessons about sex and the use of condoms, and Rafe had understood the importance. Humans were conditioned to utilize condoms to protect them from disease and unwanted pregnancies. Wahyas had no worries for either.

The decaying scent of sickness and disease curbed their instinct to couple. As for unwanted pregnancies, Wahya males could only impregnate the females they claimed with a bite.

Male wolfans used condoms because human females expected it, and it sent a message to Wahyan females that the male wasn't interested in a mateship.

"Are you listening?" Tristan waggled a box stamped Fire and Ice in front of Rafe's face.

He definitely didn't want his cock sheathed in anything that would light it on fire or freeze it off.

He knocked aside Tristan's hand.

"Trying to help out a brother."

"You're not helping."

Tristan laughed and put the box on the shelf. "Who's the lucky woman?"

Rafe answered with a stare.

"Loretta?" Tristan leaned forward, nearly nose to nose with Rafe.

"What the hell are you doing?"

"Checking for a twinkle."

"Back off. My eyes don't have a damn twinkle."

Tristan's grin took up most of his face. He uttered one word. "Grace."

Awareness rushed Rafe's senses. Her fragrance filled his nose, the softness of her mouth tingled his lips, her laughter rang in his ears and the deep jade pools of her eyes looking up at him, warm and trusting, made his heart sputter.

"We have a winner." Tristan's deep-bellied laughter broke the spell. "Grace not only puts a twinkle in your eyes, she can damn near make you drool. Wipe your mouth, bro."

"I'm not your bro." Rafe swiped his sleeve across his face. Not one wet spot.

Tristan laughed again. "If you were, I would've taught you which condoms to buy." He picked up a tame-looking box and handed it to him. His expression turned serious. "My advice—unless you're playing for keeps, keep your cock in your pants around Grace. Fuck Loretta, instead." He slapped Rafe's shoulder. "See ya later at the rendezvous point."

Tristan strolled toward the front of the store dangling a box of deli chicken from his fingers while Rafe silently cursed.

He didn't want to play anything with Loretta. But neither Rafe nor Grace were ready to play for keeps, either.

Rafe raced through the woods. Most nights he wolf-ran for the exercise, because he couldn't sleep or he wanted a drink. Tonight he ran because he had a mission.

He zigged past a tree and leaped a fallen log. His paws barely touched the ground before he zagged around another.

The barbs on the electrified fence around the Walker's Run wolf sanctuary glittered in the moonlight. Normally he checked in with the sentinels. Tonight he couldn't.

Rafe's muscles bunched and stretched beneath his fur as he launched over the six-foot barrier into the sanctuary. The best jumper in the pack, he hadn't lost that skill. The sentinel recruits barked orders for him to halt and identify himself.

With lightning speed, he shot past them. Howls of an intruder alert broke the quiet evening. Every one of the greenhorns charged after him.

Idiots!

Blossom-laden branches snagged bits of Rafe's fur as he barreled through the wild berry bushes. The sweet smell of budding fruit wasn't nearly as tantalizing as Grace's feminine musk.

God, how his heart, his mind, his body constricted with need just thinking about her. The need to be soothed and comforted, the need to be wanted, the need to be fulfilled. Most of all, the need to be held, lost in her embrace.

Damn, damn, damn!

Rafe charged into the creek. The cold rush of water stung despite his thick fur. He paddled hard against the current.

There had been times when he wanted the river to overcome him. Not tonight, though. Tonight he fought his way to the other side.

Smooth pebbles pressed into his pads as he slunk out of the water. He turned back to his pursuers.

"Rafe, you ass! What the hell?" Hanson's irritated voice pinged Rafe's mind.

He shook the water from his fur. *"Who's protecting the perimeter?"*

A collective gasp sounded in Rafe's head. In unison, the group turned and hightailed it toward their posts.

They weren't a bad bunch, but if Rafe had been a rogue decoy, the pack would've been vulnerable. Brice and Tristan, waiting at the entry point, would make sure these recruits did not forget tonight's lesson.

Instead of returning to the rendezvous point, Rafe ambled along the riverbank allowing the adrenaline from the chase to subside. He wished the havoc in his head could dissipate as easily.

He didn't need to close his eyes to feel Grace's warmth and energy. He had yet to taste her fully, but her soft, supple lips were made for kissing and he found her sweet musk so provocative that he could almost smell her in the evening breeze.

Wait—

He stopped midstride and lifted his nose to filter the myriad of scents.

Oh, yeah. Definitely Grace.

What the hell is she doing out this late?

Fire shot through his veins and his legs engaged in an all-out run. She needed to be locked in her room. Away from dangerous predators.

Away from him.

Chapter 25

The rhythmic squeak of the swing sounded like a distorted lullaby. Grace had listened to the hypnotic drone for more than an hour.

She couldn't stop thinking about Rafe's kisses. Or why, when he'd dropped her off tonight, his lips had whispered across the shell of her ear as he said good-night, but that was it.

To say she was disappointed was like saying the Taj Mahal was a nice house.

She opened the photo app on her phone and thumbed through the pictures. There were a lot. Most of those taken over the last few days were selfies of her with Rafe in the background, her and Rafe huddled together, and some with just Rafe. In each one, she recalled exactly where they were and what they were doing at the time.

She selected a different album. The photos mostly consisted of scenery, buildings, the inside of art museums and other places she couldn't remember unless she looked at the tags. Sliding from one image to the next evoked no particular emotional response.

Switching back to the current album, Grace felt a smile stretch her mouth as the picture of her and Rafe at the scenic overlook appeared. She set it as the wallpaper image for her phone.

Yeah, yeah. She liked him.

They had chemistry in spades, but neither was quite sure what to do with it. Aside from the physical attraction, something else was taking root. Neither wanted to commit to an actual relationship, yet they naturally gravitated toward each other. When she needed something, he was the one she called on, and he never failed to respond. Most times, she simply wanted someone to talk to in the middle of the night. He always answered and never hung up even when she simply rambled on about nothing in particular. Knowing he was on the other end of the line seemed to anchor her whenever she felt the most adrift.

She'd never experienced such a strong connectedness with her previous bed buddies, and she and Rafe had yet to move beyond kissing. She hoped things between them wouldn't become too serious or complicated whenever they started having sex. They would, she knew they would. Some things were inevitable. And because of the inevitability of things, she believed they would never make it as a real couple. He was an oak, firmly planted; she was a leaf flittering in the breeze. Eventually something would take her away from here, from him.

A rustling in the woods drew Grace's attention. Silver tendrils of moonlight flitted across the dark water of the river, but she saw nothing. Yet something moved. She felt its presence, coming quickly.

She untucked her foot from beneath her thigh and stood. Her leg stung as if a thousand needles stabbed her flesh and wouldn't bear her weight, so she sat down again.

A galloping thud rose from the footpath to the river. Grace sat motionless, not daring to breathe. The sounds of the night faded into the roar in her ears. The only thing she heard with clarity was the rush of whatever charged toward her.

She saw the eyes first. Glowing orbs of bright blue brilliance, piercing the darkness beyond the reach of the soft glow of Tiki lamps along the trail. Next came the snout, housing a set of sharp, pointy teeth.

Grace screamed and a large red wolf skidded to a stop. She fumbled around the swing, putting it between herself and the wolf.

A whimper rumbled in the animal's throat. He took a hesitant step.

Heart pounding, Grace gauged the distance from the pathway to the resort. Too far to outrun a wolf. Especially since she had to use her room key to unlock the back door to the building.

The wolf came closer, his head hunched lower than his shoulders. However, his eyes remained steady on Grace.

Something about the animal seemed familiar.

"Don't be afraid."

The crystal clarity of Rafe's voice inside her head caused a wave of lightheadedness.

She stumbled backward and despite a valiant effort to stay on her feet, she landed on her bottom.

"Are you all right?" The wolf peered at her, pensive and primed.

"Don't eat me, okay?" Grace sat perfectly still, barely daring to breathe.

The wolf eased forward.

Grace's heart pounded a hard, fast rhythm, strong enough to power a mad dash back to the resort.

If she could move.

The tip of the wolf's cold, wet nose touched the back of her hand flattened on the ground.

He looked familiar.

"You're Rafe's wolf, aren't you?"

The wolf nodded.

"Be nice. I wrecked my car instead of hitting you." Cautiously, Grace lifted her hand. He licked her palm.

As her fear eased, she grazed his ears, then buried her fingers in his fur so that her nails lightly scratched his skin.

Insanity. Maybe it was a delayed reaction from the concussion.

The first symptom was the crystal clarity of Rafe's voice in her head. She should've known the occasional intrusions were signs of a mind on the verge of a meltdown.

The second symptom was believing a wolf could actually understand her.

The third was petting a freaking wild animal as if he were an ordinary house pet.

"Um, good boy?"

He raised one eyebrow over unimpressed cobalt blue eyes.

She'd seen that look.

"I've heard dogs and their owners look alike, but I never imagined the same applied to wolves."

Her heart still thundered a fast-paced rhythm. One wrong move and she might become a midnight snack.

The wolf's paw tapped her leg. He snatched the phone off the ground next to her and launched into the swing. The force of his weight caused it to rock and he struggled to keep his footing.

"Hey." She eased toward him and caught the swing to steady it. Carefully, she grasped the part of the phone sticking out of his mouth. "Give me the phone."

The wolf's growl spread chills across her skin.

She let go of the phone. "Okay, okay. You can have it."

He pawed the spot where she had been sitting.

"It's all yours. I'm going back to my room." She took one step toward the path.

The wolf growled again and put her phone on the seat of the swing.

The fourth sign of insanity. Thinking a wolf wanted her to sit next to him on a swing.

She needed her phone. The little device was her lifeline and she hadn't backed it up to the cloud in over a week.

"Maybe I can stay a few more minutes." She sat gingerly on the swing, the phone between them.

He sat there, looking at her. So pensive and determined.

Finally, he blew a long, heavy breath through his nose. His big blue eyes following her every move.

Not that she moved much. She didn't want to startle him into an attack.

"Grace, I'm not going to hurt you."

"Rafe?" She looked around.

Too often she heard him in her thoughts. She needed to get a grip on reality before she started believing in those figments of imagination.

The wolf barked once. He nosed the phone toward her.

Grace cautiously picked it up. The image of her and Rafe was on the screen.

"Look." She showed the wolf. "I'm friends with Rafe. No biting, got it?"

The wolf thumped his tail and grinned. Grace snapped his picture.

He seemed to like the attention so she kept taking pictures. Needing more space, she had to stop to delete images from the phone's memory. She chose photos from a forgotten vacation to some place she no longer remembered.

Like Matt had said, after a while, the mountains in the background all looked the same.

The wolf's breath heated her arm as she deleted pictures. On impulse, she held up the phone. "Smile," she said, snapping the selfie.

"Wow." The wolf's expression in the picture reminded her of the one of her and Rafe at the scenic overlook. Same intense eyes peering into the camera lens, same jaw set with a hint of a smile. Even the wolf's fur looked the same color as Rafe's hair.

She looked from the wolf in the picture to the one nudging her arm. "So weird, but freaking adorable, too."

Suddenly, he sprang from the swing. Grace dug her heels into the ground to stop its wild rebound.

Perched in a half crouch, he stared up the trail to the lodge. The hair along his spine spiked. Growl after growl rolled from his throat until Grace worried the wolf might be rabid.

"Stand down." Gavin Walker stepped from the shadows. The illumination from the Tiki lamps glistened in his snow-white hair.

The wolf's mouth drew back in annoyance and his vocalization resembled a grumble, but he allowed Gavin to pass.

"Good evening, Grace. From the lodge, it appeared you were alone. I wanted to make sure you were all right."

"Yes." She smiled. "Getting some fresh air and making a new friend."

"I see."

The wolf positioned himself in front of Grace and hunkered on her feet.

"Is Cassie resting okay tonight?"

"She is." Gavin made no move to join Grace on the swing. "A little cranky because of the mandatory bed rest."

"I'm glad she's taking it easy now." Grace wiggled her toes from beneath her guard wolf's solidly planted rump.

"It seems he's taken an interest in you." Gavin stroked the wolf's ears. "He's a smart one. Too smart for his own good. Likes to break the rules. Wolves aren't allowed to leave the sanctuary, especially at night."

"Sorry." Grace tucked the phone in her pocket. "I think he came to see me."

"Indeed." Gavin rubbed the wolf's head and pinched the back of his neck to hold him. "He won't bother you again."

"I don't mind," Grace said. "He's great company. So is his owner."

"Handler," Gavin corrected. "No one owns the wolves."

"Sorry, I forgot. Rafe mentioned it earlier."

"The two of you have spent quite a deal of time together since the accident." Any emotion Gavin had suddenly blanked out of his expression. "He's quite the loner and adamant to remain so, but there are a number of single men in our community who would appreciate the attentions of a lovely, kind-hearted woman such as yourself."

The wolf growled and Grace wanted to say, "Good boy." Instead, she ran her hand along his chest to soothe him.

"Rafe doesn't mind my company and I prefer his to the dozen or so men Cassie and Brice have introduced to me over the last year." She smiled her best cheerleading smile.

"Then I wish you the best in your undertaking with him."

Somehow, Grace knew he didn't.

Gavin's hand on the scruff of Rafe's neck prevented him from accompanying Grace up the walkway to the resort.

He waited until she was safely inside before he hauled Rafe into a wooded area out of sight of prying eyes.

Rafe shifted into his human form and sat back on his haunches, shaking off the pinch in his neck.

Gavin gazed at the constellations, his face relaxed, almost serene.

The Alpha's peaceful countenance didn't fool Rafe. Gavin was angry. Very angry, so Rafe waited for him to speak.

It wasn't a long wait.

Gavin's icy glare cut right through Rafe. "What the fuck are you doing?"

"My duty. You appointed me as Grace's guardian and ordered me to become her friend."

"Taking pictures with her while in your wolf form is not what I meant."

"She likes taking pictures." Particularly of him, and

them. "You wanted her to trust us. We are wolves. Now she isn't afraid of wolves." At least, not of his wolf.

Gavin growled and Rafe fell silent.

"I've told you the sheriff is looking for reasons to investigate us. Your carelessness isn't helping. What if someone saw you?"

"They would've thought a lovely woman was playing with her very large dog." Which was why Rafe had imitated the canine behavior, all the way down to the tail thumping. However, he held back on the tongue lolling. Some things he couldn't bring himself to do.

"Have you lost your fucking mind?" Gavin snarled. "You know what it means to show a human your wolf."

He did, but Grace had already seen his wolf. There was no harm in her meeting him again.

"She hasn't seen me shift." Yet.

But on the verge of showing her tonight, Rafe wasn't sure if he was relieved or irritated by Gavin's intrusion.

"Do you intend to claim Grace?"

"No," Rafe forced out after a pause. Just because he wasn't ready for a mateship didn't mean he didn't crave Grace's company.

"Then stop confusing her. She is using you as an excuse to push away other suitors."

"I heard." Her revelation had filled him with a sense of pride and honor.

"I asked you to safeguard Grace's best interests."

"I am. Grace doesn't want a mate."

Gavin's face darkened. "Grace is close to Cassie, and she'll be close to my granddaughter. Do you understand how big a target Grace is?"

"I do." Rafe rose from his squatted position. "Particularly when you are the one holding the bow and arrows."

"Step back or step up, Rafe, soon," Gavin snapped. "I want Grace settled before my granddaughter arrives."

Rafe was reluctant to do either.

It would take a better man than he to tame Grace's spirit. Maybe not better, but different. Because Rafe didn't want her tamed, especially if she needed to soar.

Chapter 26

"Mmmmm." Rafe walked into his kitchen and slipped his arm around Grace's waist while the other skimmed past her toward the cupcakes on the table.

"Those are for Alex." She swatted Rafe's hand a second too late. He'd already swiped his finger through the frosting of the nearest cupcake.

"He won't notice if one is missing," Rafe murmured against her cheek. "Unless you rat me out, and you wouldn't do that, would you, sweetheart?"

Rafe finger-painted frosting along the underside of her jaw and beneath her ear, then proceeded to lick her skin clean.

Grace pressed her back against him, trusting him to support her weight as her legs weakened. No matter where his tongue touched, her entire nervous system short-circuited, causing immediate surrender of her body, which begged for more of the same.

Rafe reached for a second dip into the frosting. Delicious expectation curled in Grace's belly like the steam that had risen from the cupcakes when she'd taken them out of the Walkers' hot oven.

He used his free hand to undo the buttons on her blouse to one below her front-hook lace-cup bra. Next, he slathered the colored confection down the valley of her breasts.

Turning her around, Rafe gazed at her with a wicked gleam. His dilated pupils gobbled all the color to transform his eyes into large black orbs. He looked dark, dangerous and devastating.

"My, what big eyes you have," she teased.

"All the better to see your beauty." He flashed his pearly whites.

"And what big teeth you have." Grace's gaze lingered on his generous, masculine mouth.

"All the better to taste you."

At least that's what Grace thought Rafe said. She couldn't be sure since he'd growled the words.

He hauled her hips against him. She arched her back so he could lick and suck every fleck of frosting from her skin. He unhooked her bra. His tongue laved a decadent trail down her breastbone before detouring to her breast. When he sucked her nipple into his warm, moist mouth, Grace's breaths turned to pants. Each swirl across the sensitive bud caused her sex to clench until it throbbed.

With a wet pop, he pulled away, causing her to whimper. He soothed her with a soft "Shhhh," before latching on to her other breast, lavishing it with just as much attention as the first.

Unable to stop herself, she ground against him. No man had ever gotten her all hot and bothered faster than he did.

"Want to comment on the part of my anatomy that's growing by the second?" Rafe's playfulness took her breath away. Never had she seen him so relaxed and spontaneous.

She inched her fingers down his abdomen. His breaths grew shorter, faster, the farther down she went. His copper lashes fluttered lower and lower, until they closed completely with a groan as she cupped the bulge in his coveralls.

"My, my," she rasped in a sexy, sultry, siren voice. "What a big cock you have."

"All the better to fu—"

"Aa-hem!"

Grace squealed and heat flamed in her checks. Rafe's eyes widened, then his nose twitched.

"Damn it, Brice. You could've knocked." Rafe helped Grace button her blouse.

Embarrassed, she peeked over his shoulder. Brice leaned in the kitchen entryway with his arms folded over his chest. His eyes smiled in tandem with the grin broadening his mouth.

"I did." Amusement tinged his voice. "You didn't answer, so I came in to make sure everything was all right."

"We're fine." Rafe lightly tapped Grace's nose, then drew his finger down her chin to the hollow in her neck before giving her blouse a quick tug.

After checking that they hadn't missed any buttons, she gave Rafe a ready nod. He moved aside.

"Don't you dare tell Cassie." Grace glared at Brice.

"I have no secrets from my wife." Brice wiggled his brows. "Besides she knows what happens when a man and a woman who make googly eyes at each other are left to their own devices."

"Why does it matter if Cassie knows?" Rafe looked puzzled.

"She'll get the wrong idea."

Brice's gaze bounced from Grace to Rafe and back to Grace. "Oh, I think her idea hits the mark dead-center."

"Why are you here, Walker?"

"Co-op business."

"You could've called, texted, emailed."

"Yeah, but this was a lot more fun." Grinning ear to ear, Brice strolled out of the kitchen. "And very enlightening."

Grace gripped the football in a mad dash to the goal line.

"I'm open! Throw it!" Waving his hand in the air, Alex ran ahead.

"I can make it!" Grace dodged his friend Lucas, only to

collide with Alex's other friend Jeremy. They tumbled to the ground in a tangled heap.

"Grace!" Rafe's voice boomed through the park.

Jeremy's weight suddenly lifted from Grace's body and Rafe crouched over her. "Are you all right?"

"That depends." She gulped for air. "Did I make it into the end zone?"

"You sure did." Lucas peered down at her with large whiskey-colored eyes. "You were awesome!"

"She could've been hurt," Rafe snapped, shoving the trio back. "I told you boys to be careful."

"Oh, please." Grace accepted Rafe's help to stand. "Matt knocked me down harder than that when we played our made-up game of tackle croquet."

"You sure you're okay?" Worry replaced the delight in Alex's eyes.

"Absolutely." Grace hugged him. "I haven't had this much fun in a long time."

Rafe pulled her into him. "You've been playing the wrong games." He nuzzled her neck while his hands roamed her shoulders, her back, the curve of her hips, awakening every cell in her body and discombobulating her nerves at the same time.

He licked her earlobe. "Go. Sit. I'll take your place on Alex's team."

The boys didn't seem to mind the player switch, which pinched Grace's pride, although her body was grateful. Running up and down the length of the park with three teenagers had overworked her muscles. She managed not to limp over to the park bench.

As Rafe ran with the boys, Grace realized Alex and his friends had held back their strength and speed with her. They were fast, cunning, and their laughter made her smile. Well, mostly it was Rafe's laughter.

After a few minutes, the play shifted to three against

one. Every time Rafe outplayed, outmaneuvered or outran one the boys, his laughter electrified the air.

Or maybe just electrified her.

At the end of each play, Rafe's gaze landed on her, giving her heart a little flutter. The tiny glimpse of domestication rekindled a yearning for a home and family to fill it.

She snapped a picture, noticing the phone would soon run out of memory again. Later, she needed to sort through the albums and delete the old images no longer worth keeping. A few of the more recent ones, she planned to print and put in frames.

Grace smiled. She couldn't remember the last time she hung pictures. Usually, she didn't bother decorating. It simplified packing when the time came to move.

All three boys dove to tackle Rafe. He went down amidst a roar of laughter.

This, she thought. This was the sound she wanted filling the halls, if ever she had a real home.

The boys peeled off Rafe and raced to grab bottles of water from the cooler. Rafe sat up, grass in his hair, a dirt smudge across his shirt.

Grace walked over and handed him a bottle of water. Rafe downed the contents in one long gulp.

She took his hand to help him stand, but he tugged harder than Grace did and she sprawled on top of him.

Before she knew what was happening, he'd rolled her beneath him and captured her mouth in a long, luscious kiss.

A burst of warmth and immense happiness filled her being. She felt utterly content.

Strange how the phenomenon only happened around Rafe. Something about him quieted the restlessness within her. She couldn't help but wonder how long it would last.

Chapter 27

Rafe stood inside the pack's exclusive party pavilion. Separate from the resort, the building was located on the Co-op's vast community park where the pack held their gatherings. The spring festival was an all-weekend event, starting with the Friday night social.

It had been ages since Rafe attended one of the events the Alpha family hosted throughout the year. He had mixed feelings about being at this one.

The lights were dim, the air was charged with energy from the band, and the smell of sizzling steaks on the flaming grill behind a large glass window in front of the kitchen made Rafe's stomach turn on itself. Hungry, tired and all keyed up, he pivoted toward the large table reserved for the Alpha family. Brice and Cassie were snuggled in quiet conversation. Gavin and his mate, Abby, moved among the pockets of people.

Where the hell is Grace?

Scanning the crowd, Rafe focused his olfactory sense. He detected her scent after a few seconds and stopped to watch her kick up her heels in a fast-paced country one-step. With her broad smile, flushed cheeks and golden ponytail bopping to the rhythm, she was the prettiest woman on the dance floor.

His anxiety level dropping, he headed to Brice and Cassie's table.

"Who are you and what have you done with my antisocial friend?" Brice smiled as Rafe took a seat opposite his friends.

"I'm here for Grace."

"I bet you are." The teasing tone in Brice's voice irritated Rafe.

Stepping forward too soon, Grace almost bumped into another dancer. From behind, Shane cupped her shoulder, pulling her back in sync.

"If you would have been here sooner, Grace would be dancing with you." Cassie's broad smile said she knew about the cupcake incident.

"She can dance with whomever she wishes." Although every time Shane touched her, every time he made her smile, Rafe dug his nails into his palms to keep from pounding his fist into Shane's face.

"Don't fight it, man." Brice laughed.

"Fight what?" A possessive, instinctual growl rumbled in his throat as Shane spun Grace into his arms and slid his hands over her hips.

Diverting his gaze to his tablemates, Rafe flattened his palms against his thighs; his stiff fingers curved like claws, pressing through his clothes, digging into his muscles to keep him impaled in his seat.

"Serendipity. When a human female sees a wolfan male naked, they end up mated." Brice winked at Cassie. "It's a proven fact."

"That kind of talk isn't a damn bit funny." Especially considering the pull he felt toward Grace. All smiles, mostly, tender and kind. She deserved a far better man than he was.

"From this side of the table, it certainly is." Brice's grin broadened.

Cassie sucked in a sharp breath, leaned forward and grabbed her belly.

"Cas?" Brice paled.

"I'm okay." She blew a long breath. "The baby has a strong kick."

"Should I call Doc over?" Rafe's gaze targeted his father across the room in a conversation with Ronni and Alex.

"No. I'm fine, the baby's fine. There's nothing to worry about." Cassie's eyes looked a little tired, but otherwise she appeared okay.

"I'll be back." Rafe made his way to the dance floor. He gripped Shane's shoulder and pulled him away from grinding against Grace.

"Whoa," the younger wolfan said.

"Take a hike." Rafe didn't say anything else, considering his thoughts were primal and less than coherent.

Shane's eyes narrowed. One brow crept up. Amusement curled one side of his mouth. "I think Rafe intends to have the next dance."

"Okay." Grace smiled up at him, slightly winded but obviously having a good time.

Shane gave Rafe a slight nod and left them in the middle of the dance floor.

"Better late than never." A trace of annoyance weighted Grace's tease. "I thought you had changed your mind about coming."

"I got a last minute roadside assistance call. A mother and three kids broke down near Brasstown Bald. Didn't want them waiting in the dark for someone to come from Hiawassee."

"I'm glad you're here now."

"Me, too."

The band changed tempo and Rafe eased Grace into his arms.

"I didn't like seeing you with Shane."

"I noticed." Grace snuggled closer as the sounds of a sultry ballad swirled around the room.

Rafe left no distance between them. Gently molding

her body to his, he allowed her scent to filter deep into his lungs. Only then did the snarling chaos in his head quiet, allowing a single thought to emerge.

Mine!

God help him.

God help them all.

"It's beautiful up here." Grace stepped forward, drinking in the night beauty. Below them, civilization. Above them, constellations.

"Careful." Rafe's arm roped her waist and he lifted her off her feet. "Don't get close to the edge. It's a mighty long way down the mountain."

He stepped backward, taking her with him.

He set her down. The soft sweep of his cheek against her neck turned to featherlight kisses. A nip in the air added to the goose bumps his touch created.

They sat down on a blanket he'd unfolded on the ground.

"What is this place?" She leaned back against his chest and tipped her face toward the sky.

"Walker's Pointe." His voice lowered. "One of the highest peaks around here. On a clear day, you can see several states, depending on the direction you look."

The warm press of his palm against her belly made it tingle. He kissed behind her ear, nibbled her lobe and down her neck.

His fingers trailed beneath her shirt. Warm, rough and without hesitation.

His scent, fresh, clean, masculine, filled her lungs. She loved the perfect fit of her in his arms.

He unhooked the front clasp of her bra, his thumb caressing the curve of her breast. The muscles in her stomach tightened and her sex clenched. She knew where this would lead. And she couldn't wait.

She pushed his hand away, then pulled off her shirt and tossed it over her head. Her bra was next.

Rafe scrambled to whip off his shirt and it became a competition to see who got naked first.

It was a tie.

"God, you're beautiful," he whispered reverently, laying her down.

She didn't know how he could see much of her. The moon was clouded over and there were no lights.

Maybe he pictured her by touch, as he caressed every inch of her body.

She pulled his face to her lips and teased him with a near kiss. He seized her mouth, his tongue slipping inside to duel with hers. Each parry and retreat heightened her awareness and sensitized her to every brush, every stroke, every caress.

Sealing his mouth over hers, he kissed her madly, deeply, thoroughly, until she was breathless. Cupping her breast, he strummed his thumb across her sensitive nipple.

Grace lightly scored her nails down his back. Encouraged by his sensual hiss, she ran her palms across his shoulders, then down the soft swirls of hair on his upper torso. Beneath her touch, his muscles quivered. Or maybe her hands simply trembled after the slow, sensual lick he gave to the sensitive spot behind her ear. She rocked her hips against him.

Capturing her hands in his fist, he brought them to his lips and kissed her inner wrists. "Not yet," he said in a hoarse whisper.

His mouth found her peaks and he swirled his tongue across one budded nipple and then the other before gently sucking one into his warm, wet mouth. Grace arched, gripping the back of his head. A moan rumbled in the back of her throat, raw and needy.

Rafe responded with a deep, sexy growl that caused delicious shivers to run wild through her body. With a soft pop he released the tip of her breast to press light kisses along her collarbone and up the column of her throat. She became lost in the sheer vibration of his lips moving across her skin. He pinched her nipples and she cried out, sinking her nails into his muscular back.

Without pause, he inched his calloused palms down her ribs; her muscles were coiled so tight that she felt her body would snap. He laved the planes of her stomach and nibbled her inner thigh, moving closer, closer to the spot where she really wanted him to be. He touched her with his tongue, sending shivers up her spine and down to her toes. His fingers slid between her folds and pushed inside her, sliding in and out in a slow methodical rhythm that charged every feminine cell in her body.

He brought her right to the precipice of ecstasy and withdrew his fingers. She started to protest, until she realized he was simply moving into position.

A sliver of common sense nearly blinded her.

"Wait!" She slapped one palm against his chest while her other hand protected her mound.

Rafe held still but she sensed the restraint was costing him dearly.

"Condom."

He didn't say anything at first, and she couldn't make out the expression on his face. Finally, he said, "Be right back."

He rose and dashed to the truck. He whipped open the door, shielding his eyes from the light and fumbled in the glove compartment.

"Got it." He ripped the foil packet with his teeth and rolled on the condom.

He slammed the door and darted back to her.

His lips found hers as he crouched over her and surged inside her. The sudden invasion caused her to cry out, and his girth stretching her inner walls made them both gasp.

He held his hips still, despite the tremor in his arms and legs. She took a deep breath to steady her nerves rather than to steel against any pain. Initially shocked by his thickness and quick entry, her body eagerly adapted.

Her fingers glided down his back, squeezed the globes of his ass and she ground her pelvis into his. He kissed her fiercely, then thrust hard and deep.

The sensations washing over her were like nothing she'd ever experienced. It was as if Rafe's being seeped inside her and reached all the way to her soul.

Grace's breath caught in her throat as a fierce orgasm rocked her core. She clung to him, and he threw back his head and howled.

She might've howled, too, if she'd had the strength, but her body felt like a wet noodle.

Rafe's chest heaved from his rapid breaths. "You okay?"

"Yeah," she said softly, her own breaths coming easier.

He claimed her mouth in a soft, sweet kiss that left her warm and fuzzy even after he withdrew to dispose of the condom.

She sat up and gathered her clothes. "Um, could you help me find my bra?"

"Pretty sure it sailed over the edge of the cliff when you slung it behind you."

"You're kidding."

"Nope." Rafe's voice rumbled with laughter. "You were so hot for me, your clothes flew off."

"You were hot for me, too." She felt her cheeks flame. "I didn't toss my clothes over the side of a mountain, did I?"

"If I could see your face right now, I'd probably slap it." She shimmied into her pants and pulled on her blouse.

"You probably would."

Chapter 28

The flashing lights behind them illuminated the inside of the tow truck.

"Oh, you're gonna get a ticket," Grace teased.

Rafe glanced at the speedometer. "I'm five miles under the speed limit."

Flipping the turn signal on, he pulled off the road onto the shoulder.

"I feel like a teenager caught making out."

Rafe looked at her, a slow sweep over her mess of tangled hair all the way down to her bare feet. She did have her pants on fairly straight. The blouse, now missing buttons, had seen better days.

"You look the part."

Rafe shut off the lights and engine, and asked her for his wallet and registration stowed in the glove compartment.

By the time Sheriff Locke reached the window, Rafe had his driver's license, insurance card and vehicle registration in his hand.

A blinding light shone in Rafe's face.

"Evenin', Carl." Rafe handed the sheriff all the documents before he asked.

A twitch of irritation curled Locke's upper lip. "Do you know how fast you were going?"

"Forty in a forty-five zone."

Locke grunted. "What are you doing out this late?"

"Late?" Grace piped up. "It's ten-twenty-three. I haven't been driven home this early since I was seventeen."

Surprise registered on the sheriff's face. He whipped the beam of his flashlight on Grace. She shielded her face behind her hand.

"Grace Olsen?"

"That would be me."

The flashlight beam swept her head to toe. Slowly, methodically. Pausing on her chest and torso for longer than she thought appropriate.

"Wyatt. Step out of the vehicle."

Rafe relaxed his hands and climbed out of the truck.

"Walk to the front of the vehicle."

Rafe complied.

"Is there a problem, Sheriff?" Grace asked.

"Has anyone tried to hurt you, coerce you or assault you this evening?"

"No, sir."

"Are you in any jeopardy or danger? Do you fear for your life?"

"No, sir."

"You should. I warned you to stay away from him."

"I appreciate your concern, Sheriff. I'm perfectly well, in mind and body, and can make my own decisions."

"Do you have any knowledge or suspicions about the Walker's Run Cooperative or any of its members?"

"No, sir."

"You sure about that? You haven't observed any unusual behavior in Wyatt, the Walkers or any other Co-op member?"

"No, I haven't. Have you?"

"Miss, I'll ask the questions."

"I'm curious because you've approached me twice and I'd like to know what your concerns are."

"You'll find them out soon enough. Do you mind if I search the vehicle?"

"Ask Rafe. It belongs to him. He'll tell you to call his

lawyer. I have him on speed dial. Would you like me to call him?"

"Have a nice evening, miss."

The sheriff talked to Rafe at the front of the vehicle for a few minutes. Then they walked back to the truck.

"Watch yourself, Wyatt."

"Always do." Rafe climbed into the truck, buckled his seat belt. The sheriff continued on to his car.

Rafe's gaze searched her head to foot. The muscles in his face and jaw relaxed. "What did he say to you?"

"He asked a bunch of questions." Grace squeezed his fingers. "He did not like that I was with you."

"It's late on a Friday night and I'm a recovering alcoholic with a DUI history. Considering how rumpled your clothes are, maybe he wanted to be sure you were safe."

"He's also suspicious about the Co-op. There's nothing illegal going on, is there?"

"No." Rafe cranked the engine, turned on the lights, put on the blinker and eased onto the road. "We strive to be environmentally friendly, we keep our wolf pack healthy and safe, and we focus on supporting our families and community."

"Then why is the sheriff so concerned about the Co-op?" Grace noticed the patrol car following at a safe distance.

"He's an outsider. From his perspective, the Co-op is a secretive organization that he hasn't been able to crack. He thinks he's doing his job by investigating us." Rafe didn't seem to harbor any annoyance.

Grace frowned at the sheriff's car as it continued on the highway after Rafe turned onto the private road leading to the resort. He pulled to a stop at the valet station, climbed out of the tow truck and came around to her side to open the door.

His Southern manners had started to grow on her. Opening doors, the way he walked close and lightly touched her back, and he never simply dropped her off. He always walked her to her room. Made her feel protected and cherished.

In the crowded elevator, he stood behind her with his arms wrapped around her, buffering her from unruly resort guests who'd had too much to drink in the lounge downstairs. When they arrived at her floor, he stepped around her and made a path through the people so she could easily exit.

He laced his fingers through hers as they strolled to her room. Out of habit, she handed him the card-key. Somehow the reader never worked for her when Rafe accompanied her.

"Want to come in?" Good. Her voice sounded as nonchalant as she was pretending to be.

"Not tonight."

Disappointment dropped into her stomach. Maybe she'd imagined the intimate connection she'd felt as they made love.

She really needed to get a grip on her emotions before she ended up with another broken heart.

"Oh, okay." Before Grace turned to enter the suite, Rafe's hands grazed her waist before settling on her hips. Her insides fluttered like a dozen butterflies trying to escape their cocoon.

Chills, the good kind, swept over her skin as he nuzzled her neck. His lips skimmed the curve of her jaw up to the delightful spot behind her ear that instantly turned her bones to mush.

He backed her against the open door. Smart move, since she could barely stand.

Grace stared up into his eyes and felt herself falling into the depths of the dark blue pools. She didn't have time to pull herself out before Rafe gently held her face in his hands and leaned in for a kiss. The sound of waves crashing against the breakers pounded in her head.

Rafe's firm lips whispered softly over her mouth. He took his time. Patient and calm. And Grace delighted in his every nibble.

A tiny sigh escaped her lips when Rafe broke the kiss and nuzzled her cheek. "Good night, sweetheart."

With dreamlike vision, she watched Rafe walk into the elevator. "Bye," she mouthed, before he was hidden behind the shiny brass elevator doors.

Chapter 29

"Did hell freeze over and I miss the memo?" The security guard at the entrance to the Co-op's outdoor park cracked a big smile.

"Maybe so," Rafe said good-naturedly.

Grace expected they would show ID but they simply kept walking through the checkpoint.

"What good is a security guard if people can waltz right in without being checked."

"Kenneth knows who belongs and who doesn't."

"What if someone has a gun or a knife?"

"If we were at a public event, that would be a concern, but not here. We don't shoot or stab someone when we have a disagreement."

"Don't tell me. You let your wolves battle it out," Grace said jokingly.

"Well—"

"I was kidding." She clasped his arm. "Please tell me that isn't what you do. That's animal cruelty."

"Gullible." A crooked grin quirked his mouth. His arm bumped hers and he slipped his hand into hers as they walked.

The grounds were vast and the scale of the picnic larger than any she had attended. Huge tented pavilions were set up with a variety of foods, including barbecue, hot dogs, hamburgers and a several spits roasting pigs. Areas were roped off for children's events, including a clown performing magic tricks, story-telling and a bean-bag toss.

"Rafe!" A slightly more than middle-aged woman, standing between two other women, waved.

He stopped and a subtle tension crept into his posture. Grace could almost feel the tightness spreading to her body.

"What a nice surprise to see you here." The woman approached and gave him a hug. "You must be Grace." The woman's smile was warm and genuine. "I'm Cynthia Reinhardt."

Bells went off in Grace's mind and a slight unease settled in her stomach. "Nice to meet you."

"Is your cousin and her son coming today? I'd love to meet them, too."

"Ronni is working this morning. She'll be here for the baseball game." Rafe adjusted his ball cap over his eyes. "Alex spent the night with his friend, Lucas, and is coming with Lucas's family."

"Lovely. I do hope you all have a wonderful time." She swallowed and Grace glimpsed a flash of sorrow in Cynthia's eyes. Her shoulders dropped as she turned to walk away.

"Oh no!" Panic tinged the note of aggravation in her voice. She stepped hurriedly toward the man fast approaching. "Clay, stop."

He didn't. He kept barreling toward them.

"Clay," Rafe growled, tucking Grace behind him. "You need to back off."

"You filthy cur!" Clay shoved Rafe's shoulder, but Rafe's body merely absorbed the shock.

"You said you weren't coming," Cynthia's voice rose. "You promised, Clay. You promised!"

"How can you tolerate this?"

"Go home, Clay. Get control of your grief before it destroys you." Outwardly Rafe appeared to be the picture of calmness. Inwardly, Grace felt a churn of intense emotions that didn't quite feel like her own.

"Let's find Brice and Cassie." She tugged Rafe's hand.
As Rafe turned to follow her lead, Clay intercepted.

"You're aren't going anywhere with her."

"That's enough." Tristan barged between them. Fingers
spread, his wide hand slapped against Clay's chest. "If you
can't play nice, Clay, you'll have to leave."

Clay's face darkened. Spittle formed in the corners of
his mouth. "You're all a pack of mongrels."

"Why don't we take a ride to the clinic." Tristan tipped
his head and two men, plainclothes security guards, made
their way through the small crowd that had gathered.

"There's nothing wrong with me."

"Just go with them, Clay." Cynthia rubbed her temple.
"You need help."

"Come on." Rafe steered Grace away from the scene.

She looked back to see Tristan accompanying the security guards dragging away Clay, his face twisted in a
vicious scowl.

"He's a powder keg ready to blow."

"He's a broken, angry, grieving man." Sadness laced
Rafe's voice. "I used to be him."

"Not anymore." Grace playfully bumped against Rafe.

"Nope. Not anymore."

Clutching a tray of drinks, Grace climbed the bleachers.
The picnic had been in full swing since eight that morning. Now it was nearly two in the afternoon and in all that
time, she'd hardly had a break.

She and Rafe had played horseshoes, joined the sack
races, watched an archery competition and had eaten a
barbecue lunch. But, he'd disappeared half an hour ago to
meet Ronni at the entrance while Grace waited at the con-
cession stand for drinks.

Where are you?

"Grace!"

She turned and saw Ronni coming up the steps behind her.

"Hey, I thought Rafe was with you."

"He stopped to talk to Loretta."

"Oh." Grace's stomach flipped. Her gaze darted between pockets of people milling around the grounds and bleachers. She found Rafe, cozied up next to Loretta in the far right section in the first set of bleachers.

She felt a rush of jealousy and, buried beneath it, disappointment.

Wow. It hadn't taken him long to change his mind.

A sudden sense of Rafe's being filled her. He looked over his shoulder and caught her staring.

"Have a little faith in me, sweetheart."

He held her gaze with such expectation that she answered with a nod.

His smile loosened the tightness in her chest.

Weird. So very weird. If hearing Rafe's voice in her head was a symptom of the concussion, she thought the effect should've faded by now. And she found it curious it was only Rafe's voice she heard, never anyone else's.

"Mind if I sit with you? I haven't met many people yet and Alex is playing in the game."

Grace's attention returned to Ronni. "I'm sitting with Cassie and her family, but we have plenty of room."

"I can find another seat. I wouldn't want to intrude."

"You're not intruding. I'll introduce you."

"Alex had a great time yesterday," Ronni said as they climbed the steps.

"Rafe and I had a lot of fun, too." Grace led Ronni midway up the bleachers. So far, the only ones sitting in the reserved row were Cassie and Abby, her mother-in-law. Grace made the introductions as she passed Abby her soda and gave Cassie a bottle of water.

"Nice to finally meet you." Cassie smiled at Ronni. "I've

wanted to invite you, Alex and Rafe to dinner, but Gavin said you're busy taking night classes."

"I am." Ronni returned a smile.

"We'll plan a small dinner party when your classes are finished," Abby said.

"Grace!" Rafe bounded up the steps, two at a time, to get to her. He took off his shades and hooked them in the collar of his T-shirt. "You're sunburned." He dusted his thumb across Grace's cheek.

"I forgot to put on sunscreen."

He took off his cap and placed it on her head.

"Thanks." She pulled her ponytail through the opening in the back. Lowering her voice, she asked, "What were you talking about with Loretta?"

"You." Rafe leaned toward Grace. "I made sure she understands the way things are now."

A heated, hungry look darkened his eyes. His arms braced against her hips.

"What are you doing?"

"Reassuring you."

"I don't need reassurance."

"Then maybe I do."

Previously, Grace might've dismissed fleeting thoughts spoken in Rafe's voice as imagination, but when it happened with him right in front of her face and his mouth never flinched with movement...well, she wasn't quite sure what to make of it.

"Kiss me. Like you did last night." His eyes darkened and a seductive smile played on his lips.

A wicked heat flashed through Grace's body.

Her nipples pebbled, desire pooled in her lower belly. She licked her lips, parched from the sudden heat wave.

"Take it down a notch or two."

Grace tore her gaze from Rafe. Cassie grinned at them like a fiend.

"The team's getting ready," Abby said to Rafe. "I hope your suit fits. You never gave me your measurements so I had to guess."

Rafe glanced toward the baseball field and back to Grace. *"I can think of a better way to spend the afternoon."*

"Oh, no." Grace wagged her finger. "You're not copping out now. I want to see your ass in those tight uniform pants, running the bases."

Humor lit Rafe's eyes and his entire face smiled. He touched his nose to hers while they stared into each other's eyes. He gave her a peck on the lips and stood.

"Make sure my ass is the only one you watch, sweetheart." The gravelly rumble in Rafe's voice nearly made her come.

He was halfway down the bleachers when she yelled out, "Hey, Wyatt!"

He turned back.

"Make sure your ass is the only one worth watching."

His smile turned lethal. The heat in his gaze seemed to cause the outdoor temperature to rise.

Or maybe just her body temperature.

Then he winked.

Grace's breathing went wonky.

"You were right. Your chemistry with Rafe is explosive." Cassie grinned. "I knew you were perfect for each other."

"He's lonely. I'm single." Grace shrugged.

"Some of the best relationships start out that way, hon." Ronni patted Grace's knee. "Especially with men like Rafe."

"Oh, we're just friends."

"Well, that's a step forward."

"What do you mean?"

"When I first asked Rafe about you, he said you were a friend of a friend," Ronni said. "Now, you've moved up to friend."

"That didn't take long." Cassie peered at Grace with sharp, inquisitive eyes.

"What?"

"A few days ago, you said he didn't want to be your friend."

"He changed his mind."

"*You* changed his mind." Cassie turned her head.

Grace followed her friend's gaze toward the locker room. Rafe hesitated, his hand on the door. He turned, locking his sights onto Grace and a sense of his very presence filled her. Smiling, she wiggled her fingers at him. He nodded and went inside.

"Maybe he'll change your mind, too."

"About what?"

"About everything."

Chapter 30

"Stirrriike." The umpire's boom echoed around the base-ball field.

"Damn it, Brice! Knock the goddamn ball out of the park!" Rafe rocked on his feet and scowled down the third baseline toward home plate.

"I'm trying!"

"Not hard enough," Tristan chimed in from his position on first base.

With the score seven to seven in the bottom of the eleventh, two runners on base, and two outs, they were fighting hard to avoid another inning of overtime. Wolfans never stopped at a draw. They played until someone won.

Rafe didn't care who won anymore. Tired and sweaty, he could no longer pick out Grace's scent from the crowd. His nerves coiled as he wondered if she had left the bleachers, bored with the game.

The pitcher wound up. Rafe wiped the moisture from his brow and crouched into position.

The fastball rocketed from the pitcher's hand. Brice's bat splintered and the ball exploded down the third baseline. Roaring, the crowd jumped to its feet. Tristan took off for second base while Brice headed to first.

Rafe stayed put, tracking the ball as it drifted south of the baseline. His adrenaline rush stalled.

"Foul!"

Tristan and Brice turned back at the umpire's call.

Rafe caught his first glimpse of Grace since the seventh

inning. Still wearing his favorite hat, she waved furiously. The worried clench in his gut eased.

"Looks like we got a time-out," the third baseman taunted. "You know what that means."

The catcher pushed up his face mask and trotted to the pitcher's mound, probably to discuss an intentional walk. A power hitter, Brice only needed to get the ball into the outfield to bring Rafe home for the win.

"Ah, hell!" Hands on his hips, Rafe kicked the dirt and paced a tight circle around the base. If Brice walked, Tristan would advance to second. The bases would be loaded with two outs. The next batter was a wolfling who didn't have the strength to knock Rafe home. Another inning loomed.

Rafe shook out his arms to cast off the antsy sting beneath his skin. The game ceased being fun when they passed the three-hour mark. Now they were pushing four with no runs scored in the last two innings.

The catcher returned to home plate. Time-out completed, the pitcher tossed the ball and the catcher stepped to Brice's right.

Shaking his head, he stepped back from the plate and stretched. The irritation on his face matched Rafe's own.

Desperation, or something close to it, seized Rafe and a reckless plan formed in his mind. He stared hard at Brice. Although they couldn't communicate telepathically in their human forms, Brice must've sensed something because he gave Rafe a slight nod.

Rafe crouched into position.

The pitcher, grinning like a man unaware all hell was about to break loose, lobbed another ball outside the batter's box. Rafe sharpened his vision on the catcher's hand.

The moment the ball cleared the catcher's fingers on the return throw, Rafe ran.

The third baseman shouted the alarm. Cheers went up from the field and the crowd roared to its feet. Rafe swore above the ruckus he heard Grace yelling, "Run, Rafe, run! You can do it! I know you can!"

The ball smacked the pitcher's glove. He reared back and launched the ball like a cannon toward home. Adrenaline surged through Rafe's veins, wide-open and full throttle. He needed every ounce of power to outrun the ball traveling more than a hundred miles per hour.

The ball rocketed past the halfway mark. Rafe kept running. The catcher readied his mitt to swallow the screaming ball.

Heart pounding, Rafe dove at the plate. With all the dirt flying in his face, he couldn't see if he beat the ball home.

"Safe," the umpire yelled.

"Thank God." Rafe plopped his head on his arm.

Seconds later, Brice jerked him to his feet and bear-hugged him. "We won! We won!"

Tristan, Shane and the rest of the team swarmed. The crowd poured out of the bleachers and onto the field. Rafe bounced between teammates, the opposing team and the pack spectators. He endured handshakes, congratulatory pats and more than a few undesired butt pinches.

"Grace?" Rafe sifted through the mass of people. "Grace!"

Her scent rose above the myriad of smells.

"Rafe!" Barely a whisper in the collective buzz, her voice pinged his auditory sense.

The angst he experienced on the field seemed nothing more than a mild itch compared to the sharp-edged need that cut through him.

Whether alarmed by the fervor in his eyes or the twisted snarl on his lips, people opened a path before him, only to fold in behind him. Relief swallowed his voice as Grace barreled into him.

"I thought I'd never find you!" She threw her arms around his neck. Her breasts jostled his chest with each bounce of her happy little dance. "You were great! I knew you would run! I could feel it. Oh, my God! You won! You won the game."

Rafe's heartbeat kept time with the discordant flounce of Grace's ponytail. Funny how he'd notice such a random thing. One action totally irrelevant to the other, yet fully harmonized. He wondered what other synchronizations would manifest when the mate-bond fused them as one.

It would happen, eventually. He could no longer deny the inevitable. Nor did he want to.

His hands slipped down her back to cup the curve of her buttocks and he hoisted her against him.

"What are you doing?" The hesitation in her big green eyes made him want to erase all her doubts, even though he shouldn't.

"Stealing a kiss. You're the whole damn reason I stole home." Rafe devoured her mouth.

She clutched his shoulders, squeezed his hips between her thighs, pressed deeper into his chest and returned the kiss, claiming him with her lips, her tongue.

Legs locked around him, she dragged her lips from his mouth, and branded him with each soft peck along his jaw. Her teeth grazed his earlobe and she nipped him.

Fire licked through his veins. An undeniable need erupted in his core. The howling in his mind blocked any doubts about the future before they surfaced. Here and now, Grace was all that mattered.

Grace's backside knocked against the door. Rafe's hands roamed her body while his hot kisses seared a trail from her lips, beneath her jaw and along the column of her throat.

After the game, they'd raced to his vehicle and returned to the resort. The Co-op festivities would last way into the night. She and Rafe had their own idea of festivities.

They'd sprinted across an empty lobby to the elevator,

stumbling into the car while lip-locked. If the ride to her floor had been a long one, they never would've made it with their clothes on.

Rafe still had his tight uniform pants. She'd unbuttoned his shirt in the elevator but he wore his dark blue T-shirt beneath it.

He'd tossed the cap she wore in the truck and pulled the band from her hair, which now hung loosely around her shoulders. Most of the buttons on her shirt were undone and his fingers made quick work of the last one.

They stopped long enough to get the door open. Once inside the suite, Rafe kicked it closed. Both of his shirts came off at once.

Grace slipped out of her blouse, kicked off her sandals and wriggled out of her shorts.

Rafe toed off his shoes and stripped out of his clay-stained pants.

"Aww, I wanted to see your ass strutting around in those tight pants." Grace protruded her lower lip in a pout.

"I'll model them later."

He stalked toward her, naked. Fierce, determined, sexy. His eyes narrowed on her. "Did I give you that bruise?"

He slipped off her bra strap, his fingers lightly tracing the dark purple mark on her shoulder.

"I got it when I fell playing football with the boys."

"You should've told me you were hurt." His voice sounded raw, edgy, a barely contained force.

"I didn't notice it until this morning. Don't get upset. This boo-boo isn't the first and won't be the last."

He kissed the dark spot, then unfastened her bra and dropped it to the floor. He staggered kisses across the expanse of her neck.

Goose bumps spread across her body. Rafe's warm, calloused hands cupped her breasts, his thumbs teasing her nipples to hard points.

She loved the tender roughness of his touch. How could a man so wrong for her make her body feel so right for his?

She turned in his arms and glided her hands down his bare chest, feeling the soft swirls of hair against her palms. His skin felt fever-hot.

Her nerves snapped like fine wires. He seized her lips. She arched, rubbing every inch of her skin against his. He picked her up and she wrapped her legs around him. He carried her to the bathroom and pulled off her panties before turning on the shower.

"Really? A bath now?"

"You making me hot and sweaty is one thing. Dirt and grime from the baseball game is another." He stepped into the shower and held out his hand. "There's room for two."

Grace joined him. He soaped her; she soaped him. The washing became a tickling game until he suddenly trapped her hands over her head and placed tiny kisses along her jaw and down her throat.

A soft moan escaped her lips. "We can't have sex without a condom." Her voice lacked true conviction.

He released her wrists to run his hands along her curves. His thumbs teased her nipples into two tight buds. He sucked one into his mouth, swirling his tongue around the nub until Grace whimpered with need. Then, he moved to suckle the other breast.

"We can't do this." She twisted her fingers into his hair.

He released her nipple and laved the valley between her breasts with his tongue. "Do what?"

He licked the full curve beneath her breasts as his hands kneaded the flare of her hips.

"Have sex without a condom," she panted.

"Sex can be many things." Kneeling, he lapped the water rivulets running down her belly and into the strip crowning her mound.

"Oh, God." Her head thumped against the shower wall,

her eyes closed. She wet her lips, slightly puffy from their aggressive kissing earlier.

She wanted him so badly, she didn't have the patience to go slow. If they were on the bed, she'd be riding him right now.

As torturous as it was, she forced aside her urgency to enjoy him taking his sweet-ass time to savor every inch of her.

He nudged her legs apart to kiss her mound. Her body jerked and she squeezed his shoulders for support. She dug her nails into the muscles in the back of his neck. He groaned and she wanted to say she was sorry if she'd hurt him, but all that came from her mouth was a guttural moan sounding nothing like an apology.

Gripping the back of her thigh, he lifted her leg over his shoulder and licked her gently. Each stroke of his tongue felt like he was branding her as his own.

Her hips quivered against his face when his tongue stroked her clit. Her moans deepened, became sultrier. She responded to his every touch, even when he simply breathed across her skin.

The gnawing ache between her legs grew strong. She peeked through shuttered eyes. Rafe winked at her and wrapped his hand around his cock, stroking in rhythm with the thumb on his other hand that was gliding over her clit.

God, she wanted more. Needed more.

"Rafe," she moaned.

Still fisting his cock, he withdrew the thumb teasing her opening and thrust his tongue inside her in a frantic rhythm.

Grace ground her hips against his face. Her inner walls began to spasm and she cried out his name, followed by a long series of "yesses" that triggered his own release.

As her breathing slowed and the ringing in her ears faded, Rafe placed kisses on her mound and inner thighs.

Realizing she still had her fingers tangled in his hair, she relaxed her grip and released him. He eased her leg off his shoulder, made sure she was steady, then rose before her.

"That was amazing." She clasped his face.

Rafe smiled.

"Oh, my God! I didn't think you could get any sexier than being naked, but wow. Naked and smiling, that's almost too much to handle."

Rafe gave her a peck on the cheek, then reached to turn off the tepid shower spray. Shoving open the curtain, he grabbed a towel from the rack and rubbed it quickly over Grace's body and then his own.

He helped her out of the shower and whispered in her ear. "Now, I'm going to show you all the ways I like to be handled."

Chapter 31

Laughter chasing her, Grace landed in the center of the mattress. Rafe stalked her on the bed, his movements stealthy and determined. The tiny smile lifting the corners of his mouth took the edge off his fierce expression.

He nudged her jaw, nipped her ear and nibbled her neck, making her feel like she was being tickled from the inside out.

She clawed and wrestled and rolled him beneath her. He clasped her hips, urging her to mount him and ride.

Tearing her mouth from his lips, she panted, "Wait."

Rafe balled his hands in the bedding, his body shaking. The madness of hunger and want and need swirled in his gaze. He gritted his teeth. "Hurry."

Grace reached for the condoms and took her sweet time peeling back the foil and rolling the latex sheath down his cock.

Rafe's muscles bunched and his body hardened from the strain of remaining still. "Good boy," she teased, kissing him lightly on his lips.

She guided him inside her on a sigh. With a slow grind, she slid up and down his length. "Breathe."

"I can't," he gulped, tilting his head back. "I...I—ah, hell."

Rafe grabbed her waist, and holding her tightly, he flipped her onto her back. A half squeal, half laugh escaped her throat.

"Let's see how you like being breathless." Rafe thrust hard and deep, and Grace arched to take in all of him.

She loved seeing his face in the soft glow of the table lamp next to the bed. No longer straitlaced and clean-cut, he wore a short beard along his jaw that framed his mouth. His tousled hair lent an air of wildness to his appearance.

She liked him wild and free. In moments like this, there were no restraints, only raw desire and pure instinct.

Part of her wanted to capture this part of his essence so she would always have it. Yet, if she did, it would be diminished by captivity.

His hands roamed her possessively, laying claim to every inch of her body, freely surrendered to him.

Eyes hooded, he studied her face and she wondered what he saw. She found him utterly beautiful, inside and out.

Soon their fast and furious rhythm had them panting and sweating and shattering in ecstasy. He stilled. The changes in his face, a predatory fierceness softening to tender concern, mesmerized her as their breathing calmed.

In the time-suspended moment, she felt his essence merge with hers. She had no other explanation for the feeling of absolute and utter completeness with him.

It lasted only a fleeting moment and then dissipated. He kissed her sweetly and slowly withdrew. Grace curled on her side as he disposed of the condom.

"You okay, sweetheart?" Rafe returned to bed and pulled her into his arms.

"Uh-huh." She yawned. "You, Mr. Wyatt, have tuckered me out."

"Then I suggest a power nap, Miss Olsen. The night is still young."

Grace snuggled against him, the warm curve of his body a perfect fit. Soon, the lulling rhythm of his breathing worked a tranquilizing magic.

"Mine!" Rafe's voice whispered through her mind as she surrendered to a peaceful sleep.

Rafe awoke, his every sense tuning to Grace's soft, even breaths. She exasperated his control, turned him upside down, inside out and everything in between.

God, he didn't want to crave her the way he did.

He was such a glutton for punishment and starved for companionship. But he'd take it, even if it only lasted for a little while.

All wrong for him, Grace had no roots and wasn't interested in putting any down, and Rafe certainly wasn't interested in leaving Walker's Run.

The way she doted on Alex and his friends caused a desperate longing to coil in Rafe's stomach. He didn't want a substitute family, he wanted the real deal.

He traced his lips over her bruised shoulder and skimmed her neckline to the sweet spot behind her ear. He breathed in her essence. God, how he loved her scent. A rich, buttery sweetness as intoxicating as his favorite bourbon. He'd have to quit her cold turkey, just like he had the booze, unless he convinced her to stay.

If only he could be certain the truth of his dual nature wouldn't scare her away. He should've told her the truth by now. Had intended to tell her last night at Walker's Pointe. But, he'd chosen to couple with her instead of revealing himself because deep down, he was afraid. If she had rejected him, he would've missed one of the most spectacular experiences of his life.

Aside from the ball-numbing orgasms he'd had making love to her, he liked this moment the most. When her guard was down and the mate-bond did its thing to weave their souls together. In the stillness of predawn, everything seemed perfect and right.

He'd been a fool to think he could keep her at arm's

length. Brice had nailed it; the heart wanted what it wanted and there was no stopping it.

He was falling in love with Grace and it scared the hell out of him.

Grace had no interest in love and he didn't know how long it would take for her to recognize the connection they had. He'd felt her emotional distress through the mate-bond when he politely told Loretta to find another moon-fuck partner.

Grace had seen them and misinterpreted the encounter because of her trust issues.

He didn't want to be numbered among those who had disappointed her. He wanted to be the one who was always there when she needed him.

If only she could need him for more than fetching a midnight snack or as a mere sex partner.

The idea of no-strings-attached sex had seemed doable at the time. Now her scent was stamped into his nose, her taste branded on his tongue, her essence infiltrating his being.

He was so screwed.

Nothing he could do about it at the moment, so he snuggled her soft form tucked against him. He was almost asleep when his phone buzzed with a call from Brice.

Rafe answered with silence, easing from the bed.

"I hate to wake you." Brice's voice sounded strained.

"Red?" Rafe's heart revved. He eased from the bed and moved into the living room area so he wouldn't wake Grace.

"She's fine." Brice paused. "I don't know any way to say this without it being a shock. Are you sitting down?"

"Spit it out, Walker." It was too early to dance around words.

"Your house is on fire."

Rafe's mind flew to his apartment, his quickened heartbeat accelerated. "The R&L is on fire?"

"No, your house," Brice said.

"I don't have a—"

Rafe's heart stopped. The lack of warm blood pumping through his veins caused an icy chill to spread from his stomach up into his throat and closed around his words.

"Ronni?" he sputtered. "Alex?"

"Safe and unharmed."

Rafe dropped into the easy chair.

"I would come get you, but since you thought the R&L is on fire, I guess you're not there."

"I'm with Grace." It came out as a whisper. Instead of fooling around with her, he should've paid more attention to his blood-kin. He could've lost them. In the blink of an eye, he could've lost them.

His stomach rolled. If he had anything in his stomach, it would've come up.

"Meet me in the lobby. Five minutes."

Rafe disconnected the call and sat in stunned silence until he could force the shock from his mind. He quietly returned to the bedroom, pulled on his uniform pants and T-shirt, and sat on the edge of the bed to put on his shoes.

"Rafe?" Grace patted his side of the bed and sat up. "Are you leaving?"

"Ronni and Alex need me." His throat burned with emotion he didn't know how to express. "The house is on fire. They got out but I need to be with them."

Grace kicked off the covers and slid out of bed. "I'm coming, too."

She put on her clothes as quickly as they'd flown off the previous night. Her wanting to be there with him, with them, touched him far more deeply than he cared to admit.

"Sweetheart." He stilled the flurry of her hands misbuttoning her blouse. "I'm meeting Brice in the lobby. I have no idea what to expect when we get to the house. When I know more about what's going on, I'll call."

Having her at the fire would divide his attention, and

he wasn't sure what his own reaction would be when he saw the house. If he had a meltdown, he'd rather Grace not witness it.

"I want to help."

"Wait with Cassie. I'm sure she's up." He smoothed the wrinkles in Grace's brow with a kiss. "I need to concentrate on Ronni and Alex. If you're there, I'll be distracted."

He stopped her protest with a soft kiss. "I'll come back when I can."

Rafe left without looking back. He couldn't bear the disappointment shimmering in Grace's big green eyes.

Chapter 32

"How did the fire start?" Rafe dropped into the leather passenger seat of Brice's Maserati.

"We don't know yet. The fire investigator will give us a full report." Brice spun the car out of his parents' driveway and took off. There wasn't any traffic this early. Even if there had been, it wouldn't have slowed Brice.

"I heard what happened with Clay yesterday. He's been hounding my dad to force Ronni and Alex out of the house. I can't help wondering—"

"No," Rafe cut him off. "Lexi loved that house. Clay wouldn't have the heart to torch it. This has to be an accident." He slammed his fist against the armrest. "Goddamn. How much more can go wrong?"

Every which way he turned, he was failing in his personal life. It was like bad karma had dropped him in the middle of a racquetball court with an automatic throwing arm pitching nonstop curve balls from an endless supply of shit.

"Everything will be fine. Mom designated one of the empty rental cabins as a temporary home for them. When the fire investigation is complete, Dad will arrange for the house to be rebuilt."

"I could've lost them." Rafe knocked his head against the headrest. "I barely know them and I could've lost them."

He'd invested more time in a woman destined to leave him on a whim than in getting to know his own family.

Once Grace got her car back, her life would return to normal. His, though, would never be the same.

He needed to leash his inner wolf and focus on his family. They would be around a lot longer than Grace.

"Last chance to change your mind." Brice stopped at the turn to Rafe's former house.

Rafe rubbed moist palms against his thighs. "Do it."

Brice inched the car up the long driveway clouded with smoke. An acrid smell seeped inside the car through the air-conditioning vents.

Rafe didn't look at the house until he'd taken several breaths and climbed out of the car. Lifting his gaze, he realized that he hadn't taken enough time to prepare.

What had once been a fairy-tale cottage with gingerbread trim, gables and shutters, now was nothing more than blackened boards, blown-out windows and ashy rubble.

Rafe choked on the breath caught in his throat.

Pain stabbed his chest like a fiery, twisted blade. His eyes stung and watered. He gasped for air, only it couldn't slip past the lump in his throat to fill his lungs. His body alternated between cold and clammy, and hot and sweaty with every heartbeat. Brice's steady hand on Rafe's shoulder kept him from sinking to the ground.

"Rafe!"

Wrapped in a utility blanket stamped with the Walker's Run Co-operative's volunteer fire department logo, Alex bolted toward him. Ronni trailed behind.

"Are y'all all right?" Rafe hauled Alex into a bear hug.

"I'm so sorry, Rafe." Ronni took Alex back into her arms. "I don't know how the fire started. I didn't leave anything turned on or burning when we went to sleep. I swear."

Dressed in jeans and a T-shirt, Tristan stepped out of the opening where the front door had been. He dropped his shoulders, lowered his head and trudged toward Rafe. "It's a total loss," he said quietly.

The ordeal had already drained the color from Ronni's skin. The gravity of the news caused her face to go ghostly pale.

"Don't worry." Rafe rubbed her back. "I'll take care of everything."

"We've been nothing but trouble." Ronni let out a halting breath. "Can't shake this bad luck."

"I know the feeling." Rafe brought her close, letting her cry on his shoulder. "Don't worry. I can replace the house. I can't replace y'all."

As her tears dampened his shirt, Rafe's body alternated between hot and cold. Relief and fear.

Ronni and Alex were his responsibility, and they'd lost everything they'd worked to rebuild and the few items from their life in Kentucky they hadn't wanted to part with when they moved. Gone. All of it, gone.

Before they arrived, he'd hired cleaners to tidy everything and an inspector to check the wiring, the gas lines, the roof and everything else a house inspector checked. Everything should've been in good working order.

Still, he'd failed them just like he'd failed Lexi. He couldn't protect them because he hadn't detected the danger.

He was useless as a family man. Simply not cut out for it all.

"You're a good man, Rafe Wyatt," Ronni sniffed.

"Yes, he is." Grace walked up beside him.

Her essence filtered through him and loosened some of the heaviness in his chest.

"Hey," he said, because no other words came to him. Just a rush of emotions too jangled for him to identify.

"Hey." Her arms wrapped him in a hug, but it was the warm embrace of her essence that comforted him the most.

"How did you get here?"

"I badgered Shane into bringing me. I wanted to be

here for you. I can't imagine how difficult it is to see the house like this."

"You're a good woman, Grace Olsen." Rafe kissed her temple. *"And God help me because I'm falling in love with you."*

"This is too much." Ronni cupped her hand over her mouth and Grace cleared away the wrapping paper torn from a huge box. Packed inside was a professional sewing machine. "I mean, thank you, Mrs. Walker, but I can't possibly accept."

"Nonsense." Abby smiled. "I heard you're a talented seamstress. After things settle down, I have a list of projects I want to discuss with you."

"I suggested she open a business." Grace sat next to Ronni on the floral print couch in the cabin the Walkers had provided for temporary housing. Alex had gone off with his friends and Ronni had entertained a steady stream of visitors all afternoon. Word spread quickly through the Co-op, and within minutes of Alex and Ronni's release from the hospital people began arriving to give them assistance.

The generous outpouring of food, clothes and other household items reminded Grace of how the military families would gather whenever a new family moved in, when the time came for them to leave or when they received news, good or bad, about their loved ones on active duty. She missed those days. Not the multiple moves, but the sense of community, knowing no matter where they landed a group would be there to welcome them into their temporary home or help send them on their way.

After too many years of being adrift, Grace wondered if the time had come to park herself long enough to get rooted. Cassie had been a tumbleweed until life dumped her in Maico. Although not quite stranded by her car accident, Grace had been afforded the opportunity to stop, look around and discover life at a more leisurely pace.

"I have all I can handle working at the diner, going to night classes and raising Alex." Ronni traced the picture of the sewing machine on the box. "It's a nice dream, though."

"There's no reason to work at the diner if you'd rather not," Abby said.

"I don't want to freeload off Rafe. He does a lot for us, as it is. Waitressing is all I know."

"You know how to sew. If you're going to work, make it something you enjoy." Cassie smiled.

"You could work from home, make your own schedule, only choose the projects you wanted to do. I can create a business website, design business cards, advertising flyers." Grace would do everything pro bono. How could she not? Especially since Rafe was handling her car repairs and was in the process of getting an accessible car for Matt.

"Brice could help with filing the proper paperwork to make the business official," Cassie chimed in.

"The Co-op will assist with any start-up expenses." Abby practically glowed, much to Grace's surprise. Cassie's mother-in-law usually maintained a poised, aloof manner.

"Alex and I aren't official members yet."

Abby flicked her hand. "I'll take care of Gavin. He likes to think he's the big dog and usually he is. Some matters, though, he's learned to heel when I say so. This will be one of those matters."

Grace felt a small pang of jealousy over Ronni and Alex's ready inclusion in the Co-op's exclusive membership. Still, she loved how the community quickly responded to the emergency and how they took care of Ronni and Alex simply because they were Rafe's kin.

Independent in her own right, Grace didn't need to be taken care of, but she longed to be part of something substantial. Not merely a face on someone's TouchBase friends list.

At least she had Cassie. And no matter the distance, Cassie's little girl would always link them.

She would also link Grace to Rafe, too. Cassie wanted Grace and Rafe to be involved in her daughter's life. Something about that made Grace smile.

She truly enjoyed Rafe's company. Things had been strained at first, but now, when they weren't together, she often found herself counting the minutes until she would see him again.

She'd even indulged the fantasy of becoming something more meaningful to him than a casual lover. Overindulged, actually. This morning, her imagination had run wild with Rafe's voice invading her thoughts to say he'd fallen in love with her.

She doubted the reality because they were too different. She'd disrupted his natural order and he had to reconstruct it around her impulsiveness. He did so without much complaint.

He had the patience of a saint, she'd give him extra kudos for that instead of brownie points, since he was allergic to chocolate.

A cold, harsh thought crossed her mind. If whatever she had with Rafe turned into something more meaningful, she'd have to give up her all-time favorite treat.

He'd probably be worth it.

"I sure as hell am worth it!"

An inexplicable sense of Rafe's being filled her. He wasn't simply in her head, she felt him to her very core.

She rubbed her temple. If the peculiar mental experiences didn't stop soon, Grace would ask Doc for a checkup and possibly another brain scan. Maybe he'd missed something in the exam following the accident.

"Are you okay?" Cassie spoke softly as Ronni and Abby engaged in a conversation about redecorating the Walkers' home. "You seem distracted."

"Weird thoughts and sensations." Grace waggled her bottle of water at Cassie. "No coffee in two days."

"Are you sure it isn't something else? Or *someone* else?"

"No, why?"

"Come on." Cassie gave her an incredulous look. "The entire Co-op saw the fat, juicy kiss he gave you after the game. Everyone was talking about it. I'm surprised you didn't hear them. Oh, wait." The flat seam of her mouth quirked as she struggled not to smile. "You didn't hear them because you couldn't. You and Rafe disappeared for the rest of the evening."

"Fine! We had sex." No sense denying the truth when her heated cheeks were broadcasting it.

"Duh!" Cassie giggled.

"It does not mean we're in a relationship. We're just having fun."

"Best advice, don't fight the inevitable. The struggle can become quite painful. Might as well skip straight to the good part."

From Grace's perspective, she and Rafe were enjoying the good part. She hoped the fire wouldn't change things.

Chapter 33

"**N**o way in hell." Rafe spat at the large, steel kennel. His gut clenched, and his muscles hardened all the way to his jaw.

"The sheriff specifically asked to see your wolf." Tristan's mouth turned down. "People have reported a wolf prowling at night, destroying property. Wolf tracks were found at the scenes."

"Not mine," Rafe snapped.

"He knows your wolf escaped the sanctuary the night of Grace's accident," Gavin said. "It's natural for him to think the perpetrator is the same wolf."

"I haven't been outside the sanctuary in my wolf form since that night."

"I understand, but I've stalled this demonstration for as long as I can. In light of recent events, it's in the best interest of the pack to show the sheriff that the Co-op will assist fully with his investigation."

"I'm not doing it."

"The sheriff believes your wolf is dangerous." Gavin exhaled an audible, frustrated breath. "I want to prove you aren't."

"I *will* be a danger to the first person who tries to shove me into that goddamn pen."

"Dad." Brice ground his teeth. "You can't seriously expect Rafe to do this. We don't cage our own kind."

Except when feral, rabid and dangerous.

All of which Rafe felt at the moment.

His heart raced, his mind swirled, his vision dimmed, his breathing dissolved into pants.

"Take it easy, son." Doc's hand rested on Rafe's shoulder. Strong and steadying.

"It'll only be for a few minutes, Rafe." Gavin stepped forward. "I'm not happy with the arrangement, but the sheriff insists. The most expedient way to end this witch hunt is to allow him to see how docile our wolves are toward people. Beginning with yours."

A bad feeling crawled up Rafe's spine. He wasn't docile at all, and if he had to go into that pen, everyone would see.

Never cage a wild animal. Never.

"Want me to play nice and sweet?" Rafe cut his eyes at Gavin. "Don't put me in a cage."

"Let me open negotiations with the sheriff," Brice said. "This doesn't feel right."

Tristan wouldn't meet anyone's gaze. "I'm not in favor of this, but it's what Locke insists on. He wants Rafe's wolf secured while he assesses whether or not the wolf is dangerous. He'll seek a subpoena if you refuse."

"Let him." Brice pinched the bridge of his nose.

Rafe toed the ground. Any involvement with the courts was risky. Even if Brice and his uncle's law firm routinely dealt with the judicial system in Atlanta.

"The sooner we get this over with, the better." Gavin opened the cage door.

Rafe's every instinct fought against it. He simply could not, would not, put himself in a cage.

"Gavin, don't make him do this." Doc stood next to Rafe, mirroring Brice's angry scowl.

Gavin ignored them both, fastening his hard, intense gaze onto Rafe. "This is for the good of the pack, Rafe."

"You're caging one of us, Dad. Because a human asked you to do so. Rafe isn't sick or feral. Forcing him into a cage is unconscionable. The pack won't react well to this."

"If Rafe does this willingly, there won't be an issue."

"You've got a problem, then. I am not going to be caged."

"Damn it, Gavin." Doc stood toe to toe with the Alpha. "He's your godson."

"Which is why I haven't ordered Tristan to forcibly put him inside, but my patience is waning. We will cooperate fully with the sheriff's department to avoid any reprisals. We will not give Locke any further cause to nose around in our business."

The muscle in Gavin's jaw twitched. His hardened gaze slid toward Brice. "One wolf's pride isn't worth putting the pack's safety at risk."

Brice's brow scrunched as he stared at the cage. Rafe could almost see and hear the wheels turning in his friend's clever mind, playing out a dozen or more scenarios within seconds. He rubbed his jaw. "I'll go inside the pen with him."

Gavin's ears reddened, then purpled, and the color painted his entire face and neck.

"No," he and Rafe shouted simultaneously.

Rafe wouldn't allow his Alpha-in-waiting to be caged. His loyalty had always belonged, first and foremost, to Brice.

If Brice was willing to submit to the cage, it meant he'd come to the same conclusion as his father. The best way to deal with the sheriff was to give him what he wanted.

What the man wanted was Rafe and his wolf.

Knots formed in his stomach. "This is not going to go as well as he thinks," he said to Brice.

"I have the same feeling."

Rafe slipped out of his clothes, balled them up instead of folding them and tossed them to his father.

"I've got your back, man." Brice nodded slightly. Frustrated anger burned in his eyes.

Rafe crouched on the ground, looking at the serene blue

sky above him and tried to block out the thoughts of how this could all go horribly wrong.

He turned his gaze to Gavin. If the Alpha felt any satisfaction, it didn't show in his eyes.

"I won't forget this," Rafe warned.

"Neither will I." Gavin nodded.

A current of energy pulsed along Rafe's nerves, shooting tiny electrical impulses that pinched his skin. There was a sudden shift in awareness as he morphed from man to wolf.

The wolf wanted to run. Hard, fast and without looking back.

Doc knelt in front of Rafe and rubbed his ears. "You'll be all right, son. I promise."

Brice walked beside Rafe to the cage. Tristan opened the door. Both of them looked as uncomfortable as Rafe felt.

He padded into the cage. The door clanged closed and the lock dropped, driving panic into his stomach. An involuntary cringe rippled down his back.

An instinctual growl rolled up his throat.

Doc squatted beside the cage. "Calm yourself. We don't want you snarling when the sheriff arrives."

Refusing to face forward, Rafe turned in a tight circle and lay down. Paws tucked under his chin, he exhaled a heavy breath from his snout and closed his eyes. He wished he could nap through the humiliating demonstration, but Wahyas only held their wolf form while conscious.

He heard the crunch of tires on the dirt road, the hum of a V-8 engine, and the cold silence of his dad and three wolfans in human form standing on the outside while he was trapped on the inside.

Poetic justice?

Maybe.

After all, a beast lurked inside him. If it ever got out, a cage would be the least of his worries.

Car doors shut. Voices blended. Rafe didn't much care

about what was being said. He wanted this degradation to be over.

It seemed an eternity passed before the sheriff and a lady deputy stood by Tristan next to the kennel.

"Where's Wyatt?" The sheriff swung his gaze around the men gathered.

"He's dealing with a family matter. Doc is here on his behalf," Gavin said.

Squatting, the sheriff peered at Rafe. "So, this is the wolf that shredded a man into a bloody pulp."

The hackles rose along Rafe's spine.

"He was protecting his family," Doc snarled.

"The incident was investigated. The hunter was trespassing. He shot two Co-op members, killing one of them. The wolf's actions were defensive," Gavin replied matter-of-factly. "The sheriff and the DA's office agreed."

"There's a new sheriff in town now." Locke's gaze pinned Rafe. "Seems Wyatt has a penchant for luck with the courts. Things get swept under the rug. No charges were filed when he drove off the road at Wiggins's Pass, drunk out of his mind. And he just happened to be in the woods when a resort guest wrecked her car because his wolf darted into her path."

Rafe really didn't like the way this demonstration was going.

"What's the real story?" The sheriff rattled the cage.

Rafe swallowed a growl and forced himself to shrink away.

"Don't harass him." Brice stepped up. "If you intentionally provoke him—"

"He'll bite me? Rip my throat out?" Locke stood.

"You'll be in violation of the wolf protection order issued to the Walker's Run Cooperative, signed by the governor," Brice said coolly. "A sheriff who breaks the law won't remain sheriff for long."

"Is that a threat?"

"A promise."

Rafe snorted. Brice never made a promise he couldn't keep.

Locke walked around the perimeter of the cage. "He looks sick."

"He's pouting because he's penned," Gavin said.

"I have his paperwork if you want to see it." The cold, hard edge to Doc's voice hadn't mellowed. "Latest shot record, last physical exam. He's in excellent health."

Something jabbed Rafe's side, hard. He scrambled to his paws, whipping his muzzle around, barely restraining the growl scaling his throat.

Locke poked his baton toward Rafe's chest.

Rafe stepped backward, his rump grazing the inside side wall of the cage.

"Don't do that again." Brice stepped into the sheriff's personal space, forcing the man to look up. At nearly six and half feet tall, Brice could be a formidable force when he chose to be.

"Making sure he's not sedated."

"Our wolves are docile. Tranquilizers are rarely necessary." Gavin approached the side of the cage where Rafe's wolf form pressed against the slender, aluminum bars so flimsy that one or two good shoulder dives would bust them wide open.

"But you have used them." The sheriff tipped his head. "On this one in particular."

"During an extraordinary situation we hope never happens again." Gavin's fingers slipped through the slats and stroked behind Rafe's ear. Some of his agitation eased, but it annoyed him that he could be manipulated by a gentle petting.

He should've nipped Gavin's fingers to protest. Of course, the action wouldn't go over well with the sheriff.

"I want his paw prints to compare with the ones we found at the botanical gardens and the public library."

"Here." Doc handed the sheriff a copy of Rafe's wolf prints, on file in his medical chart.

"I'd prefer to take a fresh set." The sheriff nodded to the lady deputy.

"This will be interesting." She approached the cage with a handheld scanner and knelt next to Gavin. "Never had to use this on a wolf."

She whistled. "Come here, boy."

What the hell? I'm not a dog.

Yet, here he was, locked inside a pen, padding toward her as commanded.

If anyone tried to put a collar on him, he'd bite off their hand.

"Whoa!" Her head tilted and her gaze targeted between his hind legs. "You don't neuter them?"

Rafe froze.

"We encourage our wolves to mate. When they select one, they're together for the rest of their natural lives."

"But his mate was killed, right?"

"Yes." There was a sorrowful note in Gavin's voice.

Rafe pressed his snout against the cage and the deputy stroked his muzzle. "Sorry about this, big guy, and sorry about your mate."

"He can claim another one," Gavin said. "He's being stubborn, even though it's high time for him to settle down again."

The Alpha's gaze heated Rafe's fur, still Rafe refused to make eye contact. Instead, he watched the woman work the handheld scanner through the thin bars of the cage. She lifted his left front paw.

"He isn't the one." She looked over her shoulder toward the sheriff.

"You got his prints that fast?"

"He's got a thick scar on his left front paw pad. The molds we made at the scene didn't show any ridges from a scar."

"Get his prints anyway."

Rafe heard a car drive up but couldn't see anything other than the woman deputy and the back of Gavin's jeans-clad legs.

He sensed Doc's presence behind the cage. Tristan and Brice walked away, presumably toward the newly arrived vehicle.

Offering his right front paw, he wished the lady would go a bit faster. The cage was closing in and it was all he could do to not fight his way out.

The deputy had a difficult time scanning his back paws. She kept twisting his leg odd ways until he yelped.

Grace's scent reached him about the time her voice did, in a high-pitched squeal. "You put him in a cage?"

Phone clenched in her hand, she broke free of the huddle around her and darted to the kennel. Kneeling, she pressed her hands against the bars. "You poor thing."

Rafe eased to her and touched his nose to her palm, breathing in her scent.

"He's been a trouper." The lady deputy rubbed his ear and stood. "Got 'em." She held up the scanner and walked toward the group headed to the cage.

"Shouldn't be much longer," Doc said. "Sit tight."

Having Grace within reach eased a lot of his anxiety, although he'd rather she didn't see him caged.

He stuck his snout between the bars.

"I'm so sorry, big guy." She cupped his muzzle. "When the deputy said I had to identify the wolf who caused my accident, I had no idea they would do this to you."

"Ma'am, step away from the cage. He's a dangerous animal," a male deputy said. Rafe hadn't seen him earlier, so he must've been the one who brought Grace.

"He won't hurt me." Grace kissed Rafe's wolf nose.

Her trust reinforced his resolve. He needed to tell her the truth, show her all that he was. He couldn't wait another day.

"I said, step away!" The deputy grabbed Grace's shoulders and harshly yanked her to her feet.

Startled, Grace yelled in fright and she struggled to get free of his grip.

Rafe's tenuous restraint on his wolf's instinct broke.

He barked, he growled, he threw himself against the kennel door.

Shouts were raised, shoving seemed imminent. All Rafe cared about was Grace.

As her panic rose, so did Rafe's primal need to protect her. He rammed the kennel door, over and over again.

Doc's commanding voice faded in the chaos.

Rafe heard a loud pop. Then another. And another.

He kept slamming against the cage but his force lessened as his body slowed. His vision blurred and he lost complete coordination in his legs. He collapsed, unable to stand.

The only things working were his ears and those rang clearly with Grace's voice screaming, "You shot him. Oh, my God! You shot him."

Chapter 34

Grace nearly knocked Doc over as she slid to her knees.

Rafe's wolf lay crumpled on his side. Struggling to remain open, his arctic blue eyes followed her every move.

"Will he be all right?"

"As far as I can tell, he's not bleeding," Doc said.

Doc slowly opened the cage side door and reached inside. The wolf growled a warning.

"Easy, son." Doc inched closer. Grace moved to the side, giving him more room.

The wolf snapped and snarled.

"So help me, if you bite me…" Doc's voice sharpened.

"He needs to see Grace," Brice said, approaching at a fast limp.

Doc pivoted to allow her to scoot forward. "Try to get him to come closer so I can examine him."

"You won't bite me, will you?" she asked the wolf.

"Right now, I suspect you're the only one he won't bite," Brice said.

The wolf snorted. As if that were possible.

Doc helped Brice drape the cage with an old tarp, blocking the view of the commotion between Gavin, the sheriff and his deputies.

"All right, buddy." On her hands and knees, Grace poked her head into the pen. "Come here."

He diligently tried to stand but his body wouldn't cooperate and he collapsed. Each time his eyelids lowered, it took longer for him to raise them.

"Grr...ay...sss." Rafe's slurred voice whispered through her mind.

"Rafe?" She glanced around but didn't see him.

The wolf stretched his front left leg toward her. She took his paw in her hand, rubbing her thumb against a thin, hard ridge across his pads.

"Hey. He has the same scar as Rafe, in the same spot."

A tingly current nipped her palm and zipped through her body.

In the blink of an eye, the furry paw she held morphed into a man's calloused hand. Her gaze flew to the wolf's face. Rafe stared back at her.

Grace's heart stopped midbeat, her lungs froze midbreath, trapping a lump in her throat. Her ears rang with voices or static or maybe the sound of madness. An icky, clammy chill coated her skin.

"Grrr...aayy...sss." Rafe's voice rang in her head but his lips never moved. *"I—"*

His eyes rolled upward and his entire body went limp.

No, no, no! Please God, no.

Her stomach seized so hard acid spewed up her esophagus.

A large hand clamped over her mouth and she was quickly hauled back from the cage.

"Don't scream," Brice's soft, stern voice filled her ear. "If you do, the sheriff will come over to investigate. What do you think he'll do when he finds Rafe tranqed inside the cage instead of a wolf?"

Gagging, Grace tugged at his hand and thrashed against his light restraint. It wasn't a scream she needed to let out. She elbowed Brice in the ribs until he released her.

She crawled a few feet away and vomited.

Death, the thought of someone dying, or close to dying always caused a revolution in her stomach. She'd seen too many death messengers in their dress uniforms walking up to the doors of neighboring houses, fearing one day it would be her door they knocked on and hung a black wreath over.

"I'll take care of her." Brice knelt next to Grace and called back to Doc. "You take care of him."

Brice's hand rested on Grace's shoulder. "Breathe slowly and try to calm yourself," he said gently.

Calm? How could she remain calm at a time like this?

A wolf transformed into Rafe—right in front of her freaked-out face. Her mind got stuck in one thought.

Rafe was a wolf.

The freaking wolf who caused her accident.

"This isn't happening," she kept muttering to herself.

"Grace. Everything happening is as real as it gets," Brice said. And here she'd always thought he was a reasonable sort of fellow. "Pull it together, Grace. Rafe needs you."

"He's not dead?"

"He was hit with tranquilizer darts."

"Oh, God." Another bout of nausea struck.

"Easy." Brice's thumb slipped beneath her ponytail to massage the base of her skull.

"That's not helpful."

"Yeah, Cassie says that, too." He removed his hand and handed her a handkerchief. "My dad always did that for me and it made me feel better. Maybe humans are different."

The words sunk in.

"Oh, my God! You're a…a werewolf, too?" She scooted away from him.

"We're not werewolves," Brice snapped. He swallowed a breath and began again. "We're called Wahyas and our species has maintained a fairly harmonious existence with humans since the beginning of recorded time. You don't need to be afraid of us."

"Cassie—"

"Is human." Brice's mouth pressed in a firm line. "She

has always been and always will be human. Wahyas are born, not turned."

"Does she know what you are?"

"Of course she does."

"She should've told me." Grace shook her head. "Why didn't she?"

"We had a plan…" Brice's voice trailed.

"What?" She jerked away from Brice when he offered to help her stand.

"I'm still the same person, Grace. Just like Rafe is. Neither of us will hurt you."

She suspected he told the truth. If either had wanted her harmed, there had been ample opportunity before now. Besides, the sheriff and three deputies were nearby in a heated discussion with Gavin.

In all likelihood, he was a werewolf, too.

A cold, hard tremor shook her entire body.

"Grace, I know this is a shock. This isn't how we wanted you to find out about us."

"When were you planning to tell me?"

"We wanted to explain everything before Brenna arrives. But when Rafe showed an interest in you, we decided to see what developed between the two of you. We didn't want to complicate things."

"What do you call what happened here, if not a complication?" Grace watched the sheriff's department vehicles slowly leave.

"An unfortunate situation." Brice frowned. "I trust you with what you've seen. Understand what a great responsibility this is. We're an evolutionary species, similar to humans, but we keep the truth of our existence secret because the world isn't ready for us. For Chrissakes, look at what Locke did to Rafe's wolf while he was caged."

As confused and hurt by the secrecy as she was, Grace forced herself to compartmentalize the situation so she could deal with a more urgent matter. "I want to see Rafe." She needed to know he was still alive.

"Good start." Relief softened the clench in Brice's jaw.

They hurried back to the cage. Rafe was curled on his side, breathing hard and fast.

"Let him scent you." Brice gently nudged her forward. "It'll calm him."

Hesitantly, she stroked Rafe's cheek. He turned his face to nuzzle her palm. He whispered her name like a reverent prayer and a faint smile appeared on his lips.

Doc held three darts in his hand. Still kneeling by the cage, he glared at Gavin. "You saved my life once and I swore I would always be at your side. And when you convinced the Woelfesenat to let me adopt Rafe, I believed nothing would ever break our friendship. But I swear, if you ever do this to my son again, I will fucking kill you."

The fierce, drop-dead seriousness in his eyes, and the frigid sharpness of his voice iced Grace's veins. He was the kindness, gentlest soul she'd ever met, and yet she believed he would absolutely carry out his threat.

Gavin knelt next to Doc and took the darts. "On my life, this will not happen again."

"We need to get him out of there," Tristan said.

"He's heavily sedated but not in any danger." Doc stroked Rafe's head. "Bring him to my house. He'll never forgive me if I hold him in the hospital for observation."

"I'd like to come, too," Grace said. She and Rafe had a lot to discuss when he woke up.

Chapter 35

"I'm so sorry." Cassie sat at Doc's kitchen table. Her face was scrunched, her eyes brimming with tears. "I didn't want you to find out like this."

"You didn't want me to find out at all." Grace sipped her coffee without waiting for it cool. The hot liquid scalded her throat, though Grace barely acknowledged it beneath the searing truth that her best friend had conspired against her.

And Grace had thought only men couldn't be trusted.

It hurt that Cassie had kept this secret. Hurt to have been left out of something so important. Hurt to think she'd been played for a fool. Grace hadn't been taken into Cassie's confidence, she'd merely been presented with the illusion of inclusion.

"I wanted to tell you," Cassie said softly. "It's complicated and frightening, and I wanted to ease you into it."

"I've lived all over the world, Cassie. I had to adapt to foreign cultures, foreign food and foreign politics as a way of life. I didn't need to be handled with kid gloves."

Angry and numb, mystified and curious, Grace had no idea how to reconcile the myriad of emotions running amok inside her. "Brice and Rafe, what are they exactly? Werewolves?"

"They're called Wahyas. They get touchy when someone uses the term werewolf."

"Wa-hi-yas?" Grace said the term slowly.

"They evolved alongside humans, but at some point in the ancient past, humans hunted them to near extinction.

After that, they keep their identities and abilities secret for good reason."

"How many others?" Grace asked.

"There are packs worldwide. Locally, most of the members of the Walker's Run pack are Wahya. Me, Doc and a few others are human."

"Rafe was adopted by a human?" Grace swallowed.

"Yes." Cassie tucked a loose strand of hair behind her ear. "Humans and Wahyas can coexist. They aren't that different from us."

Cassie's hand rested protectively on her belly. "Does knowing Brenna is a wolfan change the way you feel about her?"

From the moment she learned of Cassie's pregnancy Grace had regarded the little one as family. No matter her heritage or ability to sprout fur and howl, the baby was Cassie's daughter. And despite the ruse, Cassie was Grace's friend.

"Of course not. I'm not upset about what she is, or what her father is. I'm upset because everyone conspired against me."

"We conspired *for* you, Grace. Never against you." Cassie worried her lip between her teeth. "It was always our intention to reveal everything before we asked you to be Brenna's godmother."

"Godmother?" Grace's heart pinched.

Cassie nodded. "When we told Gavin, he insisted we wait until Brenna was born to explain everything to you. He wanted the pack to get to know you and for you to know them before we told you everything. He thought it would be easier that way."

Cassie reached for Grace's hand. "I trusted you, but some secrets aren't mine to share. Gavin is the Alpha. We have to respect his wishes."

"Maybe you do." Grace snorted. "I still have free will."

"Pinky sisters through thick and thin?" Cassie held up her tiniest finger.

Discovering a community of wolfan shapeshifters living among humans stretched the limits of Grace's coping abilities. She wasn't sure how much more she could take, but Cassie was a friend she loved like a sister and Grace wouldn't let a wolf pack come between them.

"Absolutely." Grace hooked her pinky around Cassie's finger and laughed. "Although when we made this promise in the second grade I never thought we'd end up in the midst of a group of wolf people."

Brice knocked on the wall before he entered. "Rafe is awake and asking for Grace."

"I'll call you later." She squeezed Cassie's hand and shot Brice a scathing look.

"Grace," Brice said softly.

"I'm not speaking to you, except to ask—how could you put Rafe in a cage? He's your best friend. I would never let someone do that to Cassie. And I seriously doubt Rafe would allow someone to do that to you."

"Your right. He didn't. I offered to go into the cage with him. He refused." Brice rubbed his palm against his brow. "Nothing like this will happen again. You have my word."

"Considering all that's happened, your word isn't worth two cents to me, right now."

Doc stopped Grace in the hallway outside Rafe's room.

"He's groggy, but won't suffer any lasting effects from the tranquilizers." Doc squeezed her arm. "He cares about you, Grace. He's worried what you'll think of him. Try to keep an open mind."

"The wolf pack should've kept an open mind about me." She laughed harshly. "I understand necessary precautions, but you and the wolf pack shouldn't ask something of me that you weren't willing to give yourselves."

"Don't punish Rafe for our Alpha's decisions, Grace."

"I won't." She would, however, hold him accountable for his own decisions.

Doc retreated downstairs.

Grace entered the bedroom, not sure what to expect.

Rafe sat up but his body swayed from side to side. His gaze was unfocused. "Grace?" A note of panic tinged his voice.

She moved next to him. "I'm here."

He clumsily cupped her cheek and pressed his forehead to hers. "Are you all right?" His words ran together in a slur.

"Physically, yes." She pulled away. "For Pete's sake, Rafe. You should've told me what you are before we had sex."

Grace leaned against the long dresser at the foot of the bed.

"I wanted you to know from the start." Rafe flattened his hand on the mattress. "Gavin and his goddamn schemes. Sometimes I want to wring his neck."

"Cassie said he's the Alpha."

"He likes to meddle and manipulate to get what he wants." Rafe rubbed the developing bruise on his side.

"Why did he cage you? Was it because of me?"

"No, sweetheart. The sheriff is a suspicious man. He's been asking to see my wolf for a while. Gavin thought if the sheriff saw that my wolf posed no danger, he'd finally leave us alone. If we're ever exposed, things will get really bad for our kind. The public at large isn't ready for us yet."

"In a global sense, I understand the need for secrecy. On a personal level, I'm disappointed neither you nor Cassie trusted me."

"I do trust you and I want you to know me, Grace. All of me." Sincerity shimmered in the vast blue of his eyes. "But this isn't a secret I can confess the first time we meet. I wouldn't have hidden my true self indefinitely. We ran out of time before I could tell you."

He was right. It still hurt, but he was right. The time she'd had to get to know him had been brief.

Rafe sat patiently, waiting. He didn't try to persuade her with pressure or reasoning. He simply spoke his truth and waited for her to decide.

Still, he wasn't blasé about the situation. His jaw muscles were tight, tension wrapped around his body as if steeling him against whatever may come.

"You swear you were going to tell me?"

Hope flickered in his eyes. "I intended to tell you when I took you to Walker's Pointe, but things happened between us and I got distracted. I planned to take you back there, tonight. It's secluded and peaceful."

"And you could throw me off the cliff if I freaked out too badly." She tried to look stern, but the appalled expression on Rafe's face disrupted her attempt and she laughed.

"I wouldn't hurt you, Grace." He sounded affronted. "Even if you can't accept what I am, I would never hurt you."

She didn't doubt he would not harm her physically. Her heart, however, would reserve judgment.

She edged toward the bed and sat on the foot of the mattress. "Can I see your wolf again?"

"Tell me when you're ready." He pushed aside the sheet and tucked his legs beneath him.

Ready as she could be, Grace nodded.

Just that quick, it happened. No flash of light. No bone-cracking transformation. No shedding of skin.

One second she was looking at Rafe, and the next a red wolf sat in his place. He hunkered down, inching forward on his paws. Never taking his gaze off her face.

When he reached her, he lifted his nose to touch her hand twisted in the bedsheets. She touched his wolf form, half believing it was an apparition. Yet she felt the solidness of the wolf's body, the softness of his fur.

His chin rested on her lap.

As Grace's fingers slipped through the wolf's fur, the copper strands became Rafe's hair.

"Wolf or man," he sighed, repositioning himself beside her. "I'm still me and both of us want you."

"Are you two separate beings?"

"More like a shared consciousness. I'm him and he's me, but sometimes we have a difference of opinion."

"How?"

"The wolf has wanted you ever since we met at Brice's birthday party. All along, he sensed that you are our mate. I ignored the instinct to claim you because I needed to get my life together."

"Claim me?"

"Wahyas crave love, just like humans. Many of us won't claim a female until we fall in love and a mate-bond forms. A claiming occurs when a male binds to a female during sex, with a bite, here." He traced his finger over the place where her neck and shoulder met. "It's like getting married, except there is no divorce under wolfan law. The only thing that breaks the claim is death. But the mate-claim only binds our bodies. A mate-bond syncs our hearts and souls. It allows a couple to hear each other's thoughts, know their feelings. It's like a part of them lives inside you."

Rafe held their hands against his chest, and Grace's heart ached.

"Sweetheart, what's wrong?"

"This claiming and bond stuff freaks me out."

"Put it out of your mind." His gaze drifted from hers. "Life is one day at a time. We can be, too. If all you want, if all you need me for, is a friend with benefits, I'm still in. I'll take you any way I can have you."

He gently pulled the band from her hair and her skin began to prickle with expectation.

The muscles in her stomach tightened and her sex

clenched. She knew where this would lead if she didn't stop him.

Her heart drowned out the insanity. No matter what, the man next to her was Rafe.

The man who sat with her in the ER so she wouldn't be alone.

The man who brought her ice cream at midnight.

The man who turned on all the lights so she wouldn't have to walk into darkness.

Did it matter that he could change into a wolf?

Her body didn't think so, because it responded to his touch the same way it always had, arching toward him when she should've run the other way.

When his lips touched her mouth, the kiss didn't turn into the usual frenzy. It was slow and tender, long and deep.

She'd never wanted a man as much as she wanted him. Beyond the physical, he touched her on a level she'd been afraid to let anyone reach.

She molded her hand around his erection and stroked his hardness. "Condom?"

"Don't need them. I can't get you pregnant unless I claim you." He ran his tongue over his eye teeth. "Biting during sex introduces the male's scent hormone into the female and triggers his ability to father children with her."

A comfortable warmth rushed through her body, making her feel as if she was being hugged from the inside out. She thought of the laughter as Rafe and the boys played in the park. They weren't her kids, Rafe wasn't her husband or her mate. Yet he anchored her, provided her stability, and was the most dependable person she'd ever met.

Someday, she might be ready for his bite. But today was not that day.

Chapter 36

Rafe inched closer to Grace, slowly cocooning her in his arms. In his spirit, he sensed the small chasm between them. Her emotions were warring inside her.

He staggered kisses across the back of her neck. Re-establishing a physical connection between them could help calm her internal storm and bridge the gap before it grew any wider.

She sighed, tilting her head forward, unwittingly exposing the spot where her neck and shoulder joined. The spot that instinctively enticed a male wolfan to bite.

He wouldn't push for more than she could give. Time was on their side.

He slowly exhaled and Grace's shoulder twitched beneath his breath. He licked the curve of her neck, tasting the natural sweetness of her skin that a human male couldn't detect.

"I am what I am, Grace. Can you accept that I'm different?"

She sighed, leaning against him. "The problem isn't that we're different races."

Technically, they were different species but he held his tongue.

"How can I trust you again?"

"I'll earn your trust back. No matter how long it takes." He gently turned her chin toward him. "The last few days with you have meant the world to me. There are other things about me I want to tell you, but I don't want to freak you out more than you already are."

She turned toward him, creating a physical space between them as they sat face-to-face on the edge of the bed. "Shapeshifters, mystical bonds, what more could there be?"

Grace's skin coloring turned ghostly. "Oh, my God. Are vampires real, too?"

"I've never encountered one." As far as he knew. "It's possible other species are hiding in plain sight like we are."

"That's not reassuring."

"I'm the same person you've known, Grace. I was wolfan yesterday, the day before and so on. Only now, you know about this side of me. Your discovery doesn't change who I am. It only changes your perception of reality."

"What other reality am I missing?"

Rafe's heart sped up and his mouth went suddenly dry. "Wolves aren't the only creatures Wahyas can shift into. It rarely occurs, but inside each of us is the potential to regress into a Wahyarian. From the research I've done, the Wahyarian could be the origin of the multiple werewolf myths in human folklore."

"Werewolves exist?" Grace's eyes widened.

"Not for long. When a wolfan regresses into their primitive state, the Woelfesenat—our wolf council—puts them down."

"As in…" Grace made a slicing motion across her throat.

Rafe nodded. "The beast is why we tend to be highly sexual. The hormones released during sex keep the wolfan hormones in check, especially during a full moon."

He toyed with Grace's fingers, long and elegant with painted pink nails. "Loretta has been my moon-fuck partner since my wife died. Our encounters were always in wolf form."

"Why?"

"I didn't need or want anything more." Rafe lifted his

gaze to Grace's eyes. God, he wanted to lose himself in the depths of those beautiful, shimmering green pools. "Until I met you."

"Are you proposing that I should become your new full-moon partner?" She crossed her arms over her chest and scrunched her mouth, but her eyes were smiling too much for her to look stern.

"Well," he leaned forward, bracing his hands on either side of her legs. "We don't need to limit the benefits to the full moon and I definitely won't be in wolf form. Sex is more fun and a helluva lot more satisfying as a human."

"Is that so?" A soft breath parted her lips.

He seized the opportunity to claim her mouth, sliding his tongue inside.

Her tongue teased the tender underside of his and he nearly broke out in a sweat from the blister of heat that flashed through his body. He captured the little fire starter between his teeth and gently sucked.

Grace's groan, low and deep, and as primal as that of any she-wolf, rose from the back of her throat, rumbled along her tongue and into his mouth for him to swallow, burying it deep into his being. As she straddled him, her thighs locked around his hips and her arms tangled around his neck.

Rafe slowly pulled his mouth from hers. If he didn't, they'd both pass out from lack of air.

"After what's happened, I shouldn't want you," Grace panted. "God help me, I do." She dropped her head against his chest.

Before his mind completely clouded in a thick haze of lust, he scooted them to the center of the bed.

"Kiss me again," Rafe said. He loved her kisses, passionate, feminine, yielding.

Cradling the back of her head, he urged her forward until her soft lips whispered across his mouth. She moved along his jaw to his ear. The tentative flick of her tongue against his lobe and the delicate nibble around the shell almost made him howl.

She caressed, kissed and studied every inch of him, head to toe.

"You have really nice feet." The fingernail Grace dragged down his arch felt as hot as smoldering coal and triggered a powerful surge that shot straight to his groin. "Oh! You like that, do you?"

Struggling to rise on his elbows, Rafe replied with a heavy pant.

Her fingers closed around his ankle. A wicked gleam lit her eyes. Reflexively, he pulled back his leg. Grace held firm.

"Uh-uh." She waggled her finger and sucked it into her mouth. Twisting it slowly, she pulled it out and moved it toward his foot.

His breathing stopped. Every muscle in his body primed in expectancy. When she stroked her wet fingertip across his sole, Rafe's body jerked as if he'd stepped on a live wire.

He collapsed on the bed, eyes fixed on the ceiling, and tried to remember how to breathe. Grace would damn near kill him before he had a chance to thrust inside her.

She slowly removed her shirt and shimmied out of her shorts. He had no objections to the clothes dropping to the floor.

Wearing only her lacy bra and panties, she straddled his hips. "Did you know your feet were that sensitive?"

It took him a minute to force out a scratchy, "No."

Her delighted eyes crinkled and her smile went from brilliant to stellar. She tugged his arms and Rafe sat up, surprised that he could since his nerves felt like they had exploded.

The little pink tongue that parted her lips, and the hunger in her eyes as she palmed his shoulders and chest, made him curse the nights he'd said good-night at her door.

The sweet musk of her desire almost cost Rafe his control. He held onto his sanity because he really wanted Grace to get whatever she needed out of this little power play.

Rafe balled his fists into the bedcovers to keep from rolling her beneath him and driving into her wet heat.

Few male wolfans wore underwear. Most found the garment itchy and too confining. However, Rafe more than appreciated the lacy pink lingerie clinging to Grace's curves.

She stretched along his body, and one leg nudged between his thighs. Her hand inched lower and lower across his abdomen, causing an involuntary twitch in his groin.

"Awww. Looks like something needs some attention," Grace purred.

She squeezed his sac and Rafe saw stars. The current he felt in his feet now pulsed the length of his shaft.

Her thumb stroked the tip of his cock until he leaked from the slit.

Sweat beaded along his hairline and a pebble of water rolled down the side of his face. "Grace," he croaked.

She licked his tip. His hips bucked and her laughter wrapped him in a sultry caress.

"Grace!" Rafe lifted on his elbows.

The delight on her face faded into uncertainty and she bit her lower lip.

"Sweetheart." He gentled his voice. "Another time and I'll let you suck me dry. Right now, I need to be inside you."

He unhooked her bra and flung it across the room. With a firm grip on her waist, he positioned her so that he could suck a dusky peak into his mouth.

Grace moaned and rocked her hips. If he didn't control her writhing, he'd never make it inside her.

"Hold on, sweetheart." Rafe locked his arms around her and rolled her beneath him. Before he got comfortable, he dragged her thong down her thighs. She lifted her legs to help him remove the flimsy scrap.

As much as Rafe wanted to savor every inch of her golden skin, that would have to wait for another time. Kissing her furiously, he slowly parted her folds to stroke her nub.

She rocked her hips to speed the tempo. "Now, Rafe. Now!"

Aligning his body to hers, he rubbed his cock through her folds to gather her wetness before burying himself to the hilt.

"Oh, God," she groaned, lifting her hips to absorb his thrusts.

After that, the world became a dizzying array of Grace's mewls and moans, and every touch that made her writhe and scream in pleasure was imprinted in his brain. When the spasms along her inner walls signaled her orgasmic release, his own followed.

It took a few moments for his awareness to return. He rolled to his side, and she turned to face him.

Grace flashed an impish smile that made everything inside him turn to mush. Then, she snuggled against the curve of his body, melding her flesh into his. Her heat warmed his skin and penetrated his pores.

He was nearly asleep when he sensed the sadness well inside her.

"Knowing all this doesn't change things," she whispered. "I can't—"

"Shh." Rafe stroked his knuckles along the contour of her cheek. So soft and delicate. "The here and now is good enough."

Despite how well Grace seemed to have taken the revelation, she'd suffered a major shock to her view of reality. She needed time to truly come to terms with what she'd experienced. Time to learn she could trust him with her heart.

Rafe was a patient man. He would give her all the time she needed.

Chapter 37

Grace knocked on the mammoth door to Gavin Walker's office. Her heart pounded against her breastbone, fast, furious, scared.

He was the Alpha. El head honcho, the big dog. Piss him off and—

So be it.

"Come," he called from behind the closed door.

Grace gulped a big breath, swung the door wide and stepped inside his office.

"Ah, Miss Olsen. What a lovely surprise."

He didn't look surprised. His sharp, assessing eyes and all-business smile suggested he was expecting her, although she'd only made the decision to confront him on her way to pack her belongings.

"I have a bone to pick with you." She left the door open, in case she needed to run, and advanced toward the monstrous desk covered in papers.

He stood and Grace's heart missed a beat, suspended midstrike, expectantly waiting for his next move.

"Please, have a seat." He waved his hand toward the two captain's chairs in front of the desk.

"Thank you. I'd rather stand."

His gaze slid to the open door and back to her. A predator assessing his prey's intent to flee. The tease of a smile appeared in his eyes. "As you wish." He retook his seat.

"Aren't you going to ask about Rafe?"

"My dear, I know how Rafe is faring. I kept in constant

touch with his father last night and this morning. Reports are he'll have no lasting effects from yesterday's incident."

She gripped the back of the captain's chair she stood behind. "You have nothing else to say?"

"What would you like to hear?"

"An apology, to him, would be a nice start. You caged him like an animal and he got shot."

"I won't apologize for the actions I take to protect my pack. The demonstration was necessary to thwart a sheriff office's investigation prompted by your accident."

"So, you're not sorry?"

"I stand by my decision. I do, however, regret the shooting. Should there be further interaction with law enforcement and our wolves, I'll insist that all weapons, including tranquilizer guns, will be stored in the trunks."

"Do you even care about Rafe?"

"I care about all of my pack members, especially Rafe. He's my godson, my son's best friend and a vital member of my pack."

"I reiterate. You put him in a cage."

"He went willingly because he understood the ripple effect of a human law enforcement agency investigating a wolfan pack." Hands resting on his desk, Gavin laced his fingers. "You aren't pack so I don't expect you to understand. Pack members do as I ask because they know it's my duty to serve and protect them."

"Cassie said you're the reason she didn't tell me about Wahyas." Chin pointed, head high, Grace held his gaze. "I can understand your caution when Cassie and I reconnected, but it's been a year and a half. You should've trusted me with the truth."

"It's been a lifetime for the human residents of Maico and most still don't know our secret. I prefer to err on the side of caution, Miss Olsen. I make no apologies. The manner in which you learned the nature of our existence is unfortunate. I hope you understand the devastating effects this information could have on the people you've met and grown close to at Walker's Run." His calculating blue eyes pinned her and her grip on the chair back tightened as he stood.

"A cage is the least Rafe will contend with if the human population at large suddenly discovers us. He'll be poked, prodded, subjected to testing. His life will no longer be his own. My pack, our entire species would forfeit their freedom and, likely, their lives. All it would take would be a slip of the tongue to the wrong person at the right time." Gavin stalked toward her.

He always seemed like a nice, polite, Southern gentleman and a doting grandfather-to-be. Now, she noticed he moved with the stealthy grace of a predator and his sharp, icy gaze made mincemeat of her previous impression.

"Your world must be cold, dark and frightening, Mr. Walker, to see everyone as an enemy. Doubting the intentions of those among you who deserve your trust and respect. Frankly, I don't want to be drawn into such a narrow-minded existence. But Cassie is the sister of my heart and I will continue to be part of her life."

"I hoped you would." He gestured to the chair she clutched. "Please sit. I don't want us to be enemies."

Grace forced out the tight breath balled in her lungs and slid into the seat. Gavin sat in the second chair, the tension in his body easing.

"I have no objection to your relationship with Cassie," he said. "I had hopes of inducting you into the pack. The easiest, most expeditious way would be for you to accept one of our single males as your mate."

"Not interested." Especially since once she committed, there was no way out. What if one or both changed their minds? They would be stuck. Until one of them died.

"So Rafe has repeatedly informed me." Gavin's mouth turned down.

Grace's heart dropped into her stomach. "Did you order him to be nice to me? *To seduce me?*"

A wave of nausea hit her hard. Good thing only coffee filled her stomach or it might've come back up and landed at her feet.

"After your accident, I appointed him as your guardian, to look after your best interests. Although I hoped one of our males would capture your heart, I didn't want you to become inundated with unwanted suitors during your extended stay." Gavin leaned forward and gently patted her knee. "Rafe's affections are truly his own. I cannot, nor would I, command those."

The pretzel knots working their way from her stomach to her throat came undone. She hated to think what transpired between her and Rafe had been an act on his part.

"Is there a possibility—"

"No," Grace interrupted. "I would never do anything to put Rafe at risk. Or Cassie and Brice and the baby. So kindly, butt out of our affairs."

"I would be more inclined to believe you if you made an outward commitment to this pack."

"I'm not doing the mate thing with Rafe or anyone else."

"Fine, but at least consider making a permanent home in Maico, or any place within my territory. Get involved with our community, contribute to the well-being of the pack. Become more than a weekend friend with my daughter-in-law. If you do, I will officially induct you into the Walker's Run pack."

"Why would I want to join an organization that played me like a fool?" She kept his gaze even though the hard, cold edge sent a chill down her spine. "You tried to manipulate me, and forced my friends to keep secrets, to lie to me."

"I never asked them to lie."

"A lie of omission is still a lie."

"I call it survival. Wahyas continue as a species because

mankind as a whole isn't aware of our existence. To correct that misconception would lead to genocide. I won't risk the safety of my pack, my family, not even for you."

"Trust has to begin somewhere, Mr. Walker. Or your granddaughter's grandchildren will be held captive by the same fear that grips you."

"The same applies to you. Except if you continue flitting from here to there without any permanency, you will never have a granddaughter, and likely no friends of value." Gavin walked around his desk and leaned against the edge. Feet crossed, arms loose at his sides.

"You may not like my methods. You may not like me—"

"I don't."

Gavin actually laughed, then smiled. "You're plucky. It's one of the things I like about you. I have always believed that you would thrive among us."

"Why is that?"

"We have the stability and consistency and sense of belonging you've been searching for."

"But I don't belong. Or you wouldn't have ordered the people I trusted to keep secrets from me."

"A miscalculation on my part."

She noticed Gavin didn't say he was sorry, nor did he appear to be.

Several tense moments passed.

"My offer to join us has no expiration date. It will always be available to you." His fixed expression gave no indication of his actual thoughts. "So will your suite."

"I appreciate your generous hospitality. However, considering the circumstances, I'm not comfortable remaining here, for now. I need time to get my bearings straight."

Gavin's brow furrowed and his lips puckered as if words were swirling in his mouth. "Are you returning to Knoxville?"

"Yes. My brother and his partner will pick me up on

Wednesday. Until then, Doc has invited me to stay in his home."

Gavin's head tilted slightly and a sly smile played on his lips.

"Rafe won't be there," Grace said. "I asked him to give me some space."

"What about Cassie? And Alex? They've come to rely on you."

"I'll continue to visit Cassie and plan to be with her when the baby arrives." Grace's heart began to race and she reminded herself to breathe slowly. For the baby's sake, she wanted to be more than a weekend visitor who popped by every now and again. She simply didn't know how to manage her life any other way. "Alex and I can video chat for as long as he needs a tutor."

Resignation settled over Gavin's features. He pushed away from the desk. "Wherever you go, know we will always have a place for you here."

Chapter 38

Rafe smiled at the tangled sheets on the bed, and his body heated from the memory of what had twisted them into such a state. Despite their agreement that he would not spend the night, when the time came for him to leave, Grace didn't let him go.

Good thing Doc had gone to the hospital after their late supper. The racket Rafe and Grace made in the bedroom might've driven him from the house.

Rafe made the bed, snapping the sheet over the mattress. His scent combined with Grace's swirled in the room. He liked how their scents melded into one, just as they had several times during the night.

God, he would miss her.

Today and tonight was all the time that remained. She would leave tomorrow. The uncertainty of their future gnawed and burned like an ulcer on his soul.

Every instinct within Rafe demanded he convince her not to leave, to claim her and make her his, now and for always. An irritating grain of truth in his conscience kept him from doing so.

As long as Grace's eyes, her bright green beautiful eyes, held a flicker of the panic he'd felt when locked in the cage, he wouldn't claim her.

Until it faded, he'd have to be more patient than he'd ever been. Master the wolf, master the man. Master his heart. Because she needed time to come to terms with her reality shift, the bond growing between them and her skewed view of relationships.

He thought she-wolves were complicated. Human females had an entirely different level of complexity, over rationalizing and overthinking basic things. Things wolfans took for granted, such as knowing when they'd met their match.

At first, he'd resisted the truth. If not for the accident, the likelihood of a mateship with Grace would've been negligible because he would've continued to ignore her. Fate had a funny way of re-orienting destiny so that everything worked out in the end. If he told himself that enough times, maybe he'd start to believe it.

He finished making the bed, nearly stepping on the laptop discarded on the floor. Grace tended to drop things right where she changed directions in thought or action, to pick them up again later when she resumed the task. He'd found the trait annoying in the beginning, but quickly realized it was because she lived so fully in the present that when something new came up, she let go of what was in her hands to fully embrace the moment.

He wished she'd learn to do the same with her heart. The hurts she'd endured had caused calluses to develop on her tender heart. He looked at his hands and fingers, still functional despite the scars and toughened skin. He had hope for Grace. For them.

Even if she didn't.

He zipped the laptop into the nylon case he found slung in the corner and tucked the thong dangling from the nightstand lamp into his pocket.

Straightening the rest of the room, he felt a tweak in his heart. He didn't mind the mess. Going around behind her, picking up whatever she'd discarded, was his way of taking care of the little things. Of taking care of her.

Wahyan males were driven to provide for, protect and pleasure their mates.

He'd sorta skipped straight to the third one. Of course he knew he would give his life to protect her. He'd start working on the provide part.

Financially, Grace could stand on her own. He wanted to give her something she'd always wanted—a home. He smiled, knowing exactly what he'd do to give it to her.

His phone pinged and he checked Grace's text.

Back early. W/ Cassie. Headed 2 Doc's 2 p/u laptop b4 R&L.

Rafe answered.

Already have it. Enroute to p/u Alex.

A thumbs-up icon appeared on his screen, then, a second later, C U soon! followed by a smiley face with big, red kissy lips.

Sliding his thumb over the bubbles of conversation, he thought he much preferred to hear her voice over reading her words.

He also preferred to be the one she spent her last day with, shopping, having lunch, whatever she desired. Well, he didn't care too much about the shopping, but he liked spending time with her. Everything interested her and she had a way of transforming ordinary days into something amazing.

He dropped the phone into his pocket and tucked the laptop case beneath his arm. Nearly to the door, he sensed a presence in the house.

"Dad?" It was nearly two-thirty in the afternoon. If Doc had come home, something was wrong. Today was clinic day; he should be out until after six.

Standing at the top of the staircase, Rafe listened for his father's footsteps. Nothing.

Maybe he had jumpy nerves after being caged and shot.

He descended the stairs, two at a time. At the bottom, his nose twitched and he followed the familiar scent into the kitchen.

The door to the garage opened.

"Clay, what are you doing here?"

"Your father should learn to lock the front door." Clay's grip tightened around Doc's Marlin 336W rifle, usually kept in a metal storage cabinet in the garage. "And you should've listened when I told you to move your filthy blood-kin out of my daughter's house." He shoved three cartridges into the side chamber.

"What the hell are you doing?" Rafe stepped forward, his heart pumping harder, faster.

"Purging the taint that's been infecting the pack for too long." He lifted the gun, pointing the barrel at the dead center of Rafe's chest. "If Gavin hadn't brought Doc here, if Doc hadn't brought you here, my daughter would be alive and well." He advanced and Rafe stepped back. "Instead, she's dead and you're carrying on as if she never existed. Curs are living in *her* home and you've taken a human whore to your bed as if Alexis meant nothing to you!"

A righteous rage welled inside Rafe. "I loved her! With every bit of my soul I loved her! And the man I came to be with her died alongside her."

"You look damn healthy for a dead man."

Rafe's ears rang with the explosive bang. Clay had never smiled at him before. Rafe was glad to have been spared the maniacal flash of white, straight teeth in tandem with the spiteful, cold, dark eyes laughing at him.

Pain, molten and breath-stealing, flowed from his chest, into his left shoulder and down his arm. Blood soaked through his T-shirt and coveralls. He dropped to his knees.

"That's more like it." Clay clutched Rafe's throat.

His strength rushing out as fast as his blood, Rafe couldn't lift his left arm. With his right, he only managed to claw at Clay's hand.

The man's stale breath licked Rafe's face like the arid heat of a humid summer day. "I could make this quick, but I want you to suffer. I hope you last until I get back. I need to sanitize the stain your human whore has made on your mateship to my daughter. She'll be at the R&L soon, won't she?"

"Stay…away…from her," Rafe panted over halting, painful breaths.

"Like you stayed away from my daughter?" Clay fished the cell phone out of Rafe's pocked, then shoved Rafe to the ground. "I'll be back. Wouldn't want Doc to be alone when he finds your cold, lifeless body on his kitchen floor."

After stomping on the phone, Clay stepped away. "For everything Doc has cost me, he'll suffer, too."

Grace hated routines and schedules. They gave her flashbacks of her regimented childhood and made her claustrophobic.

Today, however, her pattern of going to the R&L in the afternoons felt safe and normal, and she needed both. Especially since she couldn't shake the unsettling feeling she'd had ever since Cassie had dropped her off.

Since Alex returned to school today, she planned to help him with the mountain of homework he would have for missing yesterday. She would also show him how to video chat so he could reach her anytime he needed help with his homework.

Grace set Alex's favorite cookies on a tray and carried them out of the kitchen to the customer service area. Rafe had moved the table so she could see out the window while tutoring Alex. Customers didn't use the storefront door, preferring to walk into the service bays to see him. He'd sealed the glass front door closed a long time ago, so the temporary study area didn't impede Rafe's business.

The side glass door to the work area swung open. She sat the snack tray on the table. "Rafe is on an errand. He'll be back in a few minutes."

"I seriously doubt it." The starkness in the chilling, masculine voice gave her the willies.

Grace turned around. Clay Reinhardt peered down his long, broad nose at her. His hair was mussed and his cold, fathomless black eyes flickered with something that made her skin crawl.

"Why? What's happened?"

Clay's stark, sinister laugh slithered down her spine and coiled in the pit of her stomach. "He's dead."

The blood in Grace's veins froze. "Is this a joke?"

"Do I look like someone with a sense of humor?"

Uh, no. He looked like a man touched by madness.

Grace clutched the top of one of the table chairs to use in a self-defense move if he came any closer.

Rafe couldn't be dead. She'd know it.

Grace didn't know how she would know, only that she would. Or should.

"Rafe is coming!" She had to believe that he was. She just needed to buy time until he arrived.

"He'll be here any minute. You need to wait for him in the garage." Grace pointed toward the door to the service bays.

"Rafe is *dead*. I killed him. And because he couldn't keep his paws off you and his cock in his pants, you have to die, too." Clay lunged.

Desperation, fear and fury feeding her adrenaline, Grace jerked up the chair, blocked his attack with the chrome legs and rammed the seat bottom against his torso.

He toppled to the floor. Pinning him down with the chair legs, she stomped his ankle.

Clay's painful yells turned into string of obscenities. "You bitch! I'm gonna kill you and everyone else he loves."

Grace bolted to the closest door—the one leading to the apartment, and locked it behind her.

Her heart felt cold, brittle, lifeless. Her lungs seized from the ice crystals forming along her bronchial tubes. Her ears rang with the clamor of cubes dropping into ice buckets.

Rafe wasn't dead, he couldn't be.

She ran into the kitchen for her phone, screaming at the voice dial operation: "Call Rafe! Call Rafe!"

The phone rang and rang and went to voice mail. There was no voice message, only silence.

She called 911.

"What is your emergency?"

Unable to control her hysterical screams, she yelled into the phone. "Rafe's been shot at Doc's house. I don't know the address."

"Dr. Habersham's residence?"

"Yes."

"He's a member of the Walker's Run Cooperative. Hold for their emergency service."

Grace heard a beep and thought the call dropped until a familiar voice came on the line.

"This is Tristan. Leave a message. I'll be in touch."

"What kind of emergency line is this? Rafe's been shot. At Doc's house. Please, Tristan, please. Help him."

Grace hung up and called Rafe. Her hands shook so badly she almost dropped the phone. "Please pick up. Please pick up. Please pick up."

She got his silent voice mail again.

She hung up to dial again but her phone rang. "Rafe!"

"Grace?"

Her heart sank at Tristan's voice. "Go to Doc's. Go now!"

"I'm on my way. What's happening?"

"Clay said he killed Rafe!" She sobbed as pure, un-adulterated sorrow shredded her heart.

"Grace, are you safe?"

"I'm in the apartment. I bolted the door. He can't get in."

"Stay on the line with me. No matter what, don't hang up." How could he sound so calm when her entire world had just exploded?

Tears slicked her face. Her throat was raw and she wanted to throw up.

"Grace? Everything will be all right."

Lies, lies, lies. Would the lies ever stop?

"It's not okay."

Rafe was dead and she'd never told him she loved him.

Chapter 39

Blowing through a red light, Rafe sped toward the R&L. Sheer force of will had helped him get to his feet, and then into the tow truck.

"Grace!"

Her panicked emotions flooded him through the mate-bond. Near hysteria, she wouldn't be able to sense him if she didn't calm down.

"Grace, sweetheart. I'm all right."

Blistering pain throbbed in Rafe's left shoulder. When he moved, molten agony flowed down his useless left arm. The pungent, metallic scent of blood made him nauseous. Not exactly all right, but he was alive.

He gathered his strength and put all his effort into sending Grace his essence.

A burst of energy erupted from his heart, fanned through his body and mind.

Thank God! He wasn't too late.

"Rafe! He said you were dead!"

"Not yet." He breathed slightly easier. *"Where are you?"*

"Locked in the apartment. He's still out there."

"Stay put. I'm here."

The tow truck skidded into the back lot of the garage. Rafe didn't take the time to shut off the engine. He merely jumped out and ran.

Hyped on pure adrenaline, Rafe burst through the back door. The overwhelming smell of antifreeze and motor oil burned his nostrils.

"Get out, Clay. All of this will go away if you leave now."

Clay shook his head. "She has to die, Rafe. I warned you not to whore with her. You didn't listen. Just like you didn't listen when I ordered you to keep your nasty paws away from my daughter."

A feral gleam lit his eyes. "Alexis is dead because of you. Soon you will be, too. You have to run out of lives sometime."

Leaning against the glass door to the office, Clay struck a match and tossed it inside. Fire vined the walls and raced toward the ceiling. Clay's chilling laughter twisted Rafe's stomach. "I'm finally going to put you down like the filthy dog you are."

Rafe darted to the fire extinguisher on the opposite wall, popped open the fastener and yanked the canister free. Stabbing pain exploded in his left shoulder and traveled down his arm. His hands trembled so badly that he wouldn't be able to hold it for long. He spun around.

Holding its twisted, right hind foot off the ground, a large sable wolf snarled and bared his sharp, white teeth.

"Don't do it, Clay. Just get out."

The wolf launched into the air and slammed into Rafe's chest.

Rafe hit the floor. The fire extinguisher rolled away. Smoke rolled into the garage and was likely filling the apartment.

Grace had no windows to climb out of and the fire in the office would cut off her only escape.

He had to get her out. If it was the last thing he ever did, he had to get her out.

The sable wolf swiped a paw across Rafe's face. He barely registered the nails slicing through his skin. Every instinct, every ounce of energy and strength focused on saving Grace. He punched the animal's throat and shoved him aside.

Rafe snatched the fire extinguisher from the floor, hit the big red buttons on the wall to open the service bays and darted into the office, sweeping fire retardant over the flames. Ashy, sulfuric smoke burned his eyes and throat. "Grace! I'm coming!"

Sharp teeth stabbed his leg. Rafe slammed the extinguisher against the wolf's muzzle. He managed one more sweep before the wolf dragged him down, knocking the canister out of his reach.

Grace's screams rose above the voracious roar and crackle of the fire. A dark and primal fear began to pulse in Rafe's veins.

He had to get to Grace. Had to get her out. He had to, or they'd both die.

The wolf stalked toward him and he would keep coming, would keep Rafe from saving Grace. Unless Rafe killed him.

Rafe shifted.

A sickening grin twisted the sable wolf's snout. *"You took my only child from me. She's dead because of you. You desecrate her home, her possessions and the mate-claim. Now I will destroy you, your blood-kin, and your filthy human whore."*

Rafe launched into Clay. Both wolves skidded across the floor. Regaining his balance, Rafe dove for Clay's throat and caught a mouthful of fur. Clay jerked free before Rafe could clamp his jaws.

"You set the fire at the house, didn't you? Goddamn it. Lexi loved that house."

"That's why I burned it. It was her *house. No one else has the right to live in it."*

Clay whirled around, gnashing Rafe's injured leg. Past the point of registering pain, Rafe rammed him into the upright tool chest, causing it to tip over and scatter its contents. Rafe pinned Clay beneath his weight, shifted into his human form, grabbed a wrench off the floor and slammed the tool against Clay's skull. There was a loud crack and a wet, squishy sound.

The wolf's head lolled harshly to the side, his vacant eyes glazed. Clay's body returned to human form.

Rafe's left arm felt like a dead weight. The slightest movement shot crippling pain through his body.

Rafe's heart pounded so fast that he could barely feel it beating. The raging fire was engulfing the service area. Once it reached the supply shelves, the building could explode.

He bolted through the flames into the office. The thick smoke nearly blinded him. He crawled on the floor until he found the fire extinguisher.

"*Rafe!*" Grace screamed between sobs. "I can't get out!"

"I'm coming, sweetheart." He sprayed a path of fire retardant toward the door.

Beads of sweat turned into boiling pellets and blistered his skin. The heated air scalded his nose, his throat, his lungs.

"Grace! I'm at the door!" He jerked the handle. The hot metal seared his palm and fingers. "Goddamn it!"

Something exploded in the service bay. The percussion knocked Rafe into the door and down to the floor. Shattered glass rained over his bare body.

Pain banded around his ribs. He gulped for air, only to cough up blood.

Grace's sobs tore through Rafe's soul and his inner wolf's nerve-grating whine filled his ears.

"Grace, listen to me," he said as the tethers of his humanity weakened. "I *will* get you out of here."

"No, Rafe!" Hysteria shrilled Grace's voice. "You have to leave me. Please, please go. While you can."

Sirens sounded in the distance. Too distant for the rescue workers to be of any help.

"I won't lose you, Grace." He'd rather die with Grace than suffer her loss. "I need to shift. But it won't be my wolf." The wolf couldn't save her. Only the beast could and Rafe felt the creature stirring. "Don't be afraid of me, okay?"

A sharp, electric current fired down his spine, ignited his nerves and juiced every neuron. His muscles burned nearly as hot as the fire around him.

"Grace?" He doubled over in excruciating pain. His fingers and toes elongated, and his face twisted.

"I love you." Grace's voice whispered through Rafe's mind as he fell into darkness.

Grace lay flat on the floor, a damp cloth over her nose and mouth. Thick, black smoke billowed from the ceiling.

The emergency drills for disaster preparedness her father had insisted upon when he was home were useless because she had absolutely no avenue of escape.

Her heart pounded and ached to the point of bursting. Her throat was raw from the tears she'd swallowed and the scorching, acrid air she inhaled.

Rafe's pained cries felt like whips striking her soul. She would likely die from smoke inhalation, but Rafe was trapped in a maelstrom of flames.

Above her, the treacherous fire disintegrated the ceiling tiles, its fiery tendrils reaching like octopus tentacles down the concrete block walls, devouring the peels of paint, bubbled and curled from the wicked heat.

A vicious roar, something like an injured animal crazed from confusion and pain, sounded behind the warped door. Forceful pounding was followed by a horrible wrenching, twisting noise.

"Rafe? What's going on?" But in her heart, she knew it was much too late for him to answer.

Tears streamed like blistery lava down her face. She choked on a cough. Rafe, if he hadn't escaped, had likely succumbed to the fire by now. Sorrow broke up her heart, the searing heat evaporating her essence.

In a final act of self-preservation, though it would likely not be enough, Grace began scooting backward down the corridor. She fully expected a search and recovery team to find her body in the farthest corner of Rafe's tiny apartment.

How ironic. The place where she'd felt most at home would be her final resting place. Except her last moments would be terror-filled, rather than peaceful.

She'd barely made it a few feet from the door when bits of debris exploded around the frame. Pounding, wrenching, twisting sounds competed with the roar of the hellish blaze. More debris scattered. Showers of bright orange flames seared the darkness.

A terrifying howl drowned all other sound. The door frame shattered as the metal door was ripped from its hinges. A rush of heat singed Grace's face and hair.

Loud, heavy footfalls thundered toward her. She glanced up through the smoke and her blood iced.

Eyes so piercingly blue they almost glowed stared down at her from a creature at least seven and half feet tall. Thin black lips curled back from a blunt snout filled with huge, razor-like teeth.

Thick, matted fur covered most of its body, thinning over the lower belly and groin. Its gangly arms and legs were more freak show wolf than man, and its paw-like feet spread into four individual toes with long black nails.

The beast stepped forward, narrowing its large, luminescent eyes. A heart-wrenching wail twisted from its lips.

Slender, pointed ears, seemingly positioned too low on its large head, flattened. The creature's hands were oddly-shaped, like a fusion of human fingers and a wolf's paw.

"Grr...aayy...sss..."

A rush of emotion filled her. Competing emotions she had no time to decipher. Beneath the wave was a steadfast presence she knew to the depths of her being.

"Rafe?" His name formed on her lips but the heat stole her voice.

He lifted her in his arms and cradled her against his chest, his soft mewls grazed her ear.

Kaboom!

The building shuddered and Grace screamed.

Shielding her from the snapping flames, he darted through the inferno and out of the back of the building. He gently sat her down behind the tow truck.

The abundance of fresh air caused her lungs to seize. She coughed to catch her breath and an ashy taste coated her tongue.

The creature brushed her hair from her face. Blisters and burns dotted his palms, although he didn't seem to register any pain.

"You're hurt." And not just his hands. Blood seeped from the wound in his left shoulder.

"My Grr...aayy...ss..."

Above the screaming sirens, an angry howl crescendoed from inside the fiery building. In the midst of the flames, another creature rose.

Gnashing its teeth, the werewolf stood. The tension in its body and posture were a clear warning to his opponent.

"No!" Grace wrapped her fingers into the creature's fur. "Don't you dare go back in there."

The werewolf responded with a tender guttural vocalization she found reassuring until it spun from her and charged into the raging inferno.

"Rafe!" Grace darted after him.

"No!" Tristan intercepted her, grabbing her as another, larger explosion rocked the entire block. They slammed to the ground. Tristan held her tight, despite her frenzied struggle.

"Rafe!" Grace screamed until her voice gave out, her legs gave out and all her hope died.

Chapter 40

Grace's eyes fluttered open to the blinding glare of fluorescence. An oxygen mask sat like a weighty octopus on her face. Instead of helping her to breathe, the steady stream of air nearly strangled her. She snatched off the contraption and slung it aside.

"Easy there." Grief pinched the doctor's features and sadness shadowed his eyes.

"Doc—" A sob racked Grace's soul.

"Honey, are you strong enough to come with me?"

"Where?"

"To see Rafe."

Grace burst into tears as her heart imploded.

"Shhhhh." Doc held her against his chest. "He's alive, calm yourself."

"A-Alive?" she stuttered.

"Yes. He's been shot and has burns on his hands and feet, but we need to hurry." Doc helped her off the gurney and into a wheelchair. "The hormonal changes that brought out his Wahyarian causes temporary amnesia. When he wakes up, he'll believe you're still trapped and that fear could cause the change again, making him dangerous to everyone trying to help him."

Doc wheeled Grace out of the triage bay.

"I don't understand. He didn't hurt me." She gripped the armrests as Doc raced her down the corridor.

"Because he loves you. And until he sees you and

.comprehends that you are safe, he will stop at nothing to find you."

They rounded the corner to the west wing and the double doors flew open.

"Grace!" Rafe's panicked voice nearly stopped her heart.

"Rafe!" Grace launched out of the wheelchair and ran into his room.

Cursing, he battled the restraints. The bed rails had bent in the struggle. *"Grace!"*

"I'm here." At his bedside, she clasped his arm, slick with blood and sweat. The bullet wound to his left shoulder was bleeding through the bandage haphazardly fastened to him. Perspiration covered his entire body, his hair was matted, blistery welts covered his hands, his feet, the tops of his ears, and he was still the most beautiful being she'd ever seen.

He looked straight through her, his eyes wide and wild. He didn't respond to her voice or her touch.

"He's in shock and doesn't recognize you yet. Make him scent you," Doc urged.

Grace clamped her palm over Rafe's nose and mouth. "Rafe, it's me."

He jerked away from her. "I have to find Grace," he snarled.

She grabbed his face and poured all her love into a harsh, fierce kiss.

At first, he struggled to push her away, then slowly he relaxed into the kiss.

"Grace," he sighed against her mouth. "My Grace."

He reached for her. Confusion and disorientation clouded his eyes. He yanked at the restraints, harder and harder. "Get these damn things off me."

Doc loosened the right arm straps. Rafe snatched Grace into a one-armed embrace, kissing and nuzzling her as he pressed his face against the curve of her neck. "Thank God," he said, over and over again.

A nurse injected a sedative into his other arm, still tethered to the bed. "Damn it!" He fought against the tranquilizer, straining to keep his eyes open and locked on Grace.

"Shh." She kissed his forehead. "They need to patch you up."

"Grace?" He blinked several times. "Don't leave. *Don't ever leave me. I need you. More than you'll ever know.*"

"I'll be here when you wake up," she said, emotionally and physically drained.

"Promise?" he asked thickly.

"Promise." Grace kissed his eyes closed.

After Doc confirmed Rafe was suitably sedated, he gently pulled Grace aside. In a dizzying flurry, the medical team whirled Rafe from the room.

"Where are they taking him?"

"To the operating room to stop the bleeding. He's lost a lot of blood and will need several transfusions."

"What's his blood type? Can I donate?"

"Wolfans share the same blood type. Members of the pack have already arrived to donate."

A wave of light-headedness made her knees wobble. Too much had happened in a space of time too short to process all of it. The discovery of a subculture of wolfan shapeshifters, an insane rescue from a flaming building by a werewolf and the stark realization she'd fallen madly in love were about to make her brain explode.

The soft, steady rhythm of Grace's breathing as she slept was Rafe's favorite sound—aside from her laughter, her voice, the mewls she made when she came. Ah, hell. He loved every little noise she made.

And he loved that she had such a possessive hold on him, her cheek pressed against his right shoulder, her arm draped over his chest, her leg hiked over his hip. If his hands weren't bundled in bandages, he'd wind his fingers through her hair, tilt her head back and kiss the dickens out of her.

God, he was mighty thankful Grace was by his side. Waking up alone would've scared the hell out of him.

"Mine." He dusted a soft kiss on the crown of her head. Her essence nestled deep within him, safeguarding his being. Strengthened by her presence, he'd never felt more loved.

She knew him.

She'd seen the darkness within him manifest and had not been afraid. Instead of fleeing at the first opportunity, she clung to him.

If he were feline, he'd probably purr.

For the first time, he felt free to be himself. The beast lurking beneath the surface of civility had come out when needed and retreated when the danger passed. He wasn't uncontrollable or without conscience. He had purpose and focus.

The restlessness he'd felt since childhood was gone. Maybe it had burned up in the fire that had destroyed the R&L—the last bit of his life connecting him to Lexi. R&L—Rafe and Lexi.

Strangely, Rafe felt no loss over the destruction of his business. The pack would help him rebuild. He'd call it something different this time. And the building wouldn't need an apartment.

Grace wiggled in her sleep, burrowing into him. Lightly, he rubbed his bandaged hand up and down her back until she settled.

It was time to build a home.

Chapter 41

Inside the bathroom of Rafe's hospital room, Grace shut off the water and dried her face. She'd slept in the yoga pants and a loose T-shirt Cassie brought to her last night. The clothes she'd been wearing, sweat-soaked and smoke-stained after the fire, had likely been tossed in the hospital incinerator.

She didn't care. Even if she managed to get the smell out of the fibers, Grace doubted she'd ever wear the outfit again.

She combed the tangles from her hair and pulled the strands back into a ponytail. Her appearance had seen better days but she didn't look like a wildling anymore so it shouldn't garner her too many stares while she searched for the cafeteria.

While Rafe was sleeping soundly she planned to slip quietly out of the room to get coffee. She'd cut back significantly, but this morning she needed at least a grande with a triple shot of espresso to calm her frazzled nerves and her fears.

She felt shell-shocked. Numb and hypersensitive at the same time. Inside and out.

She hated that every little noise made her jump, that everyone looked at her strangely, and silenced their whispers when she was nearby.

She needed time to regroup. To get her bearings straight again. Time to process, everything.

Grace eased out of the bathroom.

"Hello, Grace."

She jumped, and ducked behind the bathroom door.

"Grace? Are you all right?"

She balled her hands to keep them from shaking and stepped out again. "I'm fine, Mr. Walker." She approached Rafe's hospital bed slowly. "What are you doing here?"

"Doc said it was okay to stop in." Kindness shone in his eyes. "I thought you could use this." He handed her a large coffee. "I got it from the cafeteria. I hope it's palatable."

"I'm sure it's fine." Grace cautiously accepted the offering and sat in the chair next to the hospital bed. "Thank you."

She sipped her coffee. Hot, strong and sweetened just the right amount.

"Doc said Rafe's hands and feet have the most severe burns. He'll need physical therapy, but Doc doesn't expect any permanent damage in Rafe's ability to use his hands or walk."

"He's very lucky, and I'm very grateful."

"As we all are." Gavin sat in the second visitor's chair. "How are you doing, Grace?"

"Me?" Grace flicked her hand with a nervous laugh, "Not one scratch or burn. A little smoke inhalation that was treated last night, but nothing serious. I'm absolutely fine."

"I doubt that." Gavin's gaze narrowed on Grace. "I'm sure your entire world has turned upside down."

"It has, but I'll manage."

"By leaving?"

"It was always my plan to return to Knoxville." She peered at him over the rim of the coffee cup. "This started out as a weekend trip."

"Plans change."

"Mine haven't." She set her cup on the bedside table. "Look, Mr. Walker, your wolfan world isn't one I'm comfortable with at the moment. I understand you want me around because of Cassie but I have my brother to care for. Until I know he's completely independent and no longer needs my support, I need to be there for him."

"I'm not here about Cassie or your brother, Grace. I'm here because of Rafe." Gavin scratched his beard. "He loves you."

"And you know that how?"

"Rafe loves with his whole being. He doesn't know how to hold anything back. That's why his beast knew you. That's why he saved you. And that's how I know he loves you."

"Love is fickle, Mr. Walker, and it certainly doesn't guarantee happiness." Grace stood up because sitting still made her feel like ants were eating her insides. "On a physical level, Rafe and I are good together. Beyond that, I'm not sure how I can be with a man who intentionally deceived me."

"Don't fault him for following my directives."

Oh, but she did. Because she couldn't depend on him to put her needs first, when it mattered most.

Her father had put his career ahead of his family. Derek had bailed on her at the first opportunity. Matt had enlisted in the military although he knew how fearful she was that something terrible would happen to him.

Rafe chose to participate in a deceptive farce rather than tell Grace the truth.

How could she ever truly trust him with her heart when his loyalties belonged to someone else?

Grace walked to the window, peering at the stretches of color lightening the early morning sky. Tears blurred her eyes.

She craved everything about Rafe. His voice, his touch. The way his presence gobbled the loneliness.

God, she loved him.

And that was the very reason she had to let him go.

* * *

"What the hell do you mean you're leaving?" Rafe struggled to sit up. The bandages on his numbed hands made it difficult to push up and he couldn't get the controls on the bed to work.

"You knew Matt and Aaron were coming today." Grace wouldn't meet his gaze, but he could tell she'd been crying.

Rafe's heart alternated between pounding too hard and not pounding at all. "If this is a joke, it isn't funny."

"I'll be back." She offered him a plastic smile.

"When?"

"A month or so." Grace adjusted the bed for him. "I have a lot of work to catch up on and…" Her voice trailed.

"And what?"

"I need to get away from all this," she said quietly.

"You mean, get away from me." The rawness in his voice wasn't due to the smoke and heat he'd inhaled during the fire.

She nodded, turning away and hugging herself.

"You love me, Grace. I know you do. Don't pretend you don't." If he could have gotten out of bed without falling to the floor he would have. Unfortunately, his feet were blistered and bandaged, like his hands.

She didn't say anything and he no longer sensed her through the mate-bond. It felt like something had snuffed out their connection.

He threw back the sheet and swung his legs off the hospital bed. To hell with the bandages and blisters.

"Don't you dare!" A spark of life sharpened her voice.

He sort of liked her bossy side. She helped him resettle in the bed and tucked the sheet around him. In an unguarded moment, she smoothed his hair and almost kissed his cheek.

She straightened with an apologetic grimace. "I don't know what came over me."

"You love me," Rafe said plainly, simply, resignedly. "You don't have to fight it, Grace. I love you, too."

"Sometimes love isn't enough."

"Grace, I need you." He patted the bed and she sat next to him. "I understand if you need time. You've gone through a lot, but don't shut me out."

Unshed tears dimmed her eyes and he hated the pain he sensed within her.

Clumsily, he pulled her against his chest, hugging her tightly and sending all his love through the mate-bond.

He knew it existed between them, knew she could sense it. Knew her doubt had the power to destroy it.

She sighed, relaxing against him.

A warm, tingling sensation filtered through his senses. Soft and feminine, her essence melded with his.

"Can you feel it?" he asked her. "Can you feel the bond between us?"

She didn't answer.

"Sweetheart?"

"I have to go," she said hoarsely. "Matt and Aaron are waiting."

Cold blanketed him, its icy threads burrowing into the marrow of his bones. "Grace? Baby, don't shut me out."

"There's nothing to shut out." She met his gaze and the finality of her decision stole the color from her eyes and snuffed the spark he'd always seen in her spirit. "Goodbye, Rafe."

She kissed his cheek, but her lips were chilled and dry.

"Grace?" His voice cracked, his panic reaching a critical point.

His heart pounded with enough force to break open his chest. If Grace was leaving, it wanted to leave with her.

Through the mate-bond, he called out to her long after she had gone.

By the time his father stopped in to check on him, Rafe

felt completely numb, nearly catatonic. All he could think was that Clay shouldn't have missed his heart.

"Two weeks. You haven't been out of the apartment in two weeks." Matt looked her up and down. "You've barely been out of your room."

"I'm working," Grace grumbled. "I got behind, lolly-gagging around the resort. I should've come home instead." Would've saved her a heartache.

And her heart did ache. She missed Rafe. Missed how his presence comforted her. He didn't need to say anything. Simply being with him gave her a peaceful sense.

Without him, she felt tossed about, like a dinghy in a storm. Her life wasn't terrible without him. She had her business, plenty of work. But whenever she wanted to do something, see something, go somewhere or talk about something, her first instinct was to text him.

She stopped eating hot fudge sundaes because they reminded her of him. His readiness to deliver one in the midnight hour, just because she asked, was too much to dwell upon.

He'd never failed to respond to her texts. If she sent one now, she would hear from him. She knew he would.

She eyed the drawer where she'd buried her phone to reduce temptation. It was all the way across the small bedroom in a dresser against the wall. The eleven or so feet was too far to walk; she lacked the energy.

Matt wheeled farther into the room. "Time to 'fess up, sis. Something happened in Maico. You're different, and not in a good way."

"Don't want to talk about it."

"Too damn bad." Matt's voice rose. "When I came back from overseas, you didn't let me wallow in self-pity. You were worse than Dad, drilling me about what I should do, needed to do, *had* to do. Payback's a bitch. I'm not going to let you mope around any longer."

"This isn't moping." Grace gave him a halfhearted eye roll. "It's work." She returned to the design she'd created for the Maico Historical Society.

"It's the mechanic, isn't it?"

"I'm busy." She hunched over her laptop.

"I'm gonna call him and tell him how mopey you are." Matt popped a wheelie in his chair and rolled out of the room.

"You don't have his number."

"I do now." Matt returned, waving a large yellow envelope. "The building manager dropped this off."

He dumped the contents of the envelope into his lap. Two sets of keys fell out. One set she'd never seen before. The other was hers.

"There's a note." He handed it to Grace.

The slightly sloppy handwriting simply stated that the black Accord parked next to Grace's car in the lot now belonged to Matt. The name and number of a mechanic in Knoxville were listed, in case Matt needed adjustments to the hand controls that had been installed. Below Rafe's name, seemingly an afterthought, were the words, *If Grace needs anything, call me.* Followed by his number.

"That's it?" Her voice was sharp and Matt laughed.

"What were you expecting? A love letter?" He popped his front wheels in the air and turned his chair around. "Come on. I want to take my new ride for a spin."

He wheeled out of her room, head bopping to some tune running through his head.

Grace lifted the note to her nose. It didn't smell like anything, and it was stupid to have thought it might hold Rafe's scent the way his clothes did.

Not one personal sentence addressed to her.

How much lower could her heart sink?

She closed her eyes, trying to feel him. Nothing, absolutely nothing.

Squinting, she tried again.

"Are you constipated or something?" Matt's voice startled her from the doorway.

"I'm building up my nerve to let you drive." She pushed away from her desk. "You scare the daylights out of me."

"Yet you're the one who wrecked her car."

"Don't remind me." Because she might've wrecked her life, too.

Chapter 42

It will get easier, they said.

When, goddamn it? When?

Six weeks had passed and being separated from Grace, in a way, felt worse than losing his first mate. Grace was alive and only four-and-a-half hours away. Every primal instinct Rafe had beckoned him to drive to Knoxville and bring her back. To make her his, now and for always.

Instead, Rafe dragged himself out of his new red Range Rover and glanced around the crowded parking lot. His heart raced, his breathing fell out of rhythm, his mouth turned dry and his stomach seemed to fist around his throat.

He shut the truck door without locking it. If someone pilfered the brown bag on his front seat, well, that would be a good thing.

Inside Taylor's, the rumble of voices, the music, the saturating scents, the sea of faces, all weighted his senses like a heavy blanket. The weeknight rendezvous with Brice and Tristan had become part of Rafe's new routine. He didn't dare miss because they would worry, and his friends had spent too much time worrying about him.

After Grace left, he convinced himself she would be back someday.

Someday turned out to be a lot longer than expected. She continued tutoring Alex through a video chat, so occasionally Rafe caught a glimpse of her on the laptop, when he timed it just right to go into Doc's kitchen for something to drink or to retrieve something he'd purposely left on the counter.

They never talked, just exchanged awkward smiles or nods. Most days, he simply lingered out of sight, listening to her voice.

She sounded happy. Why wouldn't she? She wasn't the brooding type; she looked for reasons to be happy. Lived each moment, found delight in the tiniest things.

Unorganized and unsettled, she had completely upended his life. He loved her sense of wonder and amazement. Hell, he plain loved her.

"Where's Tristan?" Rafe slid into the booth.

Brice hiked his thumb toward the dance floor. "We were beginning to think you weren't showing tonight."

"Stopped to help a motorist with a flat." Coming back from a place he didn't purposely drive to and never should've been.

The waitress sat a frosted beer mug in front of Tristan's empty spot and handed Brice a similar mug.

Rafe's mouth watered, not for the beer in Brice's hand but for the bottle inside the brown bag sitting on the seat inside the Rover.

The waitress slid Rafe a large iced tea. "Hey, handsome. I'm off at ten. Save a dance for me?"

"Not tonight, Angeline." Rafe sucked a mouthful of his drink. The cold, sweetness wet his tongue as he swallowed, but did nothing to quench his thirst.

She winked. "One of these days, you're going to say yes."

Rafe doubted he would. Angeline was a lovely she-wolf, but she'd have sex with anything willing to hump.

He like sharing his bed, his life, with one woman. He liked sex as much as anyone, but for him it wasn't just about the physical feel-good. He craved the closeness of sharing not only bodies, but souls.

Grace's soul had touched his, and he really, really missed her.

Eventually, he'd have to have sex again. He'd missed one full moon. Tonight would be the second. He shouldn't miss many more.

He'd not gone back to Loretta. It wouldn't be fair to her, even though she'd come around to test the waters. She wanted something he couldn't give and deserved the chance to find it with someone who could love her.

"The renovations are complete," Brice said. His grandmother's cabin was where he and Cassie had met, and where they had lived, but the two-bedroom cottage wasn't large enough to accommodate the family they wanted. So they'd built up and out, keeping as much of the original homestead intact as possible. "We're moving back in this weekend. I need your help setting up the furniture."

Rafe nodded.

Brice wiped the condensation from his mug. "Grace is coming."

"She's not ready to see me." Rafe played with the paper from his straw. He hoped he would know if and when she was. Hoped he'd feel it to the marrow of his bones. Right now, he simply felt empty.

"I understand how you feel." Brice leaned forward, elbows resting on the table. He and Cassie had faced their own separation in the beginning of their relationship. "Don't give up on the mate-bond."

"I'm trying not to. But as each day passes it gets harder."

"I know it's hard. I've been where you are. Cassie and I were separated for three months before things were right again."

"That was different. You were in another country. Grace is only a few hours away."

"Be patient and believe in her, man. Be the constant she's never had."

The problem was, Grace was like a river, always moving. Sometimes changing direction, but never stopping.

After all he'd put her through, why would she change for him?

"Rafe!"

Grace sat up, clutching the sheet to her sweat-dampened breasts. Her gaze darted around the bedroom. The soft flicker of light from the TV kept the darkness at bay, but not the monsters from her dreams.

Usually when her nightmares began, a sense of Rafe's presence would flood her mind. She never saw him in those dreams, but somehow she knew he was there. Keeping her safe.

She missed him. Missed him to the depths of her soul.

He'd caused her car accident, revealed to her that werewolves really do exist, seduced her and rescued her from a burning building.

And she loved him for it. For all of it.

That was the real nightmare.

She loved him and she'd left. When he'd needed her, she'd left.

It was for his own good. If she'd stayed through his recovery, their bond would have grown stronger.

She needed it to wither away, or else he'd never find his real true love.

Grace climbed out of bed, padded to the dresser and changed into the shirt she'd borrowed from Rafe the morning after the accident. He'd left it folded on the passenger seat of her Beetle.

Grace's chest tightened. She hadn't called, texted or emailed him since saying goodbye.

Even though her heart swelled with gratitude when Matt got to drive his new car with the hand controls, she didn't call Rafe.

He hadn't called, texted or emailed her, either.

He could've attached a brief note to her when he wrote the one to Matt. A simple "Hi, Grace" would've been enough.

She got nada.

She ran her hands up and down the shirtsleeves. Usually, the simple action brought her immediate warmth. A feeling of safety and assurance.

Tonight she felt cold. Bone cold.

She fluffed her pillow, jumped back into bed and grabbed her phone off the nightstand.

She scanned through the status updates of her Touch-Base friends. With friends all over the world, she'd never felt more alone.

Unable to shake the icky residue from her nightmare, Grace sent an impulsive text.

Are you there?

Her heart thumped hard against her chest.

He wouldn't answer. It was after two in the morning. He was asleep.

Seconds turned into minutes without a response. If her nightmare had been a premonition… She shivered.

Rafe was the strongest, most steadfast man she knew. He wouldn't stumble, not after almost a year of sobriety.

In the dream, she'd felt the depths of his despair, the aching loneliness and utter futility.

But he wouldn't be alone tonight.

Tonight was the second full moon since her departure. He'd moved on to another full-moon partner by now. Or went back to Loretta.

Grace's stomach clenched.

It made her uncomfortable and sad to think of Rafe with another woman.

She curled on her side, holding the phone to her chest, wishing she could be the woman he needed.

As she dozed off, the phone vibrated and sang the Alan Jackson tune she'd set as Rafe's ringtone.

"Hello?" She sat up, her heart kicking an excited beat.

"I'm here, sweetheart." Rafe's voice was soft and raw, and melted the clinging shadows of her dream.

"I had a nightmare." She resettled against her pillow.

Rafe didn't say anything. Knowing he was there was enough. Okay, maybe not enough, but comforting.

She heard a rustle, a clink and silence. He was on the move, quiet, prowling. To the kitchen or bathroom? She heard running water.

"Are you doing okay?" Maybe she shouldn't ask, but it was something she asked any friend when reconnecting, and this was what she was doing, right? Reconnecting?

Should she do this?

Could she do this?

Rafe had said he loved her. Was it too soon?

A heavy sigh warmed her ear. He didn't say "Peachy," which was good, because he usually meant it sarcastically.

He didn't say anything at all, but his voice, his words whispered through her mind, *"I miss you."*

"Matt loves the car," she said, instead of telling Rafe how often she thought of him. "It's everything he wanted in an accessible vehicle."

Grace wiggled into a cozy, comfortable spot on her mattress and tucked the covers beneath her chin. She guessed Rafe did the same from the familiar squeak of his weight sinking into a mattress.

She imagined his warmth beneath the covers, his body spooned against her. She loved the way he slept pressed against her, a shield against her fears.

He'd told her once that something connected them on more than a physical level. She wondered if that's how he chased the monsters away in her dreams. More than that, she wondered what he dreamed.

Grace snorted awake. Her body hummed and tingled, and when she stretched, her muscles were sore. Muscles that were sore after great sex.

The sheet had tangled around her body. The shirt she'd changed into after her nightmare was on the floor.

Not again!

For Pete's sake. She'd had the most vivid, erotic dream after falling asleep talking to Rafe, and now her brain defaulted to the sexual fantasy every night.

The next morning, she'd dreamed that Rafe, instead of saying goodbye, promised in a sleepy, sexy voice, "I'll be here whenever you need me. Always."

She heard him say it every morning, seconds before she awoke.

If talking to him on the phone incited powerful sex dreams, what would happen when she saw him in person?

Chapter 43

Minutes before ten, Rafe walked into the emergency department summoned by Grace's text. It had been nearly three months since she had left him, and six weeks since they had talked on the phone.

She wouldn't stay out of his dreams, though.

Sometimes they sat together and watched a sunset or sunrise in some place she'd visited in her past. Sometimes she rode alongside him on a routine roadside assistance call, or had dinner with him at Doc's or danced at Taylor's. Wherever they were, they always had sex.

Not that he minded the least little bit.

He wanted to believe the dreams were manifestations of the mate-bond, not a coping mechanism he'd defaulted to using. The longer they went on, the worse his fear of becoming addicted to the dreams grew.

He'd tried to put an end to the nightly escapades. Each time he tried, his determination failed because, really, would he ever say no to sex with Grace? Even dream sex?

Uh, no. Hell, no.

But, he wanted more than a fantasy life with her. He deserved more, and he could finally admit that he did.

For a long time, Rafe had tried to be the man he thought Doc and the others wanted him to be. Recent months had taught him that eventually all facades fail.

Rafe had to accept who and what he was at the core of his being. From changing hairstyles and clothes, to a new vehicle and a new business, for the first time, Rafe felt comfortable in his own skin.

Through the glass inserts in the double security doors, he saw Doc talking with Cassie, Brice and Grace. Every time Grace looked over, Rafe gave her a slight nod, smile or finger wave of assurance.

When they disappeared down the corridor, Rafe circled around the back way to the wolfan waiting area in the west wing. The pack would start filtering in shortly to await the birth of the newest Alpha-heir.

He picked a comfortable spot, pulled the cap over his eyes and settled in for a long wait.

He had a lot to do in the coming days. The R&L had been rebuilt as Wyatt Automotive Services with more service bays. He needed to interview and hire a couple of qualified mechanics to help with the work. Alex had been one of the first to put in his application for a part-time job after school. The kid had an automatic in, but Rafe intended to put him through the interview process for the experience.

Ronni was finishing up some sewing projects he'd hired her to do, but with Cassie's baby coming almost a week early, Ronni wouldn't finish in time for what Rafe had planned.

People filtered into the waiting room. Some huddled near him, speaking in hushed whispers, but he knew they wanted him to speak up and give them news.

Well, when he had something to tell them, he would. Until then, he needed a nap.

Fifteen hours later, his phone pinged with a text picture from Grace of Brice holding his newborn daughter, the first female wolfling born into the Walker line since the pack's inception.

"We have a new Alpha wolfling." Rafe stood, holding up the phone so everyone could see. "Brenna Elizabeth Walker. Daughter of Brice, son of Gavin, son of Nathan, son of Abram, son of…" Rafe continued the rote recitation of male descendants all the way back to Isom Walker, the first Alpha of Walker's Run.

Celebratory howls went up in the soundproof room. Rafe tucked the phone into his pocket and started toward the door. A nurse in scrubs opened it before he reached it.

"They're waiting for you," she said.

He followed the nurse down the corridor, although he could've found his way without her guidance. Every cell in his body had honed in on Grace's presence.

As he entered the room, his heart stopped him dead in his tracks. Grace's stellar smile brightened the room. She laughed and spoke baby talk to the infant in her arms.

Longing erupted in his chest. This was what he wanted to his very core.

"This is your Uncle Rafe." She walked toward him with the baby. "Sometimes he's a little grumpy, but he'll always be there if you need him."

Rafe gently stroked Brenna's cheek. Eyes closed, she turned her head toward his hand, her pert little nose twitching for his scent. Her tiny fingers grasped his thumb, pulling it toward her mouth to suck. One eyelid slid partially open to peek at him.

"She's gonna be trouble." He grinned at Brice.

"I hope she gives her daddy hell." Gavin laughed. "He deserves it."

Abby playfully elbowed him. "We want her to be a lady, not a hooligan."

"My wish for you, little girl, is to have all the happiness your heart can hold and may it last a lifetime." Rafe kissed the baby's forehead.

"All right, everyone." Doc clasped his hands. "Let's give Brenna and her parents some time alone. They need the rest, and all of us need some, too."

"Video everything." Grace returned Brenna to her

mother. "Well, not the breast-feeding or the diaper chang-ing." Grace grimaced. "Everything else, though. The coo-ing and aahing. You know, the good stuff."

Cassie saluted, then laughed.

"Want to grab something to eat?" Rafe asked, walking Grace to the parking lot.

"I don't have the energy to go anywhere."

Rafe fished a half-eaten package of crackers from the pocket of his shorts.

"Thanks." She ate the first cracker in two bites. "Would you drop me off at Cassie and Brice's place? I'm staying with them."

"Sure."

Grace hooked her elbow around his arm. "We should talk sometime."

"We're talking now."

"I mean *talk* talk." Her eyes grew large and bright when they stopped at the Rover. "Wow, you got a new truck. Nice."

Rafe opened the door and helped Grace inside. By the time he reached the driver's side, she'd fallen asleep.

He brushed her hair from her forehead. Not even the ti-niest mark remained of the ugly bump from the accident.

Wondering if everything else that followed had been erased as easily, he drove out of the parking lot, taking his time to reach their destination.

Eyes closed and holding on to that last little bit of sleep, Grace uncurled in a full-body stretch. She breathed in the fresh fragrance of lemons and roses, her favorite scents.

Neither of which permeated the air at the resort or Cassie's new house.

Grace sat up in a room she'd never been in and yet was as familiar as her reflection in a mirror.

The larger walls were painted an eggshell color and the

accent walls were blush rose. Floor-to-ceiling windows stretched the entire length of the master bedroom.

Even the comforter matched the one she'd clipped from a magazine when she was sixteen.

This has to be a dream.

She slid slowly from the bed, turning to study the head- and footboard. Every detail, perfect.

She ventured down the hallway. Each of the four bedrooms was exactly as she expected them to be.

The receiving room was minus the brocade curtains, but otherwise decorated to perfection.

Every color detail, down to the carpet shade, was perfect. On top of and around the dining room table were large gift-wrapped boxes. The name tags bore numbers. She picked up the one labeled 1, the smallest of them all and deceptively heavy.

She wanted to open the present but put it down since it didn't have her name on it.

The large kitchen was functional and beautiful, and had large bay windows with a view of the river.

The French doors opened. Rafe stepped inside, saw her and smiled the kind of smile that sucked the breath right out of her.

Her pattering heart skipped a beat. She loved meeting Rafe in her dreams. Still, her stomach knotted. She was tired of wishing and dreaming and looking for something just beyond her grasp.

He gently took her arm and led her into the living room. Grace sat on the couch. Rafe started to sit on the coffee table in front of her, frowned at its delicate construction and sat on the stiff sofa with her. "It's time for that *talk* you wanted."

"Wait, wait, wait." She turned toward him, drawing her legs beneath her. "This isn't what our dream is for. I just want to be with you, without the heavy stuff getting in the way."

"This isn't a dream." Rafe's brow wrinkled. He leaned toward her. "Wait—you have the dreams, too?"

"Yeah, and we're in one. How else would we be in the house I clipped from a magazine when I was twelve?"

"You left your scrapbook at Doc's. So I thought…"

Grace sat there as Rafe's words sank in.

"This is real?"

He shrugged uncomfortably.

"You did all this? For me?" She shook her head. "Why?"

"I love you," Rafe said softly. "I want you to have a place to always come home to."

Grace's chest tightened as her heart swelled.

"I'd hoped we could start over. As friends, lovers, full-moon partners, whatever you wanted, with the understanding that I would be your only friend with bedroom privileges. I don't share. Not you, at least."

Grace swallowed hard.

"But I can't." He let out a tightly held breath. "I want the whole package, Grace. I want a wife, kids. Hell, I even want grandkids. I need to share my everyday life, not just moments."

"Rafe, I…"

"I built this house for you, Grace. And I filled it with all the things you dreamed of having. I added one item that wasn't on your list, a walking bridge built above the river. It leads to Brice and Cassie's house.

"Ronni has your scrapbook. She's finishing up the drapes for the living room. She'll bring it to you when the drapes are ready."

Rafe stood. "You have a home now. Whether you choose to stay, or use it only when you come to see Cassie and Brenna, it's yours."

"I don't know what to say." Emotion swelled in her

throat. Rafe had taken her dreams and turned them into reality.

"I love you, Grace. More than you'll ever know. And because I love you, I need to let you go. Goodbye, sweetheart." He kissed the top of her head.

Grace had no idea how long she sat alone in utter shock and silence.

Finally, she dragged herself from the couch and stumbled to the dining room table. She picked up the box numbered 1 and opened it.

Her fingers glided over the pink handle of a sturdy claw hammer. She picked up the box of nails next to it. The note attached read, "Put holes anywhere you want, sweetheart."

A single tear slipped down her check. She tore the paper off the rest of the boxes. Each was filled with framed prints, photos and a few paintings, all from her wish book.

Grace picked up her phone and scrolled through the contacts until she found the one she needed.

"Hi, it's Grace," she said when the call was answered. "I have a favor to ask."

Chapter 44

Rafe glared at Grace's text message.

Midnight emergency.

His damn wolf instinct to provide whatever she needed would drive him out of his goddamn mind if he didn't give her what she wanted.

He grabbed the white fast-food bag next to him, climbed out of the Rover and slammed the door.

The porch light was on.

He mounted the eight steps, two at a time. A flowery wreath decorated the front door. He rapped his knuckles against the wood.

Grace answered, wearing his shirt over a pink tank top and the pink pajama bottoms with cat faces.

He held the bag in front of her nose.

"What's this for?" She took the bag but didn't open it.

"You texted a midnight emergency."

"Right, a midnight emergency. Not a midnight snack emergency."

"There's a difference?"

Grace giggled. A smile as bright as the night's full moon lit her face.

Everything in him begged him to forget the lame-brained decision to let her go. He wanted her, needed her. Unfortunately, Grace didn't need the same.

She grabbed his arm and pulled him inside, not that

he offered any resistance. Then she locked the door behind him.

"I need help hanging some pictures." Behind the hope and excitement in her eyes, he saw uncertainty. A tinge of fear also tainted her scent.

He swallowed words that would've brought disappointment to her face. He was already there. What would it hurt to hang a few damn pictures?

"Show me."

Grace's smile went nova. Rafe's heart raced, pumping blood, fast and furious, straight to his groin.

"Let's start in the family room."

His gut clenched. Wouldn't someone uninterested in an actual family call it a den or TV room?

He followed her into the middle of the room. The walls were already plastered with pictures of Grace and her brother, Cassie and Brice with Brenna, and with pictures of him and Grace.

Rafe's heartbeat paused.

The sofa and glass coffee table from her wish book had been replaced. Sitting in the middle of the room was a leather couch and wooden coffee table identical to the ones he'd had in his apartment. A large wooden entertainment center, with a design similar to the Murphy bed cabinetry, housed a large flat-screen TV bigger than his had been. One of the glass doors on the entertainment center had been left open to show the new gaming system inside.

He sat hard on the coffee table. "What's going on?"

"I told you. I need help hanging this." Grace lifted a large frame from the couch. Beneath the glass was an enlarged print of the selfie she'd taken with his wolf.

Hope swelled inside his heart. Confusion tightened his chest to keep it from expanding.

"I want it centered over the couch." She gave him the picture. "It will make a nice focal point, don't you think?"

"I'm not sure what to think." He lifted his gaze to her face. "Why did you change the furniture? Put up all the pictures of…us?"

"This house, everything you put in it, it's everything I wished for—until I met you." She sat on the couch, her knee touching his. "I miss you. I was kinda hoping you would share this place with me."

God knew, Rafe wished he could. Wished he could be what she needed, but he simply wasn't wired that way. Nor could he pretend he was.

He'd spent most of his life trying to be what others thought he should be. He'd never be what he would have been if he had grown up wild with his birth pack and he'd never be quite as domesticated as wolfans fully integrated into human society.

He was somewhere in between, forging a new path, and he wanted a mate to join him on the journey.

"Grace, I can't play house with you."

"I don't want to play house." Grace knelt between his legs. "I've always wanted a real home. But, no matter where I've lived, after a while, I'd get antsy and leave."

"Grace, you don't need to explain."

"I do." She stroked his cheek. "Something changed when I met you. I didn't realize until I returned to Knoxville, but I'm not restless when I'm with you, Rafe. I'm restless without you."

Grace cupped the back of his neck, drawing him close enough for a kiss. She touched her lips to his mouth. It was hard and cold as steel. Somehow, she needed to make him believe.

Pouring every ounce of her being into that kiss, she bared the rawness of her soul. Unleashing the loneliness, the regret. The insecurity that she'd never be all he needed.

Rafe's hand slipped over her hip to her back, pressing her closer. He finally broke the kiss so they could breathe.

"God, Grace. I've missed you."

"Come with me." She took his hand, leading him into the bedroom. The lights were off but the full moon cast a soft silvery glow around the room.

"I want to be more than your full-moon partner, Rafe. I want to be your mate."

"Can you really do this?" He cradled her face in his calloused hands. "Once I claim you, there's no turning back."

"Good, because I don't want to go back. I want to move forward with you. Only you."

Rafe's kiss was as soft as a whisper and Grace wondered how something so ethereal could anchor her so firmly. Even as she felt her spirit soaring, his touch kept her from disappearing into oblivion.

She barely felt her clothes fall from her body as Rafe's heat warmed her inside and out. The luxurious caress of his skin bordered on pain. Maybe it really was possible to die from too much pleasure.

She didn't remember going from her feet to prone on the bed, but there she was, sinking into the softness of the mattress, Rafe crouched above her, so close his chest grazed her bare breasts. He nuzzled her neck, her jaw and the teeny, tiny spot behind her ear that apparently hid a direct line to her sex, because a sizzling charge shot straight down her spine, swirled in her belly and ignited an aching, clawing need in her womb.

In an almost desperate grope, Grace danced her hands up his muscled chest. The short hairs splattering his flesh tickled her palms. Excitement spiraled through her body. Wanting, needing him closer, she pushed her fingers over his shoulders and down the corded muscles in his back. Holding him tightly, she never wanted to let him go, again.

Rafe moaned and growled her name. The husky vibrations hooked her, reeling her hips against his. Grinding her mound slowly against his cock, she cupped his tight ass, squeezing and pressing.

"Inside me. Now!" It wasn't romantic or sweet, but the raging sexual fever had all but obliterated her vocabulary.

Apparently it had wiped out Rafe's. He responded with a primitive grunt, positioning himself at her entrance and thrusting without further enticement.

Grace's vaginal walls gripped his cock as he pushed harder and deeper inside. He locked his gaze on hers. The dark, feral possessiveness in his eyes stole her breath and the sheer ecstasy of their joining nearly drove her mad.

His kiss, his touch, his thrusts, she couldn't get enough. She panted his name, clawing at his haunches, widening her legs just so he'd slide deeper. A swirling heat flamed in her core. She arched her pelvis and anchored her legs around his hips, matching his hard, fast thrusts. Grace slid her arms around his neck. Pressed her breasts against his chest and held him in a promise to never let him go again.

Hoarse and halting, her name spilled from his lips as her sex began to spasm, releasing wave after wave of rapture like the rushing, rising waters of a torrential flash flood. Even as the intensity roared through her body, deafening her ears and darkening her vision, her skin became super sensitive to Rafe's touch.

He kissed the hollow of her throat, soft and sweet, yet the burn was almost unbearable. His lips waltzed toward the curve of her neck.

A stark panic flickered through her. This was it. She was becoming his and there'd be no turning back.

He licked her flesh, teasing her with his tongue. Driving her mad with the electric pulses it sparked.

"Rafe," she panted, fully embracing their future.

"Mine!" His bite felt like a sharp pinch and what followed was a rush so intense and so deeply intimate that

Grace's eyes filled with tears and a sob rose in her throat. It was as if all Rafe's love gushed out of him and straight into her soul. It was the most beautiful thing she'd ever experienced.

He trembled against her, very nearly collapsing, except for the locked elbows that kept him from crushing her with his weight. She curled her fingers gently in his hair.

"Wow," she said.

"Yeah, wow."

"I told you I came with great benefits."

"Hmm." He nuzzled her cheek, then rolled onto his side, gathering her in his arms. "Now that I'm the exclusive beneficiary of those benefits, I intend to explore every nook and cranny of the policy provider."

His fingers slid along the curve of her hip as he nipped and licked and kissed the curve of her neck and shoulder. "Every. Single. Morning. Every. Single. Night."

Rafe's heat wrapped around her in loving comfort. She felt his love, his joy, his strength.

He nudged her onto her back, moving over her with tender stealth. She sighed as he easily slid inside her, rocking her with a gentle, easy rhythm. Merging bodies, merging hearts, merging souls.

With Rafe, she'd never be alone.

Grace wrapped her arms around his neck, kissed him softly, sweetly. She'd never needed to find the perfect town, with the perfect house, filled with perfect things to have a real home.

She'd just needed him.

* * * * *

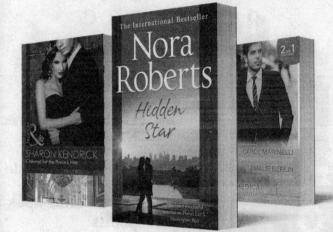